A RIGHT COZY CHRISTMAS CRIME

WENDY H. JONES   SHEENA MACLEOD   PAULINE TAIT

SUE COOK   SOPHIE SMYTHE   MARTI M. MCNAIR

ALEX GREYSON   JULIA FANCELLI CLIFFORD   STELLA ONI

DIANNE ASCROFT   LINDA MATHER   GILLIAN DUFF

MELICITY POPE

Especially for Kim

[signature]

Scott and Lawson

Cover Design by Cathy Helms of Avalon Graphics LLC

Paperback ISBN: 978-1-913372-07-1

eBook ISBN: 978-1-913372-06-4

DEDICATION

To all the members of the Sisters in Crime UK/Europe Chapter

CONTENTS

INTRODUCTION

Cozy crime is one of the most popular genres in the USA and is growing in popularity in the UK and worldwide. The genre has been described as a mixture of crime and comfort with this book being a perfect blend of both. Add Christmas to the blend and you have a large dollop of Yuletide cheer all wrapped up in a warming Christmas package. It is best served with a cup of hot chocolate, a slice of cake or even a mince pie in front of a roaring fire. Or if you live in the Southern Hemisphere relax on a beach with a cold drink and something from the barbecue. Whichever way you approach it, it is guaranteed to make Yuletide special.

Chapter One

THE CHRISTMAS CAROL KILLER

Sheena MacLeod

An annual Victorian-themed Christmas carol concert is not going to plan; choir members are dropping out due to flu. When one of the carollers is found dead inside the local charity shop with a copy of Charles Dicken's *A Christmas Carol* under his hand, co-owners of Broomsticks and Beeswax Cleaning Company, Catriona McAlister and Mei Chein, turn sleuth to find out what the dickens is going on. *A Scottish Highland Village Mystery.*

Catriona McAlister's to-do-list was growing as long as Santa's. Determined to make a start on it, she'd dragged herself from bed at the unearthly hour of 5 a.m. Less than two hours later, the kitchen was filled with the rich aroma of brandy, fruit and warming spices, from the latest batch of mince pies removed from the Aga.

Feeling somewhat smug, Catriona sat on a high stool at her breakfast bar, sipping a cup of extra-strong coffee and looking out the window. It was another cold and frosty day in Lochside, and the garden was shrouded in a thick layer of white. She added a splash of brandy to her cup for good measure. Without a doubt, winter had taken up residence in the Scottish village, and it didn't look as if it would be moving out any time soon. That suited Catriona. As far as she was concerned a white Christmas was all the more magical.

Her black cat leapt onto the window ledge and glared back at Catriona, tail swishing. He'd been tracking a robin, who had now settled onto the birdfeeder.

'Bah humbug, to you too, Oliver,' she said to him. 'Leave the wee birdie alone. Christmas is all about sharing, and you'll be getting your share of Christmas turkey soon enough. Speaking of bah humbug, I'd better be getting a move on.'

Tonight, the annual carolling concert would be held in the village square and she had the final Victorian-themed outfit steam-pressed and ready to be given out to the last caroller on her list, Leonard Scroggie. She didn't relish the thought. The assistant librarian was known around the village as a real-life Scrooge. Thinking about it, the last time she remembered him smiling was in the winter of '98 when a farmer spilled a load of Brussels sprouts from his trailer and told the villagers to help themselves.

A figure outside caught Catriona's attention and, despite the warmth of the kitchen, a strong sense of déjà vu made her shiver. In her haste to move to the window to better see who it was, she stumbled from the stool; and it had nothing to do with the brandy. Oliver scrambled out of her way.

A man was trudging along the footpath behind her cottage, his head bent down against the chilling wind. His hands were thrust deep into the pockets of a black, double-breasted coat, and he wore a woollen hat and scarf, similar to the ones Charlie had worn in the winter. But it couldn't be Charlie. It wasn't possible. Her husband had passed away six years ago. Catriona blinked twice, and the ghost-like figure morphed into Martin MacGregor, the senior librarian in the village. Despite this, Catriona's thoughts remained with Charlie and memories of Christmas's past.

A knock on the door brought her back to the present. Mei Chein swept into the kitchen and stopped dead in her tracks. 'You look as if you've seen a ghost.'

Catriona chewed on her bottom lip and gave a nervous laugh. 'I'll tell you about it later.' She looked at the clock. 'What have we got on today?' Mei and Catriona had worked together in the local bank until it closed ten years ago. Rather than relocate to another branch, they'd set up their own cleaning business, Broomsticks and Beeswax, and had never looked back.

 Mei placed a printout of the day's schedule on the kitchen table. 'A fair bit, and likely we should be making a start. But no' before a chin wag so you can tell me what had you so spooked,' she said in a Glasgow accent. Despite moving to the Highland village over twenty years before, she'd never lost the accent from where she'd grown up.

Catriona told her how seeing the librarian Martin MacGregor on the back path had triggered memories of Charlie. 'Likely it's because it's Christmas time.'

Mei enveloped her in a comforting hug. 'Aye well, that's to be expected. Nobody says you have to forget about Charlie,' she said and stepped back. 'Oh, and talking about Martin MacGregor. Wait until you hear this. What a palaver I had this morning.

3

Jenny was fair going her dinger at him, and right outside my front door as I was loading up the van.'

'Martin and his wife were arguing?' Catriona recalled the stooped figure of the librarian as he'd passed her cottage. She ran a finger down the day's cleaning schedule. 'We're due to clean the library after we finish at the Johnstone house. Perhaps we should leave the library until later. Did you hear what Martin and Jenny were arguing about?'

Mei snorted. 'Hear it? The whole village must have heard them arguing. I'm surprised you didn't. Anyway, Li came out with her camera.' Mei guffawed and slapped her knee. 'They soon moved off when they saw her take aim. Both in opposite directions.'

Catriona swept her long, red curly hair up into a messy bun. Mei's daughter, Li, was studying photography in Edinburgh and was home for the winter break. Mei would be enjoying having her back. 'Urgh! And I saw Cameron Swift taking more boxes into the charity shop yesterday. Hopefully, that will be the last of the items to be cleared from the Johnstone house and we can get in to give it a final clean-through.'

'I'm surprised Mrs Johnstone's nephew didn't want any of her things. Sad isn't it?' Mei said, before smiling. 'At least the extra money raised from selling them will help towards our latest good cause.

'Fingers crossed,' Catriona said as she slipped on her lilac Puffa coat and pulled a purple beanie down over her ears. 'I can't wait to see Donald MacLean's face when he's presented with the electric wheelchair we've placed on order for him. The years he spent out in all weathers delivering the mail played havoc with his joints.'

'An electric wheelchair is just what Donald needs to get him out and about again,' Mei said and popped the day's cleaning schedule into her bag. 'It will be lovely to see him back in the Blue Pheasant Inn.'

Catriona lifted a suit bag and followed Mei out the front

door. 'Will you stop off at Leonard Scroggie's place so I can hand in his carolling outfit for tonight?'

Catriona knocked on Leonard Scroggie's door with one hand while holding up the suit bag containing a black, Victorian-styled gentleman's cloak and hat and a red cravat in the other. The bell didn't work and the door, like the rest of the house, needed a fresh coat of paint.

Getting no answer and hearing movement inside, Catriona opened the door and called out to him. 'Leonard, it's Catriona. I've brought your carolling outfit.'

'Don't come in. Stay where you are. Erm! I'm full of that flu that's doing the rounds.'

Catriona's heart sunk to the bottom of her purple boots. Leonard was the fifth caroller to call off with flu. With only seven carollers remaining, she hoped he would be the last.

She shuffled her feet, unsure what to do. 'Are you all right?'

Leonard Scroggie let out an exasperated sigh. 'Are you deaf, Lassie? Of course, I'm not all right. I told you, I've got the flu.'

As Catriona turned to leave, Leonard Scroggie called, 'Leave my carolling outfit in the hallway.'

When Catriona climbed back into the passenger seat of their van, she rolled her eyes at Mei. 'Typical Scroggie. He's got flu and won't make it tonight, but he's paid for his costume to be cleaned so he wants it whether he'll use it, or not.'

Catriona and Mei had a full schedule and, as they made their way to Second Time Around, the charity shop in the high street, to start their cleaning day, Catriona thought about the boxes from the latest house clearance cluttering up the floors there. Until Mrs Johnstone had moved into residential care last month, Catriona and Mei had cleaned her large farmhouse twice a week and had done so for the past ten years. Mrs Johnstone's health had been failing for some time. She'd sold off the farmland and outbuildings when her husband died three years before, leaving her with only the house to manage.

'Mrs Johnstone loved to read, didn't she?' Catriona said.

'She had a big collection of old books too.'

'They've been put in the back shop for the librarians to look through, to see if any are worth taking to auction.'

Mei nodded. 'You never know. It's no' the first time Martin and Scroggie have found first or special editions amongst the books donated to the charity shop.'

'It's a shame none of her family wanted them,' Catriona said. 'I can't recall any of them visiting. Can you?'

'Well, not in the time we cleaned there. Apparently, as Mrs Johnstone didn't have any children, a nephew from Edinburgh is to inherit her estate.'

Catriona nodded. 'Hence the clearance to get the house ready for sale.'

'No point wasting time, eh!' Mei said as she pulled the van up beside the charity shop.

Noticing Cameron Swift, the local Man-With-A-Van, lugging more boxes into the shop, Catriona groaned and turned to Mei. 'The 'Blue Pheasant Inn? We could start there.'

Ten minutes later, they were carrying out a deep clean of the Inn toilets.

Their cleaning day passed quickly and Mei dropped Catriona off to get herself showered changed and have something warm to eat before they set out for the carolling concert. When they had passed the village square, green canopies had been erected above trestle tables for the food and drink. Separate, larger red canopies had been put up for the brass band and carollers to stand under. To keep the villagers warm, braziers had been readied to be lit around the square. The Christmas lights along the high street and on the large Christmas tree in the square would be turned on at 6 p.m, adding to the festive feel.

6

After Catriona had placed a full-length, Victorian-styled woollen cloak around her shoulders and tied the thick, red ribbons on her brimmed felt hat into a bow at her neck, Mei Chein arrived similarly dressed. They set off on foot, carrying two suit bags each, to hang the unused carolling outfits back up on the rail in the store room at the back of the charity shop. Then they would join the other carollers at the village square ready to start singing at seven o'clock.

When they passed the village square, the brass band was playing *God Rest Ye Merry Gentlemen*, putting Catriona in the mood for the evening of carolling ahead. As soon as she pushed open the charity shop door, Catriona sensed that something wasn't right. The lights in the room at the back of the shop were blazing. Mei made to speak, but Catriona held a finger to her lips to silence her.

They laid the carolling outfits on the front counter and made their way quietly towards the back of the shop. Reaching the open door, they both froze, Mei's mouth shaped in a round O.

Martin MacGregor paced the floor amongst scattered books, his carolling cape flowing behind him.

They quickly stepped back, but not before seeing someone else dressed in a carolling cloak, with their back to them.

'I said the last time that if it happened again that would be it,' Martin shouted at the figure. 'It's a step too far. I'm not keeping quiet this time.'

Catriona and Mei stepped backwards through to the front of the shop, where they quickly made their escape out the door.

Reaching the village square, Catriona took a deep inhalation to settle her breathing. They'd had no intention of remaining in the shop to witness a domestic taking place between Martin and his wife.

'Phew!' Mei said, 'I don't know about you but I could do with a drink after that.' She pulled on Catriona's arm and half-dragged her towards the tables set up with mulled wine.

Catriona glanced around the table. 'Is that all that's on offer? No spirits?'

'This will have to do. Just think of it as keeping with the spirit of Christmas.' Mei replied, downing a glass of mulled wine in one long gulp.

Catriona eyed the filled glasses. 'Well, I'm with you on that.' She lifted two glasses and handed one to Mei, who was waving to her daughter, Li, who was snapping pictures of the high street and the square.

As she raised the glass to drink down the warming liquid, Catriona's hand stopped halfway to her mouth. 'Mei, look! Over there. Isn't that Martin's wife, Jenny?' She nodded her head in the direction of the caroller's canopy. Jenny MacGregor stood under it, talking to another caroller.

'So, if Martin's wife is out here, which caroller was Martin arguing with in the charity shop? It couldn't have been Jenny.'

They laid their empty glasses down and made their way over to see which carollers were missing. There should have been twelve carollers. Five had called off with flu, including the assistant librarian, Leonard Scroggie. This meant there should be three more carollers, besides herself, Jenny and Mei, and Martin who was still in the charity shop.

The brass band was belting out *Once in Royal David's City*, making it difficult for Catriona to hear what Mei was saying. 'What?'

Mei raised her voice. 'I said, that's Doctor Hardcastle talking to Jenny. So, who's missing?'

Catriona frantically glanced around the square. 'I can't see Breda Burns or Cameron Swift anywhere. Can you?'

As they approached the carolling tent, Mei waved to Doctor Hardcastle and Jenny.

'Awful news that so many carollers have gone down with the flu,' Doctor Hardcastle said in greeting and tipped his black top-hat.

'Including your cousin,' Catriona said to Jenny as she retied the red ribbon on her own hat. 'I spoke to Leonard earlier. I hope he feels better soon.'

Jenny scrunched up her face in confusion. 'What? Leonard? Leonard has flu?'

'That's strange,' Doctor Hardcastle said. 'I could have sworn I saw him earlier.' He shook his head. 'But if he's home with flu, then I must have been mistaken. It's hard to tell who's who in these outfits, particularly from a distance,' he said and adjusted his spectacles.

As neither Jenny nor Doctor Hardcastle had seen Breda, the manageress of the charity shop, or Cameron, the local Man-With-A-Van, Catriona and Mei set off in search of them. They made their way around the square and walked the length of the high street. The street was set out in a semi-circle around the square with the main road separating them. The charity shop, Second Time Around, came first, then the hairdressers, Curls And Cuts, which also had its lights on. Then the Blue Pheasant Inn, a café, and a gift shop with its shutters down, the newsagent which was also closed, and a grocers which was open until 10pm. At the end of the street was the library; its stone columns reflected by uplighters built into the slabs on the ground.

Seeing no sign of the missing carollers, Catriona and Mei made their way back to the village square, stopping when they met Li.

'Have you seen Breda or Cameron?' Mei asked her daughter.

Li snapped their photo. 'Mum, you look amazing. Let me take another one.'

Catriona had to admit, Mei did look stunning in her long, black cloak and red be-ribboned hat. Her red-painted lips and the ribbon stood out in stark contrast to her jet-black hair.

'Okay, that will be a great one, Mum,' Li said. 'Oh, and no, I haven't seen Cameron at all. But I did see Breda. She said she was nipping home to change.'

'When was that?' Catriona asked.

'Gosh, I can't remember. It must have been about half an hour ago, at least. Sorry, I can't be more helpful, I was lost in my work.'

Dressed in her carolling outfit, Breda Burns raced towards them, her face white and drawn. 'Martin. He's dead. I... Ah! I've called for the police and an ambulance. I saw the lights on in the charity shop when I was passing and went in to see who was there. I can't believe it,' she said and burst into tears.

As Catriona made to move, still in shock and unsure where they should move to. Mei said, 'What do you mean dead? We saw Martin MacGregor not half an hour ago and he was fine then.'

Through her tears, and stopping frequently to gasp for breath, Breda said, 'He was on the floor in the back room of the shop. He was dead when I got there.' She took a deep breath and continued. 'There was a copy of Dicken's *A Christmas Carol* lying under one of his hands, but it wasn't our copy. It was a different one. And there was an auctioneer's receipt sticking out from between the pages.'

'What do you mean a different copy?' Catriona asked.

Before Breda could reply, three police cars pulled to a stop outside Second Time Around, their blue strobing lights flickering around the high street and village square. A policewoman escorted Breda to the side to wait to be taken to the police station to be interviewed. No doubt, everyone who'd been in or around the square would need to give a witness statement, Catriona thought.

Frozen in place, she watched events unfolding around her. As word spread about Martin, the brass band stopped playing. Jenny MacGregor ran screaming towards the charity shop, 'My husband's in there.'

With his Victorian-themed carolling cloak billowing behind him, Doctor Hardcastle, the local GP, chased after Jenny and stopped her from entering the shop which now had a policeman standing guard outside.

The following morning, Catriona sat with Mei in the lounge of the Blue Pheasant Inn sipping on a cup of filtered coffee beside a crackling log fire. It had been after 10 p.m when they'd finally left the police station after giving their statements. Catriona had a strong sense that Breda Burns might not have been telling the whole truth about what she knew. It would seem that the police thought so too, the manageress of the charity shop still hadn't been released.

'So, do you think Breda did it?'

'Why would Breda kill Martin? It doesn't make any sense.' Mei said.

'I can't help thinking about what we overheard Martin saying. Something about a last chance. And, who was he saying it to? I only caught sight of the back of a carolling cloak. Could it have been Breda?'

'I'm not sure. But if it wasn't Breda who could it have been? Doctor Hardcastle was outside with Jenny Macgregor, so it couldn't be either of them.'

'And it appears that Cameron Swift had been nowhere near the charity shop after he had dropped off the last of the boxes from the house clearance. Apparently, he'd been here the whole time in the Blue Pheasant Inn supping ale.'

Mei nodded her agreement. 'And he has witnesses to prove it.'

'I can't help thinking about what Breda said about the Dicken's book?' Catriona said and took a sip of coffee. 'I remember seeing a copy of *A Christmas Carol* at the Johnstone house. It was in the glass-fronted bookshelf beside the other old books. It would have been taken to the charity shop along with them. Do you think that was the book Breda was meaning? If so, why did

Martin have it on him? And what did Breda mean about it not being the shop's copy?'

'Could Cameron Swift have taken the book when he was picking up and delivering the boxes and replaced it with a more recent copy?'

'There's only one way to find out,' Catriona said and grabbed her bag and coat. 'Come on, your chariot awaits. Or should I say our trusted van. We're going to speak to Mrs Johnstone. I doubt if the police will. And if something sinister is going on, then we need to find out what it is before anyone else gets hurt. And no, I don't think Breda killed Martin either. But I do think she knows more than she's letting on.'

Mrs Johnstone was delighted to see them. Catriona didn't have the heart to tell the woman the reason for their visit, preferring to let her think of it as a long overdue social call. Consumed with guilt that she wouldn't have even thought of it if Martin hadn't been murdered, Catriona apologised for leaving it so long to come and see her.

'Tea?' Mrs Johnstone said and rang a bell to call on someone to make it for them. She was dressed in a green cardigan over a cream shift dress. Her thick, white hair was styled into a long plait which hung down over one shoulder, and her makeup freshly applied.

Once they were all settled and sipping the flavoursome strong brew, Catriona asked Mrs Johnstone about the copy of Dicken's, *A Christmas Carol,* that had been in her bookcase.

Mrs Johnstone beamed. 'Oh, I am so glad you found it. And that you recognised it was special. There were a few other treasures in there, but none as valuable as that one. If you've got time. I'll tell you it's story.'

Catriona and Mei nodded and then leaned forward.

'You see it is a rare edition of *A Christmas Carol.* A very special edition indeed, especially for my family. It meant so much to my mother to inherit it. And I loved it too. I do hope it finds a good home.'

Catriona didn't want to deceive the woman, but couldn't bear to tell her that the book might be missing.

Mrs Johnstone took a sip of tea before continuing. Her hand shook as she placed the cup back into the saucer. 'My great, great grandmother was an avid reader. Amelia loved nothing better than to meet the great authors of the day. Most of the antiquarian books in our family collection belonged to her, including the book you were asking about.

'Now dears, what most people don't realise now, is that Charles Dickens was a wonderful performer. He loved nothing better than to tour the country giving readings from his books, and that included tours of Scotland. Amelia attended one of these book readings. One that included Charles Dickens reading from *A Christmas Carol*. According to the admission ticket, the reading was held on the 26th February, 1869, in the George Steet Musical Hall in Edinburgh.

'Amelia had taken her own copy of the book to be signed by Dickens. And he did sign it. Arthur Smith, Dicken's tour manager, also signed the poster advertising the reading tour and the receipt for her ticket in to the reading. Meeting Dickens was one of Amelia's favourite memories.'

Mei sat back and let out a deep breath. 'Wow!'

Catriona nodded her agreement. 'I feel elated now that I even saw the book. You must have treasured it.'

'I did, and my nephew made it clear that he didn't want any of my dusty old books. Perhaps he would have changed his mind if he'd known this one was so special. It's an 1844 first edition, second issue. Not as rare as the full first edition which quickly sold out, but still a rare book indeed.'

Mei coughed, as if embarrassed to ask, before spurting out, 'Is it valuable?'

'It is. Especially as Dicken's signature is authenticated by the signed poster and ticket receipt. And to the right collector that will be very valuable indeed. It was a bitterly cold winter that year, and Dicken's wasn't well. It was his last Scottish reading tour. He died the following year.'

'Won't your nephew want the book back when he finds out its value?' Catriona asked.

Mrs Johnstone frowned. 'Then he can't have it. I deliberately didn't tell Johnathon what it was worth. Not that he ever took the time to ask me. Apart from the monetary value, the book would mean nothing to him. No, I want it to go to someone who will appreciate it. Most likely, that will be through auction.'

Catriona caught Mei's eye. They had both thought about the auction receipt mentioned by Breda. Had someone stolen the original red, leather-bound book and signed contents and put them up for auction? It would make sense of what Breda had said about an auction receipt. But who? If they found that out, likely they would find Martin's killer. Was this the 'step too far' they'd heard Martin shouting about in the shop?

'The librarian was very interested in that one when I showed him my collection of old books.'

'The librarian came to your house?' Mei said.

'Oh, yes. He called when he heard I was moving here and that my house was to be cleared. He wanted to find out which of my old books I was donating to the charity shop. He was very surprised when I told him it was all of them.'

When they left the residential home, Catriona and Mei headed to Mei's bungalow to talk. Li was there when they arrived. She was sitting on a settee in the lounge beside an open fire, sorting through photographs spread out on the coffee table in front of her.

Catriona and Mei sat on the settee opposite Li. The coffee table in between them. When they finished telling her all they had found out from Mrs Johnstone, Li added that she had also discovered something interesting.

She'd spoken to a hairdresser from Curls And Cuts, who'd been working late on the night of the carol concert. 'Robyn said she'd seen lights on in the back room of the charity shop when she'd popped out to the passageway between the two shops to empty the bins. As she'd been heading back inside, a man wearing a carolling outfit had pushed past her, almost knocking her over.'

'Was it Cameron Swift, our local Man-With-A-Van?' Catriona asked.

Li shook her head. 'No. The man Robyn saw was wearing round, gold-framed spectacles.'

'That sounds like the assistant librarian, Leonard Scroggie,' Mei said.

Catriona nodded her agreement. 'And, Doctor Hardcastle thought he'd seen him. Although, he also wears spectacles, I've never seen him wearing round, gold-framed ones.'

'Exactly, and even better,' Li said and handed them a print out of a photo she had taken in the high street. 'Look, Scroggie's hurrying away in the direction of the library.'

Catriona examined the picture. 'Scroggie had flu. He should have been at home at the time of the carolling concert. But, come to think of it, I didn't actually see him. I only spoke to him from the doorway.'

'But he asked you to leave his carolling outfit,' Mei said. 'Meaning we now have another suspect who was wearing a carolling cloak.'

'What the dickens is going on?' Catriona turned to Mei. 'We need to speak to Mrs Johnstone again... Now!'

Later that day, after Catriona and Mei had handed their evidence over to the police, Leonard Scroggie was arrested for Martin's murder. Catriona sat at her kitchen table with Mei and Li. On the floor beside them, Oliver gobbled on a bowl of chicken, his tail swishing with pleasure.

Catriona twirled a loose curl, lost in thought. When she'd

shown Li's picture to Mrs Johnstone, she identified Leonard Scroggie as the librarian who'd called at her house to look through her cabinet of old books. It hadn't been Martin MacGregor, as both she and Mei had initially thought. The auctioneers had also been contacted by Breda Burns and confirmed that the missing copy of the Dicken's book had been brought in by Leonard Scroggie to be put up for auction. The receipt, for a signed first edition, second issue of Charles' Dickens, *A Christmas Carol* plus a signed poster and ticket for the 1869 reading was made out to Leonard Scroggie and was now in the possession of the police. Likely, charges would also be made against him for theft. Catriona felt a flash of guilt for having suspected Breda.

'So, Li,' Mei said, interrupting Catriona's musings. 'We managed to speak to Jenny Macgregor. We went to her house to offer our condolences on the death of her husband. It seems that Martin found the auctioneer's receipt in Leonard's drawer in the library and had shown it to Jenny on the morning of the carolling concert. That's what they'd been arguing about when I saw them that morning.

'She'd been begging her husband not to say anything in case her cousin lost his job at the library. Martin and Scroggie had studied together at university. That's how Martin met Jenny.

Last year, Martin suspected that Scroggie had been putting a token amount into the charity shop till to pay for old books that were actually rare or first editions and then pocketing the money he made from them at auction. Martin had confronted Leonard Scroggie then about stealing from a charity. Scroggie denied it, but he stopped doing it after that.'

'Until now,' Catriona said. 'According to Jenny, after Martin found the auctioneer's receipt he said he was going to confront Scroggie. He'd noticed that the original copy of *A Christmas Carol* was missing and, suspecting that Scroggie had taken it, he'd searched through his desk at the library.'

'It looks like the rare book had proved too much of a temptation for Scroggie and he'd reverted to his old ways again,' Li said.

'It would seem so,' Mei said. 'Martin saw Scroggie going into the charity shop and followed him in with the intention of confronting him about the auctioneer's receipt. Martin found Scroggie trying to place a newer edition of *A Christmas Carol* into the back shop so that no one would notice the first edition was missing.'

Catriona nodded. 'This must have been the argument we overheard when we went into the shop to return the extra carolling outfits. By all accounts, after we left the argument turned into a physical altercation and Martin was fatally injured. Thankfully, Li photographed Leonard Scroggie after he left the shop or we might never have found out it was him.'

The following evening, the villagers gathered in the church hall. They had been invited to attend an extraordinary meeting regarding the distribution of the funds raised that year from the charity shop. The hall was packed to capacity and filled with chatter about recent events.

A carer from the home had brought Mrs Johnstone, and they sat at the side of the hall at a table beside Catriona, Mei, and Li. A large smile lit up Mrs Johnstone's face. Although she had been saddened to hear about the librarian's death, she was delighted her treasured Dicken's book would now be placed back at auction on behalf of the charity shop.

When the carollers finished singing *Silent Night*, the manageress of the charity shop, Breda Burns, took centre position in front of the stage. Beside her was a large object covered with a red sheet and bedecked with green bows.

When Cameron Swift pushed Donald Maclean into the hall in a wheelchair, Breda called for order. 'Without further ado, I would like to thank Mrs Johnstone for a very generous donation to Second

Time Around. There was, however, a strict stipulation attached to this monetary gift,' Breda said and whipped the red sheet off the large object to reveal a brand-new electric wheelchair. 'Mrs Johnstone insisted on paying for any shortfall to pay for Donald's chair.'

As Donald hobbled over to try it out, loud applause filled the hall.

Mrs Johnstone waved away the villagers and Donald's attempts to thank her.

Once he had settled into his new chair, Donald waved a hand and called out in a loud voice, 'Merry Christmas, everyone. Merry Christmas, one and all.'

BIO

Sheena Macleod is a published historical fiction author and a prize-winning and published short story writer. She lives in a seaside town on the East Coast of Scotland. She lectured at the University of Dundee, where she gained a PhD. Sheena blogs at *allaboutbooks.blog at WordPress.com* You can find her online at https://www.sheenas-books.co.uk

Chapter Two

THE HOUSE ON THE HILL

Pauline Tait

R ecently single, Jessica Winter escapes the holiday frenzy of the city for a charming cottage in the Scottish Highlands. Nestled in a picturesque and peaceful setting, she hopes to mend her broken heart. Seeking solace in an idyllic, rustic cottage, her retreat takes a turn when she discovers a body at the house on the hill. With the local police dismissive of her concerns, Jessica decides to channel her inner sleuth and solve the mystery herself. In a cozy yet suspenseful tale, Jessica's quest for answers leads her through a maze of secrets and surprises, proving that even in the most serene places, danger can lurk just around the corner.

Snowflakes gathered on Jessica's eyelashes while freezing air carried her breath into the distance in a tantalising trail that dissipated in the eeriness of her surroundings.

Smoke belching from the chimney hung low in the air. Windows, lit up and inviting, powered her frozen limbs and reminded her that Mr Anderson had promised to light the fire and stock the fridge and larder in time for her arrival.

Jessica continued to haul her suitcase up the hill. The blizzard worsening, while arctic winds wrapped around her body. All adding to the misery that had led her to flee Edinburgh for a remote cottage in the Scottish Highlands.

'Miss Winter, let me take that for you.' A hand appearing through the snow reached for her suitcase.

'Mr Anderson?'

'Call me Douglas.'

'Thank you,' she shivered, allowing him to lead the way. 'I'm Jessica.'

'Well, Jessica, welcome to Myre Cottage. The fire's stoked, heating's on and I've taken the liberty of popping a venison casserole into the oven. Esme, my wife, made it. You'll be needing a real winter warmer today.'

Jessica had heard nothing after casserole. A home cooked meal was something she hadn't had in far too long. Simon preferred to eat out. Simon preferred sushi. Simon. Simon. Simon. She quashed him from her thoughts.

'I'll leave you to it. If you need anything, you have my number. Esme's decorated the place for you. Just a bit, enough to make it feel festive until you've had a chance to sort yourself out. And remember, Esme and I are away for a couple of days from tonight.'

After thanking Douglas, Jessica closed the door on city life and began to peel the cold damp clothes from her skin. In no mood for festive cheer, she ignored the decorations, deciding a hot shower was in order. Then there was a casserole with her name on it.

❄

The following morning, the snow had stopped, and Jessica opened the curtains to deer nibbling at the lower branches of the trees. Picture perfect, it reminded her of Christmas cards her grandmother had sent in years gone by.

The bones of the cottage had finally warmed through and as Jessica prepared breakfast, she couldn't help but feel soothed by Esme's festive decorations. A tree filled the far corner of the living room. There was no obvious colour scheme to the baubles or decorations that lay scattered throughout the rooms or covered the mantel, but Jessica decided that suited the cottage. It was warm, oozed charm and, most importantly, felt homely.

Adding to the atmosphere, Jessica searched for a Christmas playlist. Singing along, she wondered when Chloe would arrive with the rest of her belongings. The mere thought brought the events of the last few weeks hurtling to the fore. Unable to suppress them, she pictured Simon flirting with the office receptionist. Jessica had known her relationship was doomed the moment the young blond had first stepped into the office. But she had thought it would be down to her annoyance at Simon's roving eye. She hadn't for one second thought he would cheat on her.

A horn, honking, plucked Jessica from her thoughts. Opening the door, she spied a shivering Chloe battling her way through the snow with arms outstretched to greet her friend. A tractor was parked a few metres behind. A man in his late sixties clambered out and hobbled towards her, his every movement accompanied by a groan.

'Hello Lass, you must be Jessica, I'm Jonesy.' He smiled, nodding towards Chloe. 'I found this one stranded at the bottom of the hill. Her van's stuck in a snow drift. Not to worry, though. We've got everything in here.'

Following Jonesy to the trailer at the rear of the tractor,

Jessica was thrilled to find all her worldly possessions piled neatly under a sheet of tarpaulin.

'Come on then', Jonesy, instructed. 'Before the snow wets it through.'

With Jonesy unloading the various boxes, cases and crates that had previously filled every crevice of Chloe's flower delivery van, Jessica and Chloe ferried them into the cottage.

And as Chloe recited the trials and tribulations of her journey north, in often white-out conditions, Jessica could feel herself relax. Second to the arrival of her friend, having all her possessions together under one roof was a much-needed comfort.

'You're really going to stay here.' Chloe made no effort to hide her concern. 'For a whole month?'

'Yup,' Jessica nodded, leading her friend further up the snowy mountain track.

'On your own?'

'I won't always be on my own. You'll be here for the first few days.'

'What about Christmas?'

'I'll be fine,' Jessica reiterated. 'I need to be away from the city. And Simon. Moving out was hard. I need time to decide what I want before I make any big decisions.' She shrugged, 'And anyway, the thought of seeing him and you-know-who together over Christmas... I couldn't bear it.'

The tranquillity of the Perthshire Highlands glistened in effervescent beauty as they continued their meander through the snow-clad forest. Their laughter echoed in the cold still air, Chloe's company and quick wit lifting Jessica from the doldrums of heartbreak until a sharp bang, not dissimilar to a car backfiring, ricocheted through the forest. Jessica spun around to locate the source. The echo faded into the forest's panic. Birds squawked overhead. Deer scarpered through the trees.

A slither of grey in the distance fleeted in and out of view. A vehicle speeding in treacherous conditions was enough to convince Jessica something was wrong.

Knowing the track would soon bring the fleeing vehicle in their direction, Jessica grabbed Chloe by the arm, pulling her behind the upturned roots of a fallen Scots Pine.

A small grey 4x4 navigated the snow-covered track as fast as the wintry conditions would allow. Its driver, hunched over the wheel, showed eager determination as he slid the vehicle into a corner before disappearing down the hill.

Escaping their hiding place, Jessica and Chloe stumbled towards the source of the bang.

Emerging from the treeline, they discovered a house, old and stately, sitting alone on the hill. It sprawled across the clearing, dominating its isolated surroundings.

The driveway had been cleared of just enough snow to allow access. Together, Jessica and Chloe followed the tyre tracks, wondering if they belonged to the 4x4 that had passed them in such a hurry. Continuing towards the house, they felt the full force of the blustering wind. The snow, becoming heavier, obscured their view until they reached the porch.

A man, late sixties, lay sprawled a few metres from the front door. The bullet wound to his chest gave the impression he had been shot at close range. Jessica felt in vain for a pulse. Noticing her friend had turned ash white. 'You call the police. I'll stay here.'

While Chloe zigzagged her way down the hill, holding her phone to the ether in search of a signal, Jessica scanned the scene.

There were no scuffle marks in the snow which, she decided, meant there had been no altercation. But the victim was lying quite a distance from the main door, suggesting he had perhaps known his killer and had stepped out to speak to him.

Noticing the heavy snow was obscuring the tyre tracks that came and went from the front porch, Jessica pulled her scarf towards her chin and began photographing what was left. She wondered if they might be crucial to the police and their investigation.

The distant rumblings of an engine approached the clearing. Jonesy's tractor coming into view moments later.

Her expression seemed to alert him that something was wrong. And as he cut the engine and struggled from the tractor, Jessica had to hold him back when he noticed the body lying on the porch.

'Detective Constable Graham Smeaton. Move aside?'

Jessica and Chloe exchanged glances. They were nowhere near the scene and if they were to move back any further, they'd be in the forest. But the DC's words seemed more an announcement of his arrival than an instruction.

Jessica watched as he strode towards the porch. His accompanying officer dutifully followed on.

'Well, someone's got him in the end.' A voice croaked from behind.

Jessica spun round. The stranger just inches from her as he navigated the snow laden branches at the edge of the forest.

'About time.' He added.

'Sorry, who are you?' Jessica asked.

'The gamie, what's it to you?'

'The who?'

'The *gamekeeper*. Not from around here, are you?' he quipped, before turning towards the porch.

'Neither are you,' she retorted, clocking his Glaswegian accent.

Stopping in his tracks, he turned, his eyes squinting and his chest out like a rooster lording over his flock. Retracing his steps, he stopped inches from her face. His breath brushed her cheek. 'Who the heck are you?' His eyes bore into Jessica's with a nastiness that caused her to flinch.

'You won't intimidate me,' she managed.

'Glad to hear it.' The accompanying officer interrupted. 'Back off Liam. There's no need for any attitude from you today.'

A quick nod towards the officer and Liam sculked towards the porch.

'I'm Constable Mark Campbell, I just need to ask a few questions.'

But a mischievous twinkle in his eye had rendered Jessica momentarily speechless.

'Your name?'

'J-Jessica Winter,' she croaked, far less coolly than she would have liked. 'And this is Chloe.'

As Jessica went on to recite the morning's events, she couldn't help but watch Detective Constable Smeaton. 'Does he know he's walking across what's left of the tyre tracks?'

Constable Campbell didn't respond, but his expression was enough to let Jessica know he didn't rate his boss overly highly. 'Can you confirm what time you discovered the body?'

'The Pathologist will confirm the time of death,' the DC interrupted.

'We found him about five minutes before Chloe called you,' Jessica continued. 'We heard the bang about ten minutes before that.'

'Anything more you can tell us?' Constable Campbell prompted, giving Jessica a reassuring smile that momentarily knocked her off piste.

'Yes, there was a grey 4x4, quite small, it-.'

'Where, here?'

'Yes. We saw it speeding down the hill, as fast as the conditions would allow. Snow was spraying in all directions. He was in a hurry.'

'He?'

'I'm sure it was a man. I only saw him for a moment, and he was wrapped up for the weather, but it was just minutes after we heard the bang.'

'I've got everything I need for now,' the DC interrupted.

Jessica couldn't help but wonder at the DC's lack of professionalism and failure to appear thorough.

'Ignore him, we'll do the job right.' Constable Campbell assured, tearing a page from his notepad. 'This is my number. Call me if you remember anything else.'

Warming themselves by the fire, coffee in one hand and a piece of Esme's homemade shortbread in the other, Jessica and Chloe chatted over the morning's events while a Christmas playlist rang out in the background.

'I can't leave you here, Jessica. Not now. I mean, there's a killer on the loose.' Chloe jumped to her feet. 'We should lock the door.'

'I think we're safer here than anywhere.' Jessica shrugged. 'Police are guarding the house and stopping all traffic from coming up the track. Not that there can be many people heading up this way. It's far more remote up here than I'd realised.'

'Let's pack up and head back to Edinburgh this afternoon.'

'Are you kidding? There's a murder to solve.' Jessica exclaimed.

'Exactly.' I love you to bits Jessica, but you don't know anything about solving a murder. You can't seriously be thinking about staying.'

'I know,' Jessica shrugged, 'but yes, I'm staying. I haven't thought about Simon all morning. Maybe a distraction is what I need? And anyway, don't you want to find out who did it? I mean, aren't you curious?'

'Curious? Jessica, a man was murdered this morning, less than half a mile from here. How is a police presence up at the house or down at the bottom of the hill going to keep us safe? Did you see how that Liam guy just appeared from the forest?'

'Yes, yes, I did.' Jessica sat bolt upright. 'What did you think of him? I mean, he obviously has a temper, and he was on edge.'

'He gave me the creeps,' Chloe interjected.

'And he was far too blasé about the fact his boss had just been murdered.'

A knock at the door made them both jump.

'Maybe we shouldn't answer?' Chloe stuttered.

'Why wouldn't we answer,' Jessica teased. 'The murderer won't exactly be going door to door.'

Chuckling at the thought, she reached for the handle.

'Constable Campbell, come in.'

'Thank you. I wanted to make sure you're both okay after this morning's discovery and see if you had remembered anything else.'

Jessica walked him through to the living room.

'You've got it toasty in here,' he remarked, warming his hands by the fire. 'And festive, I like it.'

'Are we safe here?' Chloe interrupted, sinking as far into the sofa as the worn tan leather would allow.

'Of course.' He took a seat at the opposite end from Chloe.

'Who was he?' Jessica asked, pouring a mug from the coffee machine and handing it to Constable Campbell.

'Lewis Wallace. He owned the estate, including this cottage, and a fair few of the others. Pretty much everything around here was his. Farms, houses, and most of the buildings in the village are rented from the estate.'

'Why would someone want to kill him?'

He shrugged, 'Mr Wallace wasn't the nicest man to be around.'

'That explains Liam's comments earlier,' Jessica concluded.

'Liam's just as bad, although he's more likely to thump you than shoot you.'

'Is he a suspect?'

'I can't discuss that,' he apologised. 'But everyone's a suspect until the case is solved.'

'Including us?' Chloe panicked.

Constable Campbell seemed unable to stifle his chuckle. 'We have to be open to all possibilities.' He winked.

The comment caused Chloe to retreat further into the depths of the sofa, her hands gripping her mug as though her life depended on it.

'Okay, so, who are his staff? I mean there's Liam, and Jonesy, the tractor driver.'

'Jonesy's worked for Lewis Wallace for decades. He's one of the few people that understood Lewis and more surprisingly, one of the few people Lewis liked.'

'And Liam?' Jessica prodded.

'He came here a year or so ago. Had to get away from Glasgow if you get my drift. But to be fair, Lewis gave him a job when no one else would.'

'And what about the grey 4x4, do you know who it belongs to?'

'Yeah, we do. But the DC's adamant it has nothing to do with the case.'

'What? But why? We saw it minutes after we heard the shot.'

'He has his reasons.'

'So, there's more you're not telling us?'

'There's more I *can't* tell you,' He emphasised. 'What I have told you, you'll get from his housekeeper anyway.'

'Housekeeper?'

'Yeah, Esme Anderson. She's married to Douglas. He oversees the day-to-day workings of the estate, and she is Mr & Mrs Wallace's housekeeper. Their cook as well, I think, especially when Mrs Wallace is away.'

'Away? Where does she go?'

'Edinburgh, London,' he shrugged. 'She has family in both cities and is a patron of a couple of charities, so they can take her away.'

'A lot?'

'Yeah, she's probably away two weeks in every month. But, hey, who's questioning who here?' He joked, standing to leave.

'The tyre tracks? Surely, you're not writing them off as being insignificant to the case. If you know who the 4x4 belongs to, shouldn't you be matching the tracks to the tyres?'

'It's not my call.'

'That's not what I asked,'

'Inquisitive, aren't you?'

She shrugged playfully.

'Between falling snow and the wind causing the snow to drift, we were too late to get a clean sample of the tracks.'

'So, *you* think there's a link between the tyre tracks and the murderer?' She reiterated.

'I don't think we should rule it out,' he admitted, hesitantly.

'You'll be glad to know I took photographs, before you and the DC arrived on the scene.'

The following morning Douglas and Esme had returned, and Jessica thought it was time to pay Esme a visit. Arriving at the house on the hill a little after ten, she was reluctant to knock on the front door. Not wanting to disturb Lewis's widow, she continued round the back.

The views towards the neighbouring hills stopped her in her tracks. The morning light illuminated the river in the distance. Below the snowline, it snaked through the glen, disappearing into the distance in a cacophony of faded autumnal colours and turbulent clouds.

Flurries of snow filled the air. Jessica decided it would make the ideal festive scene if she wasn't feeling so grinchy at the prospect of spending Christmas without Simon.

Her phone buzzing made her jump, but she was grateful for the distraction. 'Hello.'

'Hi, Constable Campbell here. I wanted to let you know we've made an arrest and it's looking like he's going to be charged.'

'Wow, that was quick. Who?'

'Eh well,' his tone lowered. 'It's Jonesy.'

'What? No. No way, you've got that wrong.'

'I haven't got anything wrong, thanks very much, this one's down to the DC.'

'On what grounds?'

'The bullet from Mr Wallace's chest matches a gun found lying just a mile down the track from the house. Looks like it had been thrown as the suspect fled the scene.'

'But that doesn't mean it was Jonesy who shot Lewis.'

'His prints were on the gun.'

'No, that doesn't add up. He's been set up.'

'The DC has the case wrapped.'

'Well, he's wrong.'

'Then prove it. Please.'

Knowing she had to get to the bottom of what happened, and quickly, Jessica found the courage to knock on the back door of the house on the hill.

A woman, mid-sixties, answered.

'Sorry to bother you. I'm Jessica, I've rented-'

'Myre Cottage. Yes, I know. Come on in, dear. I'm Esme, I keep the house, do the cooking, oversee the other staff.'

'Take a seat.' Esme instructed, placing a baking tray in the oven.

Jessica couldn't help but salivate at whatever was bubbling on the stove. 'You mentioned other staff?'

Yes, there's a couple of cleaners, one does the housework, the other sees to the laundry. We've waitresses, too. They come in whenever there's a function or if the family have guests staying. I suppose we're going to have to get planning for a funeral now.' Esme broke off.

'I'm sorry. It must have been a shock for you yesterday.'

'Well, yes, but how are you, dear? I mean, you must have gotten such a fright yourself. What a discovery to make. I wanted to knock on your door yesterday, see if you and your friend were alright, but I haven't wanted to leave Mrs Wallace on her own.'

'How is she?'

'She's okay. Life's going to be far easier for her now. I think she's feeling a bit guilty about that. You know, relief and all.'

'They didn't get along?'

'Good grief, no. Couldn't stand each other. It was a marriage of convenience if you know what I mean. Each bringing important connections for the other. But to each their own, as they say.'

'Have you heard they've arrested Jonesy?'

Cupping her face in her hands, Esme fell into a chair, grabbing the table as she did for support. 'They've what?'

'Constable Campbell phoned to let me know just before I knocked on the door.'

'No, no, they're wrong. He'd never do such a thing. Eric was the only one of us Lewis had any time for.'

'Eric?'

'Eric Jones.' She sniffed, 'He'll always be Eric to me, he's my big brother and he'd never do such a thing.'

Reaching for Esme's arm. 'I'm sorry. For what it's worth, I don't think he did it either. Does Eric always walk slowly, a bit stiff, as though he's in pain?'

'Oh, he's hobbled about like that for years. He has arthritis. It gets quite bad this time of year. The cold, you know. Why?' Esme asked, drying her cheeks with her apron.

'It just doesn't fit with the crime scene. He would have left shuffle marks in the snow. A few minutes after we found Lewis, Jonesy came up the hill in his tractor. I'm guessing that if he had fired the gun, there would have either been shuffle marks outside or, if he had run through the house escaping out the back door, there would have either been tractor tracks leading away or shuffle tracks leading into the forest. There were neither.'

'So, you know he didn't do it?'

'I'm sure he didn't. And I've told Constable Campbell as much. Esme, would you mind if I saw the front door from inside the house.'

'Of course.' Esme struggled to her feet. 'Follow me.'

The interior of the house was old, stately, and well looked after. A Christmas tree stood at the foot of a grand staircase that swept its way up another two floors. Vast landscapes, portraits and stuffed animal heads, which Jessica chose to ignore, covered the walls, while luxurious curtains hung at every window.

'Here we are, lass.'

'Esme, do you know the DC? I'm guessing everyone knows everyone around here. What's his reputation like, as a policeman?'

'Oh, that would be me stumbling into gossip,' Esme winced.

'I don't want you to gossip. Not at all. But anything you can tell me could help Jonesy.'

Taking her apron in her hands, Esme led Jessica into the front lounge. 'I was in here about a month ago. Mr and Mrs Wallace were expecting guests, and I was making sure everything was shipshape. You know, before they arrived.'

'Go on,' Jessica encouraged.

'Well, Mr and Mrs Wallace were in the study.' She pointed towards a closed door across the hall. 'It was Mr Wallace's private room. I'd never seen Mrs Wallace in there before.'

'What were they doing?'

'Arguing.' Esme was hesitant. 'Mr Wallace was accusing his wife of cheating.'

'Cheating? Who with?'

'Oh, I really don't know if I should say.'

'Esme, I know I'm putting you in a position, but we both know that Jonesy's innocent. If we're going to prove it, the tiniest piece of information could be crucial.'

'It was the DC.' Esme replied, reluctantly.

'The DC?' Jessica gasped.

Esme nodded. 'Mrs Wallace denied it, but he didn't believe her. Said she was lying. It got quite heated.'

'Were you aware of anything that would suggest Mrs Wallace was having an affair with the DC, or anyone else for that matter?'

Esme shook her head, 'Mrs Wallace is too, well, she's nice, you know. Far too good for Mr Wallace. He didn't treat her well, but then he didn't treat anyone well.'

'Where is Mrs Wallace now?'

'She gone off to collect their son from the station. She left just before you arrived, she'll be another twenty minutes or so.'

'And her son is coming from-.'

'London, he works for Mrs Wallace's family. He'll be taking over things here now, though.'

'Not Mrs Wallace?'

'No, the estate's always gone to the eldest son.'

'Could I have a look in Mr Wallace's study.'

'Oh, I don't know.'

'I won't touch anything, I promise.'

'You've got ten minutes, but that's all.'

Dark, dingy, and disorganised were the words that sprung to mind as Jessica opened the door. The curtains were drawn all but a few inches. A faint stench of tobacco hung in the air. A decanter, with its lid sitting to the side suggested Mr Wallace had been disturbed.

Photographs on the mantelpiece looked dated. And as Jessica leaned in for a closer look, she quickly discovered that Mr Wallace had been in the army. Most of the images were of his army life, comrades, and ceremonies. None were of his wife. Jessica was just about to move on when one photograph caught her eye.

It had to be at least thirty years old, but Jessica was sure the officer standing by Mr Wallace's side was Jonesy. Unlike the other photographs, it didn't appear to have been taken on an army base. There were no official buildings in the background or flags at full mast. Her gaze fell to a third man, standing to the other side of Jonesy. Studying his features, Jessica had an uneasy feeling.

Taking her phone from her pocket, she captured the image of the three men before turning her attention to the desk. Sitting against the opposite wall, paperwork covered every inch. A drawer sat open.

The surrounding walls were cluttered. Mostly landscapes, apart from a world map that was pinned to the wall above the desk. A section from the Middle East had been torn away.

'Jessica' Esme, interrupted, 'Mrs Wallace will be back soon, you should leave.'

'You're back. Finally.' Chloe sighed.

'What's up?' Jessica stomped snow from her boots. 'Do you fancy hot chocolate by the fire?'

'Never mind that, I've just been speaking to Douglas.'

'And.'

'He let slip that he was in the village yesterday morning.'

'That's impossible, he and Esme were away. They cut their trip short when they heard about Mr Wallace.'

'Well, I'm telling you, he was in the village yesterday morning. So was Esme.'

'He told you this?'

'Not at first. But when I pointed out that he had let it slip, he told me everything. When he and Esme started working for Mr

34

Wallace, they decided to keep their own house at the edge of the village. You see, the main workers all live on the grounds of the estate. But, Douglas said, sometimes they just needed to get away from Mr Wallace. Sounds like he was horrendous to work for.'

Pacing the floor, Jessica stopped to stoke the fire. 'Being away would have given them the perfect alibi. Mrs Wallace, too, for that matter.'

'But?'

'I'm not sure yet. Oh, that reminds me,' Jessica pulled her phone from her pocket, 'Apart from Mr Wallace, do you recognise anyone else in this photo?'

'That's Jonesy.' Chloe pointed.

'Yup, anyone else look familiar?'

'Oh, I don't know. The other guy looks vaguely familiar. He has the same creepy look that Liam had when he was having a go yesterday.'

'Yes. Yes, he does.' Marching to the kitchen. 'We need hot chocolate, and a plan of the estate.'

'Where are we going to get a plan?'

'Internet, hopefully. It doesn't have to be overly accurate, just a rough idea of the boundaries and where the tracks lead through the estate. And we need to speak to Constable Campbell.'

Later that afternoon, Jessica opened the door to Constable Campbell and Detective Constable Smeaton.

'This had better be worth my time.' the DC quipped.

'It is.' Jessica replied, holding her nerve. 'Please, take a seat.'

The DC slumped onto the sofa with a sigh as big as his stature. 'So, out with it.'

'It wasn't Jonesy.'

'How dare you.' The DC jumped to his feet. 'Who do you

think you are to summon me and tell me I've not done my job properly.'

'I'm sorry, that wasn't my intention. But I know Jonesy is innocent.'

'We're here, we might as well listen to what she has to say, Sir.' Constable Campbell interjected, nervously.

The DC reluctantly retook his seat. 'You've five minutes.'

'Jonesy was nowhere near the house at the time of the murder.'

'We found a gun, the bullet that killed Owen Wallace matched the gun. Jonesy's prints were on the gun. Case closed.'

'And Mr Wallace's prints were also on the gun.' Jessica replied.

'How did you know that.'

'Because I'm pretty sure Mr Wallace was in his study when the killer knocked on the front door.'

'And?'

'I suspect he hadn't gotten round to opening his curtains, but when he heard the knock at the door, he opened one, just enough to see who was there. That's when he took the gun from a drawer in his desk. The drawer was then left open.'

'And do you have any suspects, Miss Winter?'

'I-I have two.' She stuttered, nervously.

'Two?' The DC got to his feet to leave.

'Yes.' Taking her phone from her pocket. 'Do you recognise this man?'

With the DC refusing to look, Constable Campbell stepped forward. 'The, eh, the guy on the other side of Jonesy?'

'Yes', Jessica pushed.

'He looks a bit like Liam.'

'That's because he's Liam's father.'

'How can you know that? The DC scowled.'

'Because I've confirmed it.' A voice, stern but broken appeared from the hallway.

'It's okay, Liam, take a seat.' Jessica reassured. 'Mr Wallace and Jonesy were in the army together, that's why Jonesy was one of the few people Mr Wallace had time for. But there had been a third friend. I've no idea what happened to that friendship, but Liam's father moved away long before Liam was born. He'd always spoken fondly of growing up here, so when Liam was looking for a fresh start, he came here.

Mr Wallace had realised who Liam was and gave him a job. Not because he needed an extra labourer. I'm pretty sure something happened between Mr Wallace, Jonesy, and Liam's father when they served together in the Middle East. And I'm willing to bet that Mr Wallace covered up for Liam's father in some way. Something he paid for until the day he moved away. When Liam turned up, Mr Wallace took the chance to regain that power. Now, I can't be sure. But given the position Jonesy has found himself in, I'm pretty sure he'll talk. But you knew all that, didn't you, Detective Constable Smeaton.'

Jessica didn't take her eyes off the DC. Determined to hold her nerve, she ignored the cramping churns in her stomach.

'Now just you wait a minute.' The DC scrambled to his feet. 'I'd think very carefully before saying another word, Miss Winter.'

'Oh, I've been thinking about nothing else.' She quipped. 'You were also in the army, weren't you? You know exactly what hold Mr Wallace had over Liam's father because you were part of it.'

'Miss Winter.' The DC roared.

Stepping between the DC and Jessica, Constable Campbell urged her to continue.

Jessica could see how nervous the Constable was, but the relief at having him on side gave her the confidence to continue. A knock at the door broke the tension.

'I'll get it.' Chloe announced.

Seconds later Douglas followed Chloe into the living room.

'Any luck, Douglas.' Jessica asked.

'Oh, yeah. He's been bedded down in one of the old cottages on the other side of the hill.'

'The one that backs onto the railway station?'

Douglas nodded, 'He's gone now, probably caught a train yesterday or early this morning.'

Jessica turned to Liam, 'I'm so sorry.'

Liam was sitting with his head in his hands, 'He did it for me? Whatever you're about to insinuate, if he had a chance to get rid of Mr Wallace, he did it for me. That man treated me like a piece of meat and my dad never forgave him for that,'

'It's not quite as straightforward as you might think, Liam.' Jessica consoled. 'The DC was blackmailing your dad, weren't you.' Turning to DC Smeaton. 'Your dad felt he had no option but to do as the DC told him.'

'But why would the DC want Mr Wallace dead?' Constable Campbell interrupted.

'Because he's in love with Mrs Wallace. Isn't that right.' Jessica turned to the DC.

The following evening, Esme had gathered everyone together for a celebratory dinner in honour of Jonesy's release.

Content and full, Jessica sunk into the sofa. Esme's roast beef dinner, the Christmas tree, roaring fire, and festive music humming quietly beneath the chatter, had rendered Jessica the most relaxed she had felt since leaving Simon.

Constable Campbell took the seat beside her, 'When do you leave?'

I'm supposed to be here for another three weeks.'

Supposed to be?'

'Yeah.' Giving Douglas a cheeky grin as he topped up her glass on the passing.

'You're leaving early.'

'On the contrary, I signed a lease earlier today, I'm staying on in Myre Cottage indefinitely.'

'You are?'

Yup.'

'In that case, call me Mark.' He smiled, clinking his glass against hers.

BIO

Pauline Tait is an award-winning and bestselling children's author, romantic suspense novelist, and the voice behind *Reluctant Readers*, a weekly newsletter for parents and carers of children who are reluctant to read. Based in Perthshire, Scotland, Pauline is currently midway through writing her latest bestselling romantic suspense series set on the Scottish Isle of Skye. She is also a professional writing and publishing mentor for children's authors. Her signature six-week programme, *How to Write a Children's Picture Book from Concept to Publication*, has been praised for guiding aspiring authors smoothly toward publication, with her clients going on to win awards.

Https://www.paulinetait.com

Chapter Three

MERRY CHRISTMAS, GEORGIA

Sue Cook

C hristmas turns chaotic when trainee PI Georgia is put on the spot by her meddling mother. With missing presents to find and a quagmire of matchmaking to negotiate, Christmas will be a disaster unless she can wrap up the festive mess before the turkey hits the table. Can she and Mike, her grumpy boss, do it? Of course! But there's a nasty surprise in Santa's sack. Will this put them off their current case or provide the breakthrough they've been seeking?

Georgia and Mike are characters from a cozy crime series in the fictional small town of Wellihole, Yorkshire.

'Twas the night before Christmas and all around town
    The Griffiths clan members were settling down
    The children all sleeping, the parents on gin
    A magical day was about to begin.
    Except for young Georgia, around at her mum's
    Still wrapping up gifts for the grand day to come
    From sparkly stockings and colouring pens
    To fake severed fingers and singing red hens,
    Stink bombs and joke books and Christmassy caps
    They were two hours in, with still lots to wrap
    Oh, Mum! Georgie cried as she stared at the pile
    My poor wrists are sore. Can we stop for a while?
    So they paused for a pie and a snifter of sherry
    And before very long, the two were quite merry.
    Then giggling gaily, they started again.
    And kept right on at it till nothing remained.
    The wrapping thus finished, the tape put away
    They piled all the gifts in a toy wooden sleigh
    Where sitting beneath the fake tree they looked jolly
    All topped off with tinsel and sprigs of real holly.
    With a last good look round, checking nothing's amiss
    'Good night to you, Mum,' Georgia said with a kiss
    'It's time to go home. I'll be getting along.'
    And with everything set what could possibly go wrong?

The shriek of the landline woke me. It would be my mother. I only have a landline because she pays for it so I can't avoid her by pretending my mobile is out of battery. No one else uses it.

I picked up the receiver and pulled it under the duvet. 'Yup.'

'Georgia. That's no way to answer the phone.'

'Merry Christmas, Mum. Is that better?' I rearranged my duvet to eliminate icy draughts from my freezing bedroom.

'There's nothing merry about it, Georgie, not with what's happened.'

I did a mental eye roll. 'Oh?' My mother knows everyone and everything in Wellihole, West Yorkshire, but what sort of news would justify a Christmas morning wake-up call, especially after I'd left her only ten hours before?

She told me. 'The presents are gone.'

'What presents?'

'The ones we wrapped last night and put under the tree.'

Suddenly I was wide awake. 'What! All of them?' Two presents for each of my sibs (one from me and one from Mum), plus one to each other makes fourteen, and two for each grand-child/niece/nephew added up to around... er... Okay, I wasn't *entirely* wide awake, but how could a whole sleighful of Christmas presents disappear overnight?

'Yes, every last one. Gone. I came into the living room to switch the fairy lights back on because they're so cheerful, aren't they? And there they were. Gone.'

'You've looked?' I asked. 'Everywhere?'

'What a silly billy I am. I didn't check under the floorboards. Should I go and rip up the carpets?'

I sat up and reached for warm clothes, knowing she'd expect me to go round for moral support. At least it would be warm there. Summer and winter, her thermostat is set to twenty-two degrees. Centigrade. Me? These days I often have to choose between heating and eating.

'That's impossible,' I said, while forcing my head through the rollneck of a base layer without removing my flannel pyjamas.

'Obviously not, else they'd still be here. What are you going to do about it?'

'Me?' I paused with one arm halfway down a sleeve.

'You're the private detective, Georgie, not me.'

'Trainee,' I corrected her, then shifted the receiver to my other ear so I could push my other arm down the other sleeve before I got hypothermia.

'Georgie, you single-handedly tracked down a killer after only a few weeks in the job. A couple of missing presents should be easy. You have to save Christmas before the children arrive. I couldn't bear to see those little faces when they hear that Nan and Auntie Georgia didn't get them anything.'

Oh, that's right. Drag Auntie Georgia into it.

I could have argued that I found the killer by luck when I was hunting for goods stolen from Wright Good Pies pie factory, but this was my mother I was talking to, and reason never entered her conversations.

'I'm on my way,' I replied. 'Though honestly, Mum, I'm not sure what I can do.'

As soon as I'd finished dressing, I called Mike, my boss.

He, too, was barely awake. 'Why involve me?' he asked, not unreasonably.

'Who's coming, inexplicably, to Christmas lunch at my mother's house?' I asked. His presence at the Griffiths family Christmas lunch was, in fact, perfectly explicable. Jean Griffiths, my mum, views Mike Moore as the next Mr Georgia, as he owns his own business and is reeling from his split with his wife, Tanya, who left him for a private gynae-cologist with an enormous house and a yellow Ferrari. Mike, with his near bankrupt PI business and 10-year-old grey Mondeo, can't compete with that, and most of the time he is, frankly, a grumpy ass. I'm not surprised Tanya left him. Anyway, Mum is smooching him into marrying me, her youngest daughter and the only child so far to fail to produce grandchildren in the traditional Griffiths rabbit-like fashion.

But... No way am I admitting to her that Mike and I had a brief and surprisingly enjoyable fling after the fingers-in-pies case, as I called it, although no body parts went into the pie mix at any time. It would be another thing she wouldn't let me forget. But great sex wasn't enough, and Mike and I both realised we were unsuitable life partners. Although we still fancied each other, we were, unless desperate, keeping strictly separate bedrooms. So it was particularly galling that Mike accepted my mother's hospitality when he knew what she was up to.

I walked to Mum's and met Mike at her front gate. On the face of it, he's the most unremarkable forty-ish man you could hope to meet, one of those people you instantly forget. That's a bonus for a private detective, which is, I guess, why he cultivates his 'nothing to see here' persona. Underneath he's a surprising bundle of skills, many of which I'm sure I haven't discovered yet.

That day, he'd ditched his signature 'slept-in' shades-of-beige wardrobe and was wearing a dark green cargo jacket and complementary pine-coloured, crease-free chinos. He was less beige man and more Cotton Traders man. Mum would love that, and I suspected he knew it.

We hesitated, shuffling our feet in front of the 1960s semidetached house with its perfect paintwork, gleaming windows and new resin drive. We knew we had to enter, but crikey was it an effort of will!

'Anything new on the Atwood case?' I asked to delay the inevitable. Teddy Atwood was a local entrepreneur with many business operations. He had engaged us to prove him innocent of murder after an illegal immigrant was found dead in a detached Victorian house that had been turned into a cannabis farm. The police suspected him because he owned the house and had received an anonymous text message asking to meet him 'at the farm' where there was 'a problem'. He had duly turned up, as nearby CCTV images proved. But he didn't call in the death – another anonymous tipoff did.

Nobody believed Teddy did it: anything that involved cash under the counter and creative accounting, yes, but shooting someone on his own property? Definitely not.

Unfortunately, he couldn't prove his innocence without admitting that he knew about the cannabis farm in a house he had supposedly let to a professional family. I also couldn't see him employing illegal immigrants. Legal immigrants at or below minimum wage, yes.

'You think I've got new information since yesterday?' Mike asked. 'Christmas Eve?'

I shrugged. 'You never know.' In truth, we had hit a wall with that case. All leads had led nowhere. Neither of us thought Teddy was guilty, but we couldn't prove he was innocent, either. Soon we'd have to close the case and admit failure. This would dent the agency's reputation and our individual egos. I tried not to think about cash flow or the threat my mortgage was under. If I couldn't keep up the payments on that, I'd be moving back in with my mother.

I shuddered at the thought. One little breakthrough would make my Christmas and New Year happy.

After an awkward silence spent staring at the house, Mike said, 'What do you expect me to do?'

'Mike, I have no idea what I can do, but no way are you coming to lunch without helping me.'

We headed for the back door. Inside, my mother was ransacking the kitchen cupboards.

'Mum?'

She straightened up, looking flushed. 'Oh! Thank goodness you're here. I've looked everywhere. Twice.'

'They won't be in the cereal cupboard,' I pointed out.

'I know that. But they must be somewhere.'

We all mooched through to the living room, where the multi-coloured lights shed a happy rainbow glow on a bare cream carpet and an empty plywood sleigh.

'Any signs of a break-in?' Mike asked. 'Windows forced. Doors open? Anything else missing?'

'No, nothing.'

'At least the kids aren't here yet,' I said. We had a brief interval in which to remedy the situation, or at least prepare everyone for Santa having forgotten Nan's house. 'It would be awful if... Oh hi, you two.'

The six-year-old twins of my brother Tex had appeared in a

doorway. 'What are you doing here?' I added, more to my mother than to them.

She didn't respond.

It shouldn't be possible to have identical brother and sister twins, but I couldn't for the life of me tell Tina and Tim apart. Their mother insisted on giving them identical haircuts and now, with their reindeer jimjams and bright red, puffy eyes, it was more difficult than ever.

'Merry Christmas,' I said. They burst into tears. Looks like they already knew the situation.

'Now look what you've done.' Mum hurried forward and hugged them to her broad hips. 'Don't worry. Aunty Georgia will sort it out. Probably Santa got confused and took them by accident. Thought he'd dropped them at the wrong house or something.'

'Yes. Private detectives have a hotline to all mythical people.' I said flatly.

'What's mythical?' Tina and Tim asked in unison.

'It's like an old-fashioned superhero,' Mum said while flashing those eyes at me that meant 'toe the party line or else'. To the kids she added, 'Santa had already been when you arrived last night, hadn't he?'

They nodded, then Tina, or perhaps Tim, disentangled him- or herself from my mother and told me, 'We saw him, didn't we, Tina?' The child who had not spoken nodded.

'You saw Santa take the presents?' I asked with incredulity.

'We saw Santa,' Tim corrected. 'In the middle of the night.'

Mum gawped at them. Seems like there was one piece of gossip she'd missed.

I turned to Mike. 'Looks like we have eyewitnesses, and reliable ones, too. This will be a doddle.'

'I'm sure your Auntie Georgia will solve this in no time,' he assured them. I narrowed my eyes and got a twitch of a smile in return.

Glaring at my mother, I added, 'I thought Tex's family wasn't coming until lunchtime.'

'Well,' she began, 'you remember their mum had a teensy-weensy little procedure at the hospital?' I nodded. It rang a vague bell, though I couldn't for the life of me remember what she'd had done. There was so much to keep track of in our family.

'Last night she was feeling a bit over-tired. So after you went home, Tex rang to ask if Tina and Tim could stay here so Mummy could rest this morning.' Mum raised her hand to shield her lips from the children and mouthed 'in case he had to take her back to hospital.' 'And here they are, aren't you?'

Tim nodded. 'We seed all the presents when we got here. And we heard Santa come, and we got up and seed him, but we only seed him eat the biscuit and the sherry Nan left out, and then he went out the door and drove off in his van.'

'Van?' I echoed. 'Not a sleigh?'

'No. It sounded like a one point five litre diesel Transit Connect,' Tim said without blinking.

I blinked quite a lot before remembering that Tex owns a corporate fleet hire company, and although Tim might never be a top-grade English student, he is a junior petrol head.

'Go on,' I said. 'This is great stuff.'

'We thought he'd brung more presents,' – Tim broke off to sniff – 'but when we come downstairs this morning, they was all gone.'

'Santa stole our presents,' Tina wailed, as if I hadn't got the message.

'That must be a mistake. But can I check what Santa looked like?'

'Big. Fat.' Tina's arms traced the biggest circle they could.

'White hair,' Tim added.

'Dressed in red.'

Okay. That sounded like Santa.

'You will find him, won't you, Auntie Georgia?' they wailed in unison, eyes brimming with tears and hope, bigger and moister than that manipulative Pusscat in *Shrek*.

Jeepers. No pressure. I turned to Mike. 'How hard can it be to find a super-sized fella in a Santa suit on Christmas Day?'

'Harder than on Christmas Eve,' he replied.

I narrowed my eyes at him, but before I could respond, Tina asked, 'Are you going to search for clues?'

'You bet, aren't we, partner?'

'Always a great first step,' Mike said.

We toured the house to ensure Mum hadn't missed anything but found all the doors locked and the windows secure.

'What are these?' I asked when we discovered two bin bags of wrapped presents in the cupboard under the stairs.

Mum tutted. 'Your cousin Adam is supposed to collect those. Presents for the kids at the Methodist Church Christmas lunch, donated by the knit and natter group. The minister throws a Christmas Day lunch for single parents, especially those without other family.'

A light popped on in my head. 'When's he coming?'

She checked her watch, twisting the gold link strap a quarter of the way round her wrist to where she could read the face. 'You're right. He should have been by now. He said he might come last night. I'd better ring and check.'

Mike and I exchanged knowing glances. I hauled out my mobile. 'I'll phone him. We can take these over. Mike and I need to search for Santa, anyway.'

'Any chance of a cuppa, Jean?' Mike asked in the smooth voice he reserves for clients. 'I haven't had one yet today. We can discuss lunch while Georgia's on the phone. I made chocolate mousse.'

Adam had, of course, come round late the previous evening, let himself in with the key under the flowerpot, and taken the wrong presents.

"Why didn't you take the ones under the stairs like Mum said?" I asked.

"I was shattered, Georgie. Barely awake. Hadn't eaten for hours and my sugar levels were low. Didn't finish till gone eleven – you've no idea what it's like being a delivery driver at Christmas. I saw a heap of presents and I took them."

And so, job done, he ate the Santa snack for his low sugar. Mystery solved.

'Good job you came in your car,' I told Mike, after our teas. 'Mine is way too small.'

'Can we come?' Tina and Tim bounced to their feet and continued bouncing.

'We won't have room. Not for two big people, two little people and all those presents,' I said. 'But we need someone to watch the tree, in case Santa comes back before we catch up with him, plus someone to help Grandma with the sprouts.'

'I hate sprouts,' Tim said.

'I'll watch the tree.' Tina plonked herself in front of it, cross-legged, her chin resting in her hands, eyes trained on the six-foot, silver tinsel and LED confection that put my little spider plant draped in a few strands of curled red wrapping ribbon to shame.

Tim wasn't having that and pushed his sister over. We left them fighting and loaded the bin bags into Mike's boot.

'So, Cousin Adam,' he opened as he pulled away from the kerb, heading for the other side of town.

'Haven't seen him for several years,' I admitted. 'Was a para. Really fit. Abs to die for, yomped for days on end without breathing.'

'I feel inadequate,' Mike said.

'Don't. He's a delivery driver now. All that muscle turned to flab, making him the perfect shape for a Santa costume.'

'And he has white hair?'

I frowned. 'It used to be brown. Maybe he's going grey.'

'We all do.' He took a long look in the mirror before turning left. I wondered if he was checking his own first few silvery strands and they were making him feel his age. Let's be honest, it's the start of a slippery middle-aged slope that leads precipitously to sheep-skin slippers, comparing hot water bottles online, and looking forward to coffee and cake at the garden centre on Fridays.

I fought down the urge to rest my hand on his forearm and utter reassuring platitudes. Our relationship was complicated, and he might assume he was on for a very personal Christmas present later.

We drove the rest of the distance to Adam's in silence, the potholed streets empty as everyone else enjoyed a lie-in followed by chocolate and a Buck's Fizz eye opener in their onesies.

Adam and family live in a terraced house that fronts onto the pavement. The kerbs were rammed with vehicles because no one was at work, so we parked a hundred yards away and strolled back to rap ineffectively on the PVC door.

'Why don't people have doorbells on these things?' Mike muttered in a good imitation of Scrooge on a bad day. 'You can't knock on the stuff, and the letter boxes are rubbish, too.' To demonstrate, he smashed the gold-coloured plastic rectangle against more gold-coloured plastic with a faint 'whump'.

By heck, was he grumpier than usual today.

I yelled through said letter box to make ourselves heard above the noise of a six-person household crammed into a space built for two.

'Hey, Merry Christmas, Georgie.' Adam, beaming and filling the doorway, leaned forward and kissed my cheek.

'Same to you, coz.'

'Is this Mike?'

'Obviously,' Mike said. His eyes travelled up to Adam's thick, brown mane. 'We expected white hair.'

'White? Who gave you that idea?' Adam moved inside, and we stepped out of the cold, grey day as I explained he'd been spotted at Mum's house. We were soon all squeezed into the square back room decorated with white wood chip, a tinsel tree bigger than Mum's and Minecraft frozen on the wall-mounted TV screen. The aroma of sprouts pervaded everything.

'Hi Georgia,' his wife called from the kitchen. 'Buck's Fizz?'

'Merry Christmas, Brittany,' I called. 'And no thanks. We're working. Wouldn't refuse a coffee, though.' Mike and I were both under-caffeinated that morning. We'd normally had a couple of mugs each from his gleaming espresso machine by now, which might explain his worse than usual mood. Also, socialising would keep us out longer, making it look like we'd worked harder.

We chatted over four hot mugs and established that Adam wore a Santa costume on his Christmas Eve shift. Tina and Tim must have mistaken the fur trim for hair in the dark.

After we'd drained our mugs, it was time to do the swap.

'Where's your van?' I asked.

'Out back.' Adam jerked his thumb towards the small yard and the cobbled ginnel beyond.

A few minutes later, Mike and I were walking between the two rows of backyard walls, each with a bag of presents destined for families who had little. Adam came out of his place, startled and yelled, 'Hey!'

He sidestepped away from us along the side of the van before pounding down the ginnel.

Mike dropped his sack, said, 'Watch this,' and ran after Adam.

I assumed he was referring to his sack, not his Usain Bolt impression, so I picked it up and wrestled both bags to the back of the van. From there, I could see Adam at the far end of the ginnel, his hands on his knees, breathing hard. Of Mike, there was no sign. A tinny motorbike started up in the next street.

The van's back doors were open. I checked the model details – 1.5L diesel Connect – and felt a warm glow of pride for my little nephew with the shocking grammar.

Then, holding my breath, I peered inside... and relaxed. The bin bags were still present, though the floor was littered with gifts. Looked like we'd arrived just in time, and Christmas would still be merry.

'What happened?' I asked when the boys returned.

Adam's face was red, his hands bunched into huge, white-knuckled fists. 'I disturbed two scrotes in the back of the van. It should be empty today. How did they know?'

'It must be common knowledge you're taking presents to the Methodist Church,' I pointed out. 'I bet some of those single mums have shady ex-partners.'

He made a noise that suggested it was possible, he supposed, but he didn't believe it for a second. 'This never happened before. It must be you, Georgie,' he said. 'You attract bad karma!'

'Me? Cheeky so-and-so.'

'Who only gets jobs in companies that go bust?'

As a 'valued employee' who had suffered serial redundancy, that was too close to the truth for comfort. 'Mike hasn't gone bust,' I countered.

'Yet,' Mike muttered.

'The bank didn't go bust, either.'

'It only survived by sacking a chunk of people,' Adam pointed out. 'Including you.'

'Children, children,' Mike said. 'This is getting us nowhere. We need to check the presents. See if anything's missing.'

This made sense. I climbed into the van and took stock. Two presents for each of my sibs and each of their kids, plus one for me from my mum and one from me to her. Thirty-eight in total. I jumped out again. 'All present and correct. We must have disturbed them in time.'

We did the swap, said our goodbyes, then set off home in the Mondeo. I noticed a grim set to Mike's mouth.

'What?'

He checked his mirror. 'This wasn't random.'

'Pardon?'

'The two lads we chased jumped onto a motor scooter.' He

checked the mirror again. 'I noticed it behind us on the way over. I thought it was strange that two guys were out together on Christmas morning, but, hey, why not? Maybe they just got a new scooter.'

'I didn't see anything,' I said.

'You were looking ahead. I saw them in the rear-view mirror. They kept well back.'

'I thought you were checking for grey hairs,' I admitted.

'Grey hairs? What grey hairs?' He leaned over to peer in the mirror.

'You've only got a few. I think they look distinguished.'

He glanced at me. 'I think I got them from employing you!'

What was this? Pick on Georgia day? 'This is off the point, Mike. You were telling me about the bikers?'

'Right. They followed us.'

That seemed obvious now. 'But why?'

'As they broke into Adam's van while we were chatting, I guess they wanted something from there.'

'What could they want with a load of inexpensive kids' presents?' I thought aloud. 'And how did they know where we were going and why?'

Mike stopped at a red light, and we both stared at the large, cluttered shoulder bag I carry everywhere. It wouldn't be the first time someone dropped a bug in there. I rummaged through it and found the offending article. Mike disabled it.

This was getting tedious. I needed to buy a new bag. One that zipped up.

'Did you get the registration number?' I asked as we moved off.

'Only a partial.' He gave me four digits and letters.

'We should stop and check the presents more thoroughly,' I said. 'We don't want any nasty surprises later.' Tina, say, ripping cheery paper off a decapitated doll, or Tim discovering a selection box with each bar opened and a bite taken out. They'd be scarred for life. I'd be scarred for life, too, although I'd still offer to help Tim out with the violated chocolate bars.

Mike pulled over. We opened the boot, and he helped me keep things organised as I checked each gift for signs of tampering. Nothing. It was all very odd.

'So we did arrive in time,' I said.

'Mmm,' he replied, his lips pushed out in thought.

I knew what he meant. He didn't believe in coincidences, and my crime fiction addiction told me that no decent detective did either. Still, what could be wrong?

We made a detour to our respective homes to freshen up and collect our contributions to lunch, then delivered Christmas.

Tina and Tim threw themselves on me and declared me their superhero. My mother gave Mike a massive hug. While my little helpers and I piled the presents back into the sleigh, Mum poured out two tumblers of Buck's Fizz.

Alcohol gives my inhibitions the day off, leaving me liable to throw myself at the nearest available male. My mother knows this.

Sensing her cunning plan, but not wanting to fall for it, I set my glass aside. 'I need something to eat first, Mum.' My stomach growled in agreement.

Mum glanced at the wall clock decorated with plastic mistletoe. It said half eleven. 'Didn't you have breakfast?'

'When? You woke me up, and I ran straight over.'

She looked at Mike. 'Me neither,' he said. 'Toast would be fine. Perhaps with a little cheddar, if you have any?'

Toast and cheese it was, with a Buck's Fizz chaser. Some family members arrived with more gifts for the pile; others were coming after lunch. By the time fourteen of us had eaten every sprout, pig in a blanket and crumb of steamed pudding, we were warm, full and merry. Mike's bowl of chocolate mousse had been licked so clean it looked like it had been washed already. My discount mince pies had been earmarked for snacks after The King.

'Presents!' Mum announced to whoops from the kids. 'And we all have to thank Georgia and Mike for saving Christmas.'

She proposed a toast, to which everyone hurrahed except Mike and me. We took cursory sips and exchanged nervous glances; the horrible niggle that we'd missed something wouldn't go away.

One by one, presents were opened and found to be exactly what the recipient wanted. Steadily, as nasty surprises failed to materialise, we both relaxed. I was touched when Mike said, 'Merry Christmas, Georgia,' and handed me a squishy, shapeless gift that looked like he sat on it on the way over. I hadn't expected anything from him, and my throat choked. After a glass of wine on top of the Buck's Fizz, my inhibitions were dozing in front of the living-flame fire with their feet up. Mike, the only available man, was looking sexy.

'I didn't get you one, Mike,' I told him.

He shrugged. 'Christmas bonus from the boss.'

Inside I found three packs of ground coffee. I smiled and hugged him a bit too long. He eased me away as I was about to drop a kiss in his ear.

When I got back to my seat, my mother had topped up my wineglass and was resting back in her armchair with a self-satisfied smile.

Finally, everyone had finished opening their gifts except me. I'd been watching and waiting for the nasty shock, sipping the wine for Dutch courage.

'Come on, Georgie,' Mum said. 'We can't wait all day for you. The King will be on soon.'

Right! We couldn't keep Charles waiting. I opened some fluffy socks from Lou, cheap but fun earrings from other family members, and last of all an envelope from my mum. She had tucked the flap in rather than stuck it down. I flipped it open and took out a Waitrose Xmas card. My eyes opened wide in surprise. Food gift tokens! Even better than quality coffee, and I hadn't expected it.

As I opened the card, my mum wittered on about how I was struggling for money and thought she'd get me a token so I could treat myself to top-notch food. 'You could even invite someone over,' she added, her eyes flicking to Mike and away again. 'You should get two meal-deals for two with that.'

I stopped listening then because contained within the card was not the expected voucher. I stared at the printed words and knew we hadn't got to Adam's van in time. Looking up, I caught Mike's eye. The almost imperceptibly raised eyebrow told me he sensed something was wrong.

'Thanks, Mum,' I said. 'That's just what I need.'

I handed the card to Mike. His face remained impassive as he read: 'Drop Atwood or else. We know your family.'

Someone didn't want us proving Teddy Atwood was innocent. To me, this meant only one thing: we were getting close. Why bother to threaten us if we hadn't a clue? Unfortunately for them, that only increased my determination to succeed. If I thought we were truly washed up, I'd lose interest.

'What an unusual gift, Jean,' Mike said, smiling at Mum while handing the card back to me. 'I'll make sure Georgia does something good with that.'

My mother waffled about what a marvellous cook he was and how I'd have to drive a fair way to shop at the nearest Waitrose, but it would be worth it, she was sure. Mike listened attentively, showing no outward sign of the emotions I knew must be churning within him.

Solving Atwood's case was good publicity for the firm and would attract a much-needed bonus. Most locals would be happy, too, because although everyone knew Teddy was on the take, he was well-liked and a good landlord, providing affordable flats and terraced houses that were in reasonable shape. He also contributed a lot to local charities (offset against tax, but even so...)

But was it worth risking my family's safety? That's how Mike would be thinking. He'd decide no and tell me to drop the case.

Me? I was thinking of wreaking revenge on the toe rags who had stolen thirty quid's worth of prime food. Did they have to take the voucher when they left their threatening message? Were two lads on a bike going to shop in Waitrose? Really?

And why did they go to all that effort? They could have dropped the message in my bag along with the bug. Or pushed it through Mum's letter box while we were scoffing turkey.

True, if they'd just dropped the note in my bag, I'd probably have ignored it. Substituting a personal present with a personal threat on Christmas day with my family around? That took nerve and knowledge. That implied they knew a lot about me and my family.

Except they didn't, did they?

They got caught doing the swap and presumably had only known about the missing Christmas presents because of the bug and following us. With that information they decided to make the discovery more... dramatic. More personal. Like with the murdered lad. They hadn't needed to put Teddy at the scene. Calling in the death would have sufficed. Teddy wouldn't want police snooping around that house and asking awkward questions.

They were showmen. Confident, arrogant, maybe, and telling their adversaries that they were in control and fearless, so don't mess with them. Which fitted with young men on scooters, perhaps.

But also they thought Mike and I had enough information – or nearly enough – to solve the case. Which meant we probably had.

'I'm going upstairs for a nap,' I announced. 'All that food and wine...' Not to mention an early start, huge excitement and subtropical heat.

I shut myself in my old bedroom, lay on the single bed and unlocked my phone. The numbers on the registration plate included all the random ones, as opposed to the area and year of manufacture codes. Making plausible assumptions, I soon had a name that had already cropped up in the investigation. I made a few phone calls to the younger, more chilled out members of the Griffiths clan and confirmed a theory about young blood trying to push Teddy out of the reasonably priced, locally grown weed market. Maybe they were trying to push him out of other markets he largely controlled too. The betting shop, the second-hand car dealership and other businesses useful for money laundering.

This case was as good as solved. One quiet word in the ear of Mike's detective friend, one threatening letter dusted for finger-prints (I hadn't touched the actual note, and Mike hadn't, either), and that would be that. No one need know the police hadn't got there by themselves. Except Teddy, of course. I just had to persuade Mike of that.

Easy peasy.

I closed my eyes and smiled. This had been just what I needed for Christmas.

BIO

Sue Cook writes short and long stories for the women's fiction market. Her novels include contemporary or historical romance sprinkled with crime, intrigue or suspense. You will find her short stories in The People's Friend and My Weekly. She lives in a damp and windy corner of northwest England with her husband and five ducks. She finds writing a marvellous antidote to the urge to do housework.

https://suecookwrites.wordpress.com/contact/

Chapter Four

THE PROOF IS IN THE PUDDING

Wendy H. Jones

I n The Proof is in the Pudding, Ivy Macintosh has returned to her roots in a small Scottish village after years of working as a chef for Hollywood's elite. She's ready to embrace the slower pace of village life, especially as she and her eccentric best friend, Bunnie Chase, prepare to compete in the village's renowned Christmas Pudding Competition. But when celebrity chef Pierre Blanc, the competition's guest judge, is found dead, Ivy and Bunnie trade their aprons for detective hats. With a suspect list that stretches longer than a traditional Christmas recipe, the duo soon discover, in this village, secrets simmer beneath the surface and someone has stirred up more than just the holiday spirit.

Puddings and danger aren't words you usually hear together. Not unless Great Aunt Myrtle made the pudding but that's another story altogether, one best confined to history. Another type of history was being celebrated that day. For as long as anyone remembered, St. Jude's held the village annual Christmas Dessert Competition; rumour had it the competition was as old as Christianity itself. Mrs Mackay, who clung to the pudding organisation role like a mother with her newborn, looked as old as Christianity – and then some. Ivy Macintosh didn't give two hoots about any of this as she hurried through snow decked streets clutching a huge dish covered in a santa-decked tea towel.

'Why is there never any parking in this b...' She pulled herself up. 'Delightful village?'

'Because the council put 'no parking' signs up everywhere,' Ivy's best friend, Bunnie Chase, said, never one to avoid calling a spade a spade or the council a bunch of money-grabbing shysters. 'Hang on a minute.' She shifted her own large dish to get better purchase.

'We're definitely going to get placed this year.'

'If we ever freaking get there.'

The young women upped the pace leading to a near miss in the slip department.

'Whoa. Getting there under our own steam is better than in the back of an ambulance.'

Ivy, ignoring her friend, shoved open the door of the village hall with her shoulder, before catapulting into a scene of chaos and frazzled nerves. In contrast, the delightful aroma of sugary treats filled the room with festive cheer.

Bunnie wasn't quite so keen on Frank Sinatra blasting "White Christmas" from the speakers. 'How's a body meant to think with all this clatter going on.'

Ivy grinned as she deposited her, hopefully, prize-winning dessert on a table already groaning with entries. 'You're not. Thinking's not what we're here for, lassie. We're here to blow the competition out of the water.'

'You've no chance of that,' said a lanky man wearing a sneer like a badge of honour. 'I know Pierre Blanc personally. He has high standards.'

'I'm not sure why he chose you as a pal then, if those sorts of standards are his go to.' She turned her back on the weasel in a suit; Seamus Snowdrop and his opinions were not worth one iota of mental energy. Somehow space appeared on the table for Bunnie and her offering. Her huge tray landed on the table with a thump causing a seismic chain reaction amongst the other desserts.

'I see you two did not develop any finesse as you grew.' Mrs Mackay bustled over, bust quivering, bum swaying and clutching the obligatory huge handbag.

'Sorry, Mrs Mackay,' they said in unison. The tarragon in a pinny was their primary school teacher before she retired to terrorise the village at large and the congregation of St. Jude's in particular.

The room, already warm from over efficient central heating, shot up to Sahara levels as more hopeful entrants arrived. The mood oscillated between joyful and cranky with no time for anyone to prepare themselves either way. Someone could smile at you one minute and slap you the next.

Ivy whistled as Bunnie uncovered her creation – a magnificent snowball cheesecake with a sprig of real holly on the top. Dressed in green, red and white, her chic outfit matched it to flawlessness. 'Wow. Perfection on a plate.'

'My dear departed Grannie's recipe.'

'If that tastes as good as it looks your grannie should be immortalised and statues raised in her honour.'

Bunnie's face turned as bright as the berry on her cake. 'Let's see yours then.'

With a flourish worthy of the head chef at the Ritz, Ivy pulled the tea towel away from her offering. Silence fell as those around the table took in the perfectly spherical clootie dumpling that sat in all its shining glory, in a shimmering sea of sweetmeat. 'My mum's recipe.' Her lip quivered.

Bunnie put an arm round her. 'Your dear old ma would be proud,' she whispered in her friend's ear.

Ivy mustered up a feeble smile then whipped around at the sound of raised voices.

'You deliberately sabotaged my Bailley's trifle.' A woman wearing a denim smock and ginormous red ribbon in her hair towered over a tiny man.

'Get over yourself, it's nothing but stale cake and jelly.' Standing his ground, he glared up at her stroking his flowing white beard. 'Why would anyone want to sabotage that?' He pointed at the dessert which did look a trifle unloved.

'I'm going to kill you.' She took a step toward him before she was halted by she of the quivering bust. This was an unfortunate move as smock woman's fist took a swing at her adversary, missed by a mile and smacked Mrs Mackay squarely in the eye. It was a punch which would have Tyson Fury weeping with envy.

After a collective gasp, the room fell silent as its occupants swivelled to see what would happen next. Mrs Mackay was not famed for her sweet disposition, and this was likely to be an Oscar winning scene.

The bust ceased its quivering and grew several inches in response to Mackay's ramrod back. 'You are banned.' Thrusting her bust even higher - an awe-inspiring manoeuvre - she grabbed her attacker by the scruff of the smock and dragged her towards the door. To ensure there was no room for misunderstanding she added, 'For life.'

Once the smock had safely stomped off into the snow, her trifling trifle was removed allowing the room to return to its pre conflict euphoria. More and more people catapulted through the doors stamping their feet and blowing on their hands, ensuring the Sahara was positively cool compared to a Scottish hoolie.

'You could always rely on any event in this wee village to

rustle up some drama,' Ivy said, fanning herself with a bunch of napkins. 'Nothing's changed then.'

'Nary a thing.' Bunnie, loving the village and its foibles just as it was, had a cheery lilt to her voice.

'Is Pierre Blanc ever going to appear or is he a myth?'

'He's front and foremost on the posters, so I'll place my bet on him being fashionably late.'

'Typical celeb.' Ivy, having recently returned from a stint working as a cook in Hollywood, had had her fill of celebrities who thought they were the cream on the pudding. Many were lovely, others should be consigned to the nastiest corner of hell. She lifted the tea towel from the top of her clootie dumpling and eyed it as though it were about to leap up and defy her. 'I'm off to grab a clean cloth.' She trotted off with a determined step that brooked no nonsense.

The kitchen looked like a plague of locusts had rampaged through it and returned for seconds. The detritus of any kitchen lay hither and thither, multiplied by the number of contestants who had been titivating their entries and a bit on top to celebrate the fact it was a major competition. Ivy shuddered, grabbed a pristine cloth from an open drawer and dashed in the direction of the main room and safety. *It wouldn't surprise me to fall over the AWOL celebrity buried under a pile of rubbish. If he is here, they might find him in the next century.* Something caught her eye. What was that? She peered closer before thinking it might be a rat. Biting her lip till she drew blood she continued her dash to freedom and safety. Ivy's steely core could deal with most things, but rats were a deal too far.

She returned to the sight of said celebrity strolling through the door with a superior sneer plastered to his visage and a brace of flunkies twittering around him.

'I am 'ere. Where is it shall I put my... what eez the word?'

He glared at flunky number one who replied, 'Equipment, Chef Blanc.'

He nodded. The flunky flushed. 'Zee tools of my trade.'

The trio were escorted to a suitable spot. Zee tools, other-wise known as knives, were laid out in a reverent manner by flunky number two. They dazzled and twinkled in time to the fairy lights which adorned the room. Blanc himself adjusted a light to ensure a superior glint.

Ivy took them in. 'Impressive.' Her eyes narrowed and she whispered, 'He's judging a bunch of cakes in a rural village. What's with the ostentatious display?'

'Power trip. I've met these types many a time.' Bunnie liked the village life but that did not mean her career was provincial. She was one of the wealthiest entrepreneurs in the country and played with the big boys on a regular basis. Her look said Blanc and his display did not impress her one bit. 'I've a more imposing set in my kitchen.'

Ivy didn't doubt it.

Mrs Mackay displayed her best gracious host impression as she fussed around the celebrity chef. A glass of champagne magi-cally appeared in her hand and was handed over. He took a sip, looked down his nose and said, 'Passable. There are better vintages.'

Mackay looked like someone had kicked her new puppy then her inner teacher kicked in and her look became something else altogether.

Seamus Snowdrop smarmed up to the chef, 'Pierre, good to see you, pal.' He laid a hand on the chef's shoulder.

Blanc shrugged it off. 'It ees Chef Blanc.'

If looks could kill they'd be phoning the undertaker right now.

'Old boy's network not working so well then?' Ivy chewed her lip in an effort to hide her grin.

'Sod off.' Seamus stomped behind his creation, muttering under his breath.

'With pleasure. This is going well,' Ivy said with a festive lilt. 'Half the crowd are fighting, the other half are soaking up the Christmas spirit and I don't mean the ambiance, and our celebrity has half the contestants wanting to help him go to that great kitchen in the sky.'

'A normal day in the village.' Bunnie and Ivy laughed, literally out loud, and headed to the bar. 'Only a large Merlot will get us through this night.' Bunnie was a woman who knew her Merlot from her Shiraz and had never met a vintage she didn't know intimately.

Ivy took a large sip of a rather nice Californian Merlot, a surprise given they were in a wee Scottish village. She suspected it was a result of one of her friend's many businesses. There was never a lack of surprises with Bunnie in the mix.

Ivy took a slug of her wine. 'Is this circus ever going to start?'

'I'm not sure it—'

The strident squealing of a microphone on steroids cut through the air and cut Bunnie off.

'Ladies and Gentlemen.' The crowd being more interested in their drinks than Mrs Mackay, the response was lacklustre. She tapped the microphone. A lifetime of teaching meant she could command attention and get it. Her tone changed from pleasant to schoolmarm. 'We are here to judge these magnificent creations...' Her face, in complete contrast to her words, said she really believed the culinary offerings were less than magnificent. 'And I am sure Monsieur Blanc will be equal to the task.' She threw a sycophantic smile in the chef's direction. He returned it with his apparently signature glare. Either that or he was in a particularly bad mood that evening.

'Is he always this boorish?' Ivy said, as she pushed through bodies to get to her pudding.

'He's usually nice on the telly,' Rabbie Burns, the local butcher said, as he helped clear a path for her. As his job involved large knives there was little teasing about the fact Mrs Burns was daft enough to call her wean after Scotland's Bard. Ivy had long suspected this was why he took up butchery. Either that or he was a frustrated serial killer.

Despite Blanc's attempt to lower the mood the excitement

was palpable as the contestants lined up nicely behind their prized offerings. Or potentially prized offerings.

Blanc, with a flourish and what passed for a smile, picked up the first fork and stuck it deep into a Highland Gateau, described as a Black Forest Gateau with a Scottish twist. The look on the chef's face said he was less than impressed with the twist. The creator's (a mousey young woman called Kayleigh) lip quivered. Ivy bit her own lip as she wasn't sure whether to say there was a lot of quivering going on in this competition or lambast the chef. *It wouldn't surprise me if he ended up a corpse with one of Rabbie's knives in his chest. The culprit would be doing the world a favour.* She'd never met anyone so obnoxious and that was saying something considering some of the Hollywood stars wore entitlement like a badge of honour.

Pierre moved down the entries his unimpressed look growing ever more fixed. He glared at Seamus who glowered back, and the testosterone level grew exponentially. 'Orrible. What ees this?'

Ivy grabbed Seamus's jumper. He had a look about him that said he was about to leap the table and strangle the chef. Much as she would love to let him, she was rather hoping she would win this competition. A dead chef would just clutter the place up. And reduce the chances of winning anything. 'Leave it. He's not worth it.'

Seamus continued glowering but changed his mind on the strangling.

Eventually the chef reached the end of the line and moved slowly over to the microphone. 'I must consider thees. A chef of my 'igh calibre must take 'is time.' He scowled around the room. 'I will be in the kitchen...' he stared at his flunkies. 'Alone. I must not be disturbed.' He flounced off. Silence followed him until the door slammed shut and then the chatter almost lifted the roof.

'Who found him as a judge?' Bunnie's look said why did they bother.

'Mrs Mackay apparently. She wanted to raise the profile of the competition and create a greater buzz.'

'She's certainly created the buzz. It might be more of a profile than she envisaged.'

'For sure.'

There was an exodus towards the bar and probably the facilities given the amount of whisky, wine and beer that was flowing. Good humour and bonhomie swirled around the room.

'I love these events.' Bunnie took a generous sip of a cheeky merlot.

'Pity there isn't a ceilidh, that would really liven things_'

A scream loud enough to shake the walls brought Ivy and everyone else in the room to a dead stop. Literally a dead stop as the rumour ran through the room that their celebrity guest was, in a surprising twist, dead.

Ivy swivelled and elbowed herself in the direction of the scream with Bunnie in hot pursuit. 'Probably Chinese whispers and he's just fainted. He was having a sneaky sherbet as a side to the cake tasting.'

Mrs Mackay mustered up her finest bristle and said, 'He was cleansing his palate between tastings.'

'With vodka?' Amazement poured from every astonished syllable.

'That was water. Please stop casting aspersions on our esteemed judge.'

Having reached the prone Pierre, Ivy bent down and said, 'Our dead esteemed judge.' She stood up and looked around. 'Grab the first aid box. Anyone know CPR or the whereabouts of the community defibrillator?'

Taking in the blank stares and shaking heads she said, 'Call an ambulance and the police.' She bent down and started CPR, the words to 'Staying Alive' bouncing around her brain. Aware of a commotion she was unceremoniously shoved out of the way and a couple of muscular female paramedics took over. A man appeared from the back of the crowd. 'I'm a doctor.'

'Ivy glared at him. 'Took your time.'

Ignoring her, the mysterious doctor took over and Pierre Blanc declared dead. The paramedics took off and the police stepped in. Everyone was ushered from the room as it transformed into a crime scene.

'If we put our heads together, we might be able to solve this crime.' Ivy smiled. 'Everyone's used to us being a couple of Nosey Nora's.' She waved a warming glass of Talisker Whisky.

'I'm up for that – if there is a crime. Let's split and we can cozy up to the main suspects.' She screwed up her face. 'Who are the main suspects?'

'We need to get smock girl back in.' She has to be top of the list.'

'Given the ban, unlikely, but Simone lives next door.'

'She could have sneaked back in. Looking at the state of his body, I'd say he was poisoned.'

'More likely to be a woman then.' Bunnie never passed a chance to show her knowledge of all things criminal. It was a trifle worrying.

Ivy could never get to the bottom of why her friend knew so much. Probably watching too many true crime programmes on the telly. 'Assumptions, my dear. There are doors everywhere, all propped open with the heat.'

'Not much of a closed-door mystery then.'

They established a cast of suspects and split the room, agreeing to meet back in thirty minutes. Heading off they took care to look like a couple of women blethering about the number one topic in the room, not a pair of busybodies doing the police out of a job.

It's amazing what you can find out in thirty minutes when everyone's primed to gossip. Simone was back in their midst and professed to be shocked at the turn of events. 'I hero worshipped dear Pierre,' was her take on the matter. Her quivering lip was either beautifully acted or she was genuinely upset.

Ivy snagged a glass of White Zinfandel. 'If Mackay was dead, I'd pin it on Simone but I'm not sure what she'd have to gain by killing Pierre.'

'No scuttlebutt about her hatred of the dearly departed Pierre. However, there are some toe curling accounts about some of the others.'

'Yep.' Ivy took a sip of her wine. 'It would appear our celebrity chef stirred up some strong emotions.'

'How polite.'

'More than can be said about the chatter around the dead chef.' Ivy dragged her bestie into a corner. Not quite secluded but a valiant effort. 'Best not let everyone hear. First off, did you notice a strong smell of coffee in the vicinity of our corpse.' Her face indicated she was thinking. 'Wasn't like that when I was in there earlier.'

'Loads of people said that.'

'Was Pierre a coffee fiend?'

Bunnie threw her arms up. 'How the heck am I meant to know? I met him for the first time tonight.' She stopped suddenly before continuing. 'Mackie seems to know him better than anyone else. She's nowhere to be found though.'

Ivy's eyes opened wide. 'He was a trifle fiend.' She took in her fellow sleuth's incredulous look. 'He was. I read it somewhere.'

'Yeah. While finding out what you should make.'

'Tetchy. Pretty obvious I didn't make it. Let's focus. You didn't happen to see if any of the trifle had been scoffed, did you?' She put down her wine on a nearby chair. 'It was Bailey's trifle. That's coffee.'

'You'd need a couple of bottles for that level of stink.' Bunnie waved a dismissive hand. 'I snapped loads of photos. Might be in there.' She pulled out her iPhone; the pair crowded round it.

'Stop. Make that bigger.'

Bunnie obliged. Ivy pointed at the screen. 'See. Half-eaten. Must have been poisoned.'

'You either jumped to a rather wild conclusion or you did it.'

Whilst Ivy proclaimed her innocence Bunnie typed on her phone. 'We'll have someone testing it within ten minutes.'

'How on earth?'

Bunnie tapped her nose. 'Need to know basis.'

'Just what type of entrepreneur are you?'

Bunnie, who was having trouble looking Ivy in the eye, was spared an answer as Seamus gate-crashed their party for two.

'Your boyfriend's trying tae pin this murder on me.' Seamus took a menacing step towards Ivy, who stood her ground.

She got up so close and personal she could smell his foul breath. 'Back off. Now.' Seamus, considering his life choices, decided to obey.

Ice ran down Ivy's spine and she staggered. Her friend put a steadying hand on her elbow.

'I haven't got a boyfriend.' What she had was an ex-fiancé who was now a detective sergeant in Police Scotland. Seems like he was currently in the kitchen. In a walking, talking cliché, she was drawn to the kitchen like snow to Santa's village.

'Whoever he is, I never did this.' Seamus's faut posh accent had descended into his more realistic Dundee vernacular. Ivy was inclined to believe him; his posh accent dialled up several notches when he was lying like a cheap Chinese watch.

Ivy threw a stop me and your dead look at the bobbie guarding the door and stormed past him into the kitchen. The bobbie trailed behind like the tail of a comet.

'What idiot let a civilian...' The voice belonged to a man who could be Hugh Jackman's twin. He took one look at said civilian and added, 'Never mind. Go back to your duties.'

The policeman's face rearranged itself from worry to relief as he scurried off.

'Ivy, why are you front and centre in my crime scene?' Detective Sergeant Paul Finnigan asked.

'He was murdered then?'

Paul's eyes narrowed. 'I can neither confirm nor deny.'

Ivy changed tack. 'Seems like you're trying to frame my pal, Seamus.' Pal might be stretching it but she was after full on indignation.

'Poppycock. Now, off you trot.'

Ivy escalated from indignation to full on blazing. She bit her tongue and drew blood. No use antagonising her one possible ally. 'I see they taught you all sorts of fancy words down south.' Their engagement fell apart when he'd shimmied off to London to take up a position with the Metropolitan Police. In retaliation she jetted off to California meaning broken hearts both sides of the Atlantic. She smiled her sweetest smile although it hurt more than her heart. 'Can I just have a teensy, tiny look?'

The corner of his mouth twitched. 'You can look at as much as you like in the main hall.'

'You must have some idea of what's going on.'

His eyes softened as his dazzling blue eyes seemed to look inside her soul. 'I heard what happened with your mum. You must be devastated by her death.'

The change of both demeanour and subject hit Ivy like a jab to the solar plexus. She staggered back, gasped, then turned and hurried from the room. Bunnie chased after her.

'Why does he have to be so nice?'

'Mixture of the fact he is nice and a diversion tactic.'

The words diversion tactic had Ivy's dander soaring. 'I_'

'Hold your horses there, cowboy.' Ivy smiled at Bunnie's reference to her Californian sojourn. 'While you and the hot detective were whispering sweet nothings I was nosing around.'

'I bet you were. Spit it out.'

'Half the tragic trifle was gone, and our dearly departed chef had a suspicious trace of cream on his upper lip.' She folded her arms and leaned forward. 'Given that and the fact your boyfriend let slip it's a crime scene, I'd say you were right, Sherlock. Our celebrity has been poisoned.'

Ivy perked right up, her shoulders squared ready for battle. 'So, what are we going to do about it. Watson?'

'Why, investigate dear Mr Holmes. The game is on.'

Ivy pulled a napkin over. 'Where were the key players before he ate his last supper?'

'Key players? It could be anyone.'

'Sure could, but it would seem our celebrity isn't quite as big as his ego suggests.' She waved her arm around the room. 'Ninety-five percent of the punters had never heard of him until his name was announced. The rest either hero-worshipped or hated him.'

'And you figured this out, how?'

'Huddles, Watson. Huddles. Everyone knows everyone, so everyone has loose lips.'

'That made no sense and complete sense at the same time.'

'Focus.' Ivy knew her friend of old. It was better to keep Bunnie on track. 'So, why was he invited in the first place and why would anyone want to kill him?'

'It would seem Mrs Mackay was determined to have him as the judge.'

'I would never have put her down as a cooking aficionado although I know she did enjoy a slice of cake or two.'

'Her talents started and stopped at the persecution of decades of unsuspecting primary school pupils.' The scowl adorning Ivy's face indicated she remembered every minute.

Bunnie opened her mouth to answer before being distracted by the shrill beep of a text alert. She glanced at her phone. 'Yes, as I suspected, caffeine poison in the trifle.'

Ivy's jaw literally dropped. 'How on earth...?'

'I have my contacts.'

Ivy made a mental note to find out what her entrepreneurial

friend had been up to whilst she was swanning around with Hollywood stars. Just what sort of business was she running? She shook her head. This was neither the time nor the place to be worrying about her best friend's business dealings. 'So, it would appear someone came prepared to kill our culinary star.'

'Got it in one.'

'But who?' They stared at each other for several seconds before Ivy continued, 'That's for the murderer to know and us to find out.' She took a slug of wine and pulled the napkins towards her. She scribbled down several names – all of the contestants and the dead chef's lackies. 'It wouldn't surprise me if they helped him shuffle off this mortal coil. He must have been a bear to work for.'

'And some. They also had access to all areas and thus all the desserts.'

'Good point.' She tapped her pen on the wine glass. 'Although they could have offed him any time. No need to make it so public.' Bunnie nodded and Ivy put question marks next to their names.

'Smock lady's a definite no. She was at home telling her boyfriend her woes. He was raging fit to bust when they came back, so her alibi is as tight as the derrieres of the ducks on the castle pond.' Ivy drew a line through Simone's name.

Bunnie jumped to her feet. ' It's time to interview the main suspects.' She grabbed a napkin and snatched the pen from Ivy's hand.

'Oi. I was using that.'

Bunnie, ignoring her, scribbled down four names on the napkin and handed it to her friend. 'Go and interrogate them. In a kind and polite way of course; there's to be no torture or coercion involved.'

'This is the village hall, not Colditz. It's also packed to the gunwales with punters so how do you think I'd go about torturing anyone?'

Bunnie grinned. 'Hop to it.'

❄

Twenty minutes later Ivy returned to the rendezvous point clutching nothing more alcoholic than a couple of Virgin Marys. A clear head was needed if they were to bring this case to a successful conclusion. 'Spill.'

'Every person I spoke to had an alibi and I checked it out.' She glanced at Seamus who had magically dragged up a free chair and was making himself cosy next to Ivy. 'What's he doing here?'

'I've as much right to be here as you have. Anyway, you might need my help.'

'Need your help?' Bunnie's tone indicated that was highly unlikely.

Ivy stepped in before the Scottish equivalent of the gunfight at the OK Corral kicked off. 'Apparently he's got some juicy gossip for us.'

Bunnie leaned forward. 'Gossip I like. Come on then, out with it.'

Seamus propped his chin on his hands and smiled. 'Well...'

Ivy, who's tether had well and truly reached the end, said, 'We haven't got time for this. Solving this mystery this side of Christmas Day is what we're aiming for. If you really do have something to tell us, then get on with it or go find yourself something else to do and leave us to detect.'

'Oh, I really do have dirt to dish.' He paused as though for dramatic effect before taking in the look in Ivy's eyes. 'Did you know our Pierre Blanc is actually the more prosaic Peter White?'

Bunnie seemed singularly unimpressed. 'That's hardly earth shattering. Loads of celebrities change their names to make themselves look more impressive.'

' Ah, but there's another juicy little bit to this name change puzzle. Our dear departed Pierre and Mrs Mackay have form.'

Ivy moved closer. 'What do you mean, form?'

'There's a more sordid reason as to why Peter changed his name and his identity.' His face changed from conspiratorial to sombre. 'Peter won an international competition with a unique recipe. The clincher was the recipe was stolen from someone else. That someone else was David Mackay, the son of our Christmas pudding contest organiser.'

Ivy and Bunnie's jaws literally dropped. Ivy pulled herself together enough to say, 'What? But why would Mackay want to wreak revenge for a stolen recipe all these years later?'

'That's not the end of the sorry tale. David and Peter were lovers and David took his own life.'

Ivy leapt to her feet. 'We need to find Mrs Mackay and let Paul know.' She dashed off, Bunnie and Seamus trailing in her wake.

They'd no sooner entered the corridor then they saw their murderer. Not a bust quiver in sight she took one look at their faces, opened her handbag and pulled out a gleaming chef's knife. It looked suspiciously like one of those displayed so beautifully by the dead chef's lackeys.

'You've worked it out then?'

None of the newly formed detectives could muster up a single word.

'He deserved what he got. He killed my beautiful boy.' She advanced towards them her intent evident from the coldness in her eyes.

'You can't take on three of us,' Ivy said.

'This knife says I can.' She picked up her pace and advanced at a dizzying speed.

'Hollywood certainly didn't prepare me for this,' Ivy whispered.

'And you think entrepreneurship did?'

The knife was a whisker away from striking distance when Simone appeared with a cut glass bowl in her hand. No one quite knew what she was doing with it, but showing great skill and ingenuity, she applied it quite smartly to the top of Mrs Mackay's head. The woman screamed then dropped like a sack of neeps,.

Alerted by the hullabaloo Sergeant Paul Finnigan materialised in the hallway. He listened to the garbled tale and ordered his men to take the suspect into custody and phone an ambulance. 'You lot need to come to the station with me.' He looked at Ivy with a mixture of exasperation and tenderness. 'You could have been killed.'

'Well, I wasn't. You should be thanking me for doing your job for you.'

Paul just shook his head and walked off.

They never did find out who won the Christmas pudding competition that year, but the local old folks home feasted mightily on desserts for the next several days. They declared them all to be delicious. The proof was in the pudding in more ways than one.

BIO

Wendy H. Jones is a multi-award-winning, best-selling Scottish author of crime thrillers, cozy mysteries, children's picture books and non-fiction books for authors. She won the Books Go Social Book of the Year at Dublin writers conference and the prestigious Scottish Association of Writers, Janetta Bowie Chalice for best non-fiction book She is also an acclaimed international public speaker teaching writing craft and marketing worldwide. In addition, she is the Editor in Chief of Writers' Narrative eMagazine, a partner in Auscot Publishing and Retreats and owner of Scott and Lawson Publishing.

https://www.wendyhjones.com

Chapter Five

THE PERFECT CHRISTMAS GIFT

Sophy Smythe

I t's Christmas. The mansion is buzzing with excitement for the Christmas party of the year. But beneath the sparkle and joy, a chilling truth emerges—I've married a serial killer. For the first time in many years the whole family was complete. The estranged daughter who felt betrayed, her mysterious boyfriend who led a life in violence, the grief-stricken daughter wallowing in alcohol, the daughter willing to do anything to save her beloved horses. And then there is the butler, stiff upper lip and a murky past. And of course, the master of the house himself. Dead. Stone dead. But who murdered him?

The moment I discovered I had unwittingly married a serial killer, I knew I would be next.

The realisation coiled around my spine, and a gnawing fear settled within, forewarning me I could be the next victim in his sinister spree.

Then, abruptly, he was gone.

Who had killed him? I knew for sure someone had, and it wasn't me. He was in the prime of his life. He couldn't just have died. Gratitude intertwined with my thoughts—someone, unknowingly, had spared me from a dark and foreboding fate.

Christmas Eve arrived with a grand celebration, a festive atmosphere that masked the shadows lurking beneath. My husband had orchestrated a lavish party, inviting his children and relatives, while a jazz band set the tone.

Even though they were appalled by their father's marriage to me, his former wife's nurse, they obediently attended at his behest. I was a bit nervous, but did what any dutiful wife would do. I fortified myself for a warm welcome, whatever frosty reception they would give me, and ensured rooms prepared for their stay. Anna, of course, needed no preparation, living here already. The blue room stood ready for Eve, known for her extravagant lifestyle and financial woes. As for Lynn, a globetrotting journalist estranged from our union, I reserved the red room. I wondered if she would come. Our paths had briefly crossed at her mother's funeral, the lone encounter since her absence from our marriage. The uncertainty hung in the air, adding an enigmatic layer to the unfolding drama.

That I wasn't English nor had the translucent pale skin the English are renowned for only fuelled their resentment towards me. I stood as a barrier between them and their cherished heritage. They had coins in their eyes when they suggested selling the estate after their mother had died. Of course, Anna had vehemently opposed it. She was the horsey one. Selling the estate meant she'd lose her home and, more importantly, her beloved horses. Then he married me. I was blissfully ignorant.

It was only yesterday when I found out.

He had been hanging out with friends and at 3 am a deafening crash jolted me awake. Peering out of the window, I couldn't see anything, but the dogs barked like hell. I slipped into my peignoir and navigated the long corridor, down the winding stairs, and peered into the dimly lit hall. The butler had retired for the night, and only the table lamp cast a faint glow. I retrieved a golf club from the cupboard, determined to investigate. Armed, I descended the stairs and approached the living room window. Through a gap in the curtains, I strained to see through the misty rain, almost like fog.

'Madam?' A voice startled me from behind.

Reacting swiftly, I swung the club, narrowly missing his skull. I despised his knack for sneaking up on me.

The air was charged with tension as he stepped back. 'Respectfully, madam. It's your husband. He crashed against the wall.'

My heart raced as I processed the information. 'How is that even possible?'

'I don't know, madam.'

'Let's go outside and see.'

A cold, wet curtain enveloped the steaming engine. The front of the Rolls-Royce was crumpled. Well, not exactly crumpled, but you know what I mean. My husband leaned against the airbag, moaning.

'Sweetheart, what happened?' I struggled to open the door, brushed wet hair from my face, and tugged at his arm.

More groaning.

'Let's get him out and make sure the wall and the car get fixed.' I glanced over the fountain to the driveway and back to the house. Anna's window remained dark. How the heck could she not have heard this? Moving to the other side of the car, I opened the glove compartment and retrieved the gun.

With the butler's discreet assistance, I carefully ushered my husband to our bed. 'Sweetie, how much did you drink?'

His response was a garbled murmur.

As I unravelled the layers of his clothing, the shocking sight of bruises on his chest elicited a visceral wave of horror. 'Did you get into a fight?'

He mumbled incoherently, pleading, 'Leave me alone.'

'Not until I know what's happened.'

'Just a boy's night out. Nothing happened.'

'All right, I'll give you some painkillers and a sleeping pill so you can sleep it off.'

Dealing with the delicate task of tending to his bruised ribs —I know they hurt like hell—I carefully applied morphine plasters and administered a sleeping pill before settling down beside him.

The noxious scent of alcohol permeating from his pores made it impossible for me to find solace in sleep. In contemplation, I weighed the idea of relocating to another room, away from the unsettling aura that hung heavy in the air.

'Why?'

'Honey?'

'Why couldn't...'

'What?'

'Kill themselves.'

'What have you done, honey?'

'Why did...'

More groaning. Mumbling I couldn't understand.

'I had to...

'.. marry you, you understand?'

I sat up, utterly dumbfounded. 'Of course, honey,' I stammered, my voice quivering, and a palpable chill ran up my spine. Was it the alcohol or the morphine? I don't know. Shock and disbelief clenched at my insides as the sinister truth gradually unfolded. Piece by piece, he cryptically confessed to his involvement in the deaths of his previous wives. The details emerged agonizingly slowly, painting a grotesque portrait of a man capable of unspeakable acts. Of course, he had told me that his first wife fell from the stairs and crashed her skull. He was devastated by it. Or so he said.

And his second wife, the one I had nursed? I now reconsidered her demise. Falling off her horse, breaking her neck, and becoming paralysed—she didn't have to die. In my professional opinion, it was avoidable. She was a radiant soul, adored by her children, or so I heard. And then, abruptly, she was gone. Did he also...

That he was no saint, I knew before I married him. Like any successful businessman, he was ruthless in his pursuits. And the array of weapons in our house testified to the nature of his dealings.

My heart hammered against my throat, and my stomach twisted in knots. I staggered to the toilet, retching.

I knew with certainty. I had married a killer, likely a serial killer. Two wives before me, and I was now the third, ensnared in a web of darkness.

Would he remember what he had told me?

I wasn't sure. My breaths came in shallow, rapid bursts, and my legs felt as if burdened by a ton. Immobilised, my heart pounded in my chest, the struggle for air intensifying. I couldn't afford the risk of him recalling what he had shared. I clutched my head, attempting to think amidst the chaos.

His bruises and cryptic mutterings hinted at a troubled past filled with deception and malevolence. Fear for my safety gripped me, and I began devising a plan for escape, realising I had inadvertently become the prey of a potential serial killer. I had to get out of the house as soon as possible, but without him being suspicious. However, where could I go? No family remained, and my friends were oceans away. Any attempt to use credit cards would reveal my location. His influence spanned the globe, and I required cash.

I calculated I would be safe until the Christmas party. He wouldn't risk anything with so many witnesses around. Perhaps I could secure a ride from someone.

He awoke, burdened by a throbbing headache and bruised ribs. The once gentle, charismatic façade of my husband had crumbled, unleashing the devil within. His transformation exposed a darker, malevolent side. The revelation that he might have played a role in the deaths of his previous wives haunted me. Concealing my escalating unease, I played the part of the concerned and caring wife, all the while strategising my impending departure.

'I bet you're not feeling too well, honey. Shall we call the party off?'

'Oh, no. It's the only time of the year I have my family together. Don't you dare to call it off.'

'I just want what is best for you. Don't worry. Do you think you're up to it?'

'Yes. Of course. I'm no pussy. Just give me something for... ouch my ribs.' He bent double.

'Let me see.' I pulled his hand away and caressed his bruises. 'Some Arnica and painkillers will do the trick. You'll be fit as a fiddle.'

'I knew I could count on you. Give it to me, pronto.'

At breakfast, he was almost his own charming self that I had fallen for and I convinced myself it was the alcohol that had spoken. I shouldn't be so melodramatic. Anna joined us in riding attire. 'I'm off, daddy.'

'Remember we have a party tonight.' I said.

She ignored me.

She went over and hugged her father. 'Be a good boy.'

He winced and held his ribs.

'What's up, daddy? You don't like me anymore?' she sulked.

'It's nothing. Just a hangover.'

'You shouldn't drink so much. It seems that Eve has your genes.'

'Listen, young lady, don't talk to me like that.'

'Sorry, daddy, but mark my words, it'll be your grave.' Brusquely she turned and off she went.

The butler knew just what to serve as a pick-me-up. A vodka tomato juice with loads of tabasco and a good old English fat breakfast, kippers and all.

It seemed to do him good.

'What's up, dear? You seem a little off.'

I hadn't noticed that he was studying me.

'It's nothing, sweetie,' I evaded. 'Just preoccupied with the party. Do you think Lynn will come?'

'She wouldn't miss it. I told them all we have a family meeting. I have something important to say.'

'You have?'

He guffawed. 'They can't resist.'

I tried not to seem curious. 'I have to check if everything is alright for your party, darling. Please, take care not to overreach yourself.'

He called after me. 'I think I might have done some damage when I came home.'

'It's all taken care of, honey,' I assured him.

I was in the hall when the butler opened the door for a windswept girl and a sturdy-looking gent. 'Good morning, you must be Lynn?'

'You must be the new one. This is Steven, my boyfriend.'

'Welcome. I reserved the red room for you, but I didn't count on your boyfriend. I'll prepare the green room for him.'

'Don't be daft,' she said in a sharp tone. 'Steven is with me. Come on, Steve, let's put the luggage in the room and meet my father.'

'You'll excuse me. I have to look into the preparations for the party.'

I knew it would be difficult when I married him, but the daughters were a pain in the ass.

'Eve and Anna in?' Lynn called from halfway up the stairs.

I pretended not to hear her. She would find out one way or the other.

✳

The party pulsed with energy when the butler dramatically announced Eve's entrance. She twirled in, a cigarette dangling from one hand and a champagne glass in the other. 'Helloooo, everyone!' Her animated greeting scattered ash into the air. Thank God the jazz band played loud enough, ensuring not everyone tuned in to her antics.

'Drunk again,' I could hear Anna say. I went over to my husband and followed him as he navigated through the crowd, whiskey glass in his hand. 'Eve!' His face beamed as he hugged her. 'All together. At last.'

'Can you pay the cabbie, Daddy?' she asked before dancing away. 'Partyyyy!'

My husband grimaced, taking a sip, and another, and then emptied the glass. I could faintly hear the ice cubes jingle between two beats of the jazz band.

I had warned him not to drink with the morphine I had given him, but to no avail.

For a moment his eyes shot ice, but I doubt if anyone had noticed. Then he was again endearing as ever. I wondered if I had imagined it.

'You throw a perfect party and you are a superb hostess,' I heard a voice booming behind me. It was the mayor.

'Thank you, mayor, you're most welcome.' He was so small I had to bow my head to look into his eyes. 'Is your wife enjoying herself?'

He straightened, subtly scanning me from head to toe until his gaze fixated on my bosom. 'Of course, of course. And I must say, you look divine. Would you like to dance?'

Suppressing a shudder, I imagined dancing with him, his head awkwardly positioned against my chest. Never. 'Can I introduce you to a business associate of my husband? You might persuade him to invest in the new housing project.'

With some effort, he popped his eyes back into their sockets and followed my lead.

Intrigued by Lynn, I wiggled my way toward her and Steven, who stood near the bar with a palpable air of disdain, observing the crowd. 'Hi, Lynn. I haven't properly introduced myself.'

'I know who you are. Wife number three.'

That hurt. Putting on my broadest smile, I said, 'True. As I said, we've never met properly before, but your father told me you had the most thrilling adventures. I'm glad we finally met.' That said, I turned towards Steven. 'And a boyfriend as well. Hi Steven. You're from around here?'

'My family is from up north.' I couldn't place his accent. 'I met Lynn in Gaza where she was reporting.'

'Oh, my God. That must have been gruesome.'

'That's very euphemistic. It was hell.' He looked around. 'It's unbelievable that these people celebrate peace for all mankind. Its frivolity is disgraceful.'

'It's incredible that we are on the same planet as Gaza,' Lynn added.

'You don't approve?'

Steven's lips tightened.

'We're off tomorrow.' Lynn put a hand against his chest and kissed him on his cheek. 'We just came here, because papa said he had something important to tell us and he needed all of us here. He is not ill, is he?'

There was something off in the last sentence and the tone she had said it. I couldn't shake the feeling that it carried a hint of hope.

'Just something minor. Yesterday he bumped into the mansion's wall while driving drunk and he has some bruised ribs. But for the rest, he is fine. I got him on morphine for the night.'

'He looks as if he is in the prime of his life.' Lynn's gaze lingered on her father. Then, out of the blue, she asked, 'Do you know why he wanted me and my sisters here?'

'I don't. It must be important as he asked us all together.'

'All of us? You mean you'll be there too?'

'I will be.' I confirmed.

Anna and Eve joined us. 'So, what is this all about?'

I felt ambushed. 'Let's wait until tomorrow. I have to tell the band to play their last song.'

'Oh, this really is the countryside. It's only midnight.' Eve exclaimed, rolling her eyes.

After all the guests had departed, I escaped outside with the dogs to clear my head. I still had to figure out how to get cash and where to go. Glancing at the house with all the windows alight, I felt evil spirits clawing towards me. I shuddered. It must have been my upbringing. My grandma danced with the spirits. Or so my mother had told me. Spirits don't exist, do they? And if they did, they would flee this cold, grey, drizzling climate to warmer places like the one I came from. Yet, I could I feel their clammy hands crawling along my spine and clutching my throat. To my horror, I sensed something clawing at my legs. I jumped and looked down, only to discover it was one of the dogs begging for attention. 'Oh, my, you gave me the creeps,' I said, stroking his back. The best companions I've ever had. I'll miss them. Then the oldest one started whimpering. 'What's up, buddy? Come on, let's get some sleep.'

When I opened the door, the dogs sprinted into the house, barking and whimpering. Then, my eyes fell upon him—lying in a puddle of blood, legs awkwardly bent, face down.

Paralysis gripped me for a moment, but then I rushed over. 'Honey, honey!' Yet, deep down, I knew it was too late. Though I reached for his carotid artery, I expected the inevitable.

'What the hell is going on?' Above me, four faces were looking down. 'Papa?'

I peeked into the hall as the butler opened the front door, my eyes locked on the grotesque scene on the floor.

The chief inspector entered, eyeing the stained floor. Technicians bustled around, collecting evidence, while the doctor packed his tools into a bag.

The butler retrieved his coat. 'Madam is waiting in the salon, sir.'

The chief inspector's gaze followed the staircase spiralling three floors high towards the ceiling. 'What do you think, doc? Did he fall from up there?'

'Could be.' The doctor shrugged. 'I can tell you more after the post-mortem.'

'I know the way,' the chief inspector said to the butler.

The butler's face remained blank. 'Of course, sir.'

Entering the salon, the chief inspector expressed his sympathy. 'My dear, what an awful situation. After yesterday's party, I couldn't fathom that I would be here today for such a horrendous occasion. How are you?'

I couldn't hold the tears when he held my hands.

He reached into his pocket, offering me a handkerchief. 'Here, here.' Then, addressing the butler, 'Get her some tea, please.'

The butler noiselessly sailed to the tea table and poured the tea. 'Madam.'

Grateful, I took a seat. Sipping the tea helped me gather my composure as I recounted to the chief inspector what had unfolded the previous day after everyone left the party and how I discovered my husband.

'So, who is staying at the house at this moment?'

'Just the girls and one boyfriend and the butler of course. The housemaids are on dailies. After the party, they went to their own homes.'

'And who can testify you found the body?'

I hesitated. 'The girls and boyfriend were upstairs, and I saw the butler coming in from the side door. The dogs made a horrible noise and woke everybody. That is, if they haven't heard the thump of the fall.'

'How is it possible that he fell? He must have known these stairs with his eyes closed.'

I fell silent for a moment, then decided to confess. 'The night before the party, he was on a spree with his friends. He came home very drunk and crashed his car against the wall. He had bruised ribs, but he didn't want to cancel the party, so I gave him Fentanyl.' I explained, 'to ease the pain.'

'That's some heavy stuff you shouldn't be drinking with, right? I heard about it.'

'I warned him not to drink, but you saw him.' I sighed.

'I'd like to take everybody to the hall and do a brief experiment.' The chief inspector said.

The butler, stone-faced as ever, told us he would notify the daughters and boyfriend.

'You too,' the chief inspector told him with a definite hardness in his voice.

The butler raised an eyebrow and exited.

Once in the hall, it was difficult not to look at the place where they had marked the spot where my husband's body had lain.

We shuffled together, for once in harmony. Eve's eyes were red and small, the corners of her mouth down-turned, still reeking of alcohol. Anna's eyes were wide, with black patches on her cheeks where mascara wasn't supposed to be, hands clutched. Lynn's face didn't express anything. She must have seen more horrible scenes, but her hands clenching on Steven belied her seemingly calm appearance. Steven was the only one who more or less seemed relaxed, stroking Lynn's back. But actually, he was an outsider. And then there was me, with a stone in my stomach.

'I want you to go through the motions exactly when you discovered the body,' the chief inspector instructed us. Awkwardly, I moved to the front door and positioned myself in the open doorway. 'The dogs entered first,' I said.

'I came out of my room first,' said Anna, 'and saw you,' pointing at me, 'bending over papa.'

'How do we know you haven't pushed him?' Lynn challenged me.

'What?' Heat rushed up to my cheeks like tingling needles. 'I am the only one without a reason to wish your father dead. You were the ones who needed his money.' I bitched back.

'I signed a prenuptial,' I told the chief inspector. 'As long as my husband lived, I would have a perfect life. After he died, everything would go to his daughters.' I pointed upstairs. 'Them.'

The chief inspector rubbed his chin in thought. 'If that's the case, you have no motive…. And they do.' He looked up.

'I heard you quarrel with papa.' Eve accused Anna.

'What?'

'I saw you enter his study, and you were shouting.'

'He wanted to sell the horses.'

'I always wondered why he hadn't sold them after mama's accident,' said Lynn.

'They were mama's horses. He knew how much they meant to me,' Anna whimpered. 'Anyway, why were you eavesdropping?'

'I wasn't. He summoned me. And it was hard not to hear you yelling.'

The chief inspector coughed. 'I think it's best we all move to the salon. You, too.' He pointed at the butler, who was standing near the side door like a statue.

The butler floated behind us. 'Can I offer you tea, madam?'

Oh, this English desire for tea. As if that solves anything!

'Yes, please,' I acknowledged.

We sat in front of the fireplace, rather stiff and uncomfortable. Had Anna, in a flurry of anger, pushed her father over the balcony? I couldn't believe that. My husband was a not a heavyweight, but certainly stronger than Anna. And she was the apple of his eye. He shouldn't have done that. I mean, selling the horses. The horses were everything for her. All that was left of her mother.

The chief inspector addressed Eve. 'Why did your father summon you?'

'I bet he had something against my way of life.'

'So, you didn't speak to him?'

'After all this fighting? No, I made my way downstairs as soon as I could and left.'

'No, you didn't,' said Lynn. 'When we were settling in, I saw you entering his study.'

Eve had the grace to blush, but she straightened and said down her nose, 'I think you're mistaken. I only returned when the party was in full swing.'

The butler coughed, 'Forgive me for the interruption, sir. I remember opening the door for miss Eve at five.'

The chief inspector swivelled his head from the butler to Eve in askance.

'You don't believe this servant, do you? He would tell you anything to compromise me.'

'And why would he do that?'

'I know he stole mama's pearls after she died. And he knows I know.'

'So why didn't you report this?'

'I thought someday I could use it.' She walked over to the bar. 'I'll need something stronger. Anyone join me?'

I pitied her. After her mother had died, she could only forget herself in heavy partying, drinking, and pills. I'd tried to help her, but the sole result was that we didn't see her for months on end. When she finally showed up, all she did was sleep for a few days, begged her father for money, and left again. He said not to bother and that she would eventually come around, but I was not so certain.

'I am sure I saw you,' Lynn said. 'You also did, didn't you, Steve?'

'I saw someone,' Steven hesitated, 'but I don't know who. It could have been anyone.'

Lynn's frustration cut through the room. 'Oh, you are no use. Look at her. She looks guilty.'

'And how do we know you didn't talk to papa yourself, Lynn?'

With a disdainful look, Lynn silenced Eve. She inherited that quality from her father. That and her sense of adventure.

'Tell me why I would want to kill him. I haven't been here for over a year and then I come back to kill him? That's distasteful.'

'He might just have fallen,' I intervened. 'I don't think anybody here would kill him. But he is in a line of business with powerful enemies.'

'You just said we had motive, so what is it?' Lynn challenged aggressively.

'Well, it's you who'll inherit the money. And money is a powerful motive.' I replied, stung.

The chief inspector coughed. 'That leaves you, sir,' he said to Steven.

'Who? Me? I'm just an innocent bystander.'

'Are you? I thought I recognised you yesterday evening, and I did some researching. You are an infamous arms dealer providing weapons to terrorists.'

'Steven?' Lynn withdrew her hand and moved away. 'What the heck?'

'His name is not Steven. You didn't know, miss?'

'So why didn't papa recognise him?' asked Anna. 'As he was in the same business.'

'I'm not sure. Maybe he did, maybe not,' answered the chief inspector. 'But arms dealers have no friends, only competitors and enemies.'

'Steven? You aren't in the United Nations? Not rebuilding Gaza?' Lynn stood up and faced Steven.

That took some guts. Poor girl. It's not nice to be deceived.

'Don't believe him, Lynn, darling. You know me.' He took her hands.

'Do I?' Lynn asked in a bitter tone. 'Tell me, was that the

only reason you hooked up with me? So, you could enter this house and kill the competition?'

'You don't believe that yourself, do you? I love you.'

He looked into her eyes and made a decision. 'The chief inspector is right. But I couldn't tell you. Besides, killing the competition doesn't solve anything. It doesn't take his business away. I know it was a mistake to deceive you, but I hadn't the heart...'

'You were so involved in the Gaza case...'

'I would have told you... eventually.'

It was disgusting to watch the attempt to save his sorry life.

The butler tried to dissolve in the curtains, but the chief inspector hadn't forgotten him.

'You, sir. Did the master finally find out you had stolen the pearls and wanted to fire you?'

'Papa said that he was missing other things too,' said Anna. 'But the house was so big, he could easily have mislaid them.'

'Not your father,' I said with certainty. 'He was very meticulous and precise. Now you mention it, he indeed told me he was missing some papers. I didn't really pay attention. I don't...' I swallowed, 'didn't... intrude in his business. Weapons appall me.'

'So, did you also steal his papers?' The voice of the chief inspector cut through the salon like he wanted to chop the butler. 'And do what? Blackmail?'

'I have always had the master's best interests at heart, chief inspector.'

The butler's lips stiffened, and a twitch betrayed his unease. His hands, usually at his side, were concealed behind his back. What secrets did he hold?

'And how do you explain the missing jewels and papers?'

'I can't, chief inspector. I didn't know.'

'You sneaky liar,' Eve accused. 'You stole my mother's pearls. I saw it.'

'So you say, miss. Can I pour you another drink?'

Yes, who would believe a drunk? Mightn't she herself have pilfered the pearls to buy booze or pills?

'So you all seem to have a motive,' the chief inspector said, 'except you, madam.' He nodded to me.

I lowered my head.

'The problem is that your father was a vigorous man. At least stronger than each of you girls. So, one of you could not have pushed him. But if you worked together, you could have...

'Besides, you girls were upstairs, from where he fell. Madam here was downstairs where she had found him. You all witnessed that.'

'I can't have. I was with Steven.' Lynn protested.

'Yes, Steven, who, under false pretences visited this house. Not a very reliable witness.'

The doorbell cut through the tensioned air, and I whipped up my head.

With a nod, I gave the butler permission to open the door. I really shall fire him when all this was over. This story of missing jewels and papers didn't sit right.

The air was suffocating. We all eyed each other with suspicion.

What I didn't tell them—it's no good to tell the girls all. They've gone through enough—was that I knew my husband killed their mother. And his first wife. It was in his line of work after all. Selling arms, that is. Not killing. He let others do that for him. Until he did it himself. If he hadn't told me when he was full of alcohol and pills, I would never have guessed. And...accidents do happen.

The butler sailed in. The notary, madam. He says that he is here to read the will.

The notary entered, signalling the beginning of a new chapter, one filled with legal implications and the unravelling of my husband's enigmatic life.

As we prepared to hear the contents of the will, the tension in the room became palpable. The intricate web of deceit, secrets, and potential crimes woven into our lives demanded resolution. The notary's presence marked the commencement of a journey into the shadows of our past, where the truth awaited its reluctant unveiling.

With a jolt, I sat upright, drenched in sweat, breath caught in my throat, my heart pounding wildly. The room seemed unfamiliar for a moment until I glanced at my husband beside me.

It was Christmas morning, the sky beyond the curtains cast in a sombre grey. It was only yesterday that my husband had taken my hand and told me what he was up to. 'You've always been kind to me, love. Too kind.' He had kissed me. 'And I'm crazy about you. I've pondered how to express my love, and now, with Christmas goodwill in the air, I have the perfect gift for you. It's time my daughters learn to stand on their own feet and that they are not dependent on my money. So, I've revised my will. I want you to live comfortably for the rest of your life, even after I'm gone. I'm leaving everything to you.'

'And what about your children?' I had protested. 'It's not fair to them.'

'They'll receive a modest yearly sum to fall back upon, but the primary focus is on you.'

'So, that's the purpose of this family reunion...' I had uttered slowly. 'They won't be happy about it.'

'Don't worry, darling. Leave it to me.'

'They might contest it. You know that.'

'They can't. It's all perfectly legit.'

'It will make for an unsettling Christmas.' While I believed it wasn't the right season to address this matter, secretly, I felt elated.

'Isn't it the perfect Christmas gift?'

I had smiled and kissed him. 'Thank you, sweetie.'

It was Christmas morning, and I looked at my husband.

The snoring had gone.

I traced the bruises on his cold ribs, leaned over and placed my hand on his heart. I kissed his bloodless lips. He appeared as if he were sleeping—so tranquil, so flawless. Searching for a pulse in his neck, I found none. My husband had passed away during the night, and I, a nurse no less, had slept through it all.

As I reflected on the revelation that my husband, the man I had married, was potentially a serial killer, a wave of relief washed over me. His sudden death presented an unexpected escape from the imminent danger I had unknowingly placed myself in.

It had been a calculated risk that he wouldn't survive the combination of alcohol and pills he had consumed. But I had always excelled in mathematics. The ironic part was that I had warned him against drinking. Knowing my husband, he would defy my advice and rebel. In the end, he had orchestrated his demise entirely on his own. The perfect way to end the life of a killer.

'Thank you, sweetie. This is the perfect Christmas gift.' I whispered.

BIO

Sophy Smythe is the pen name of a doctor living in Antwerp. She wrote The Medical Code, the first in a series of medical thrillers starring Charlie Martens, MD. The second book in the series will be released in 2025.

https://sophysmythe.com

Chapter Six

THE CHRISTMAS CARD CONUNDRUM

Marti M. McNair

In the heart of snow-blanketed Jinglebell, Emma's cottage buzzes with festive cheer. Villagers mingle, their laughter and carols blending harmoniously. But the joy is interrupted when Sarah loses her precious family heirloom brooch. As Emma and Sarah search, a mysterious Christmas card hints at a deeper mystery. With the help of Fredrick, Emma embarks on a quest to uncover the truth behind the missing brooch, turning a festive gathering into an unexpected adventure.

In the heart of snow-blanketed Jinglebell, Emma Bell's cottage rang with festive cheer.

The room was filled with the scent of pine and cinnamon as the villagers mingled, their laughter and carols blending harmoniously. Emma, the town's newest resident, moved gracefully among her guests, offering mulled wine and heartfelt smiles.

As Emma circled the gathering, stopping to chat with Agnes Thomson, she noticed Sarah in the hallway. Crouched low, Sarah rummaged frantically through the umbrella and shoe stand beneath the coat pegs. Her brow furrowed and her lips pressed into a tight line as her eyes darted anxiously across the floor.

Excusing herself, Emma made her way to Sarah. 'What's wrong?' she asked.

Sarah's face was a mask of distress, her eyes glistening with unshed tears. 'I've lost my brooch,' she said, her cheeks flushing. 'It's a family heirloom . . . worth a bit of money. It's insured . . . been in our family for generations. It was stupid of me to wear it on my coat . . . but it sparkled nicely and . . .'

'Don't panic. It must be here somewhere,' Emma reassured, scanning the wooden floor. 'I always lose things in the shop and they turn up in the most obvious of places.'

Agnes noticed the commotion. 'Is everything alright?' she asked, joining the girls in the hallway. Her gaze lingered on Emma and Sarah, now searching the floor on all fours.

'I've lost my brooch,' Sarah said, sitting back on her heels and covering her face with her hands.

'Don't worry. I'm sure it will turn up,' Agnes said, giving them one last look before leaving them to it.

'That's all I need,' Sarah said with a sigh. 'Agnes is the village gossip. News of this will spread like wildfire and you can bet my parents will hear of it before they return from their vacation.'

'Is there a story here, ladies?' Fredrick Harris asked, sidling beside them, and sipping his beer from the bottle. 'I could be doing with a good scoop for the paper. Agnes said you've lost something valuable.'

Sarah rolled her eyes, 'See what I mean. You might as well have handed her a megaphone.'

As the last guest trickled out, Emma's shoulders sagged. Despite their thorough search, Sarah's brooch was still missing. The once merry cottage now felt hollow, as if shadows of gloom had crept in with the fading light to steal the festive magic.

While clearing away her good crystal glasses, Emma's gaze wandered to the marble mantelpiece, where a single envelope sat on top of the decorative ivy. Slicing it open, she found a Christmas card picturing a beautiful scene of the village. Looking inside didn't reveal the name of the sender, only a cryptic message.

To find Sarah's missing glittering piece, begin your search and do not cease. Follow the trail of clues - Who sees everything and talks the most?

Emma's brow furrowed, her mind already racing with the implications of this message – rather than the brooch being lost – someone had stolen it – and for whatever reason, wanted Emma to track it down.

Pulling her mobile from her bag, Emma called Sarah. 'Hi,' she said when Sarah answered, recounting the mysterious discovery while trying to keep the tremors from her voice. 'Can you think of anyone who would have taken your brooch, or who might have left this Christmas card for me to find?'

Sarah's voice echoed down the line. 'Everyone is so nice in Jinglebell. I can't think of anyone who would steal. You should call Fredrick. His research skills will come in handy.'

'I was thinking we should call Inspector Smyth?'

'He drank too much cider tonight and will be hungover for days. Fredrick is our best bet of getting to the bottom of this.'

'But could sleuthing be considered as interfering with a crime scene?' Emma asked.

'You're always moaning that nothing exciting ever happens in

Jinglebell. Not only that, you get to spend time with Fredrick. Why would you want to pass that up?'

Emma sighed. 'Okay, I'll think about it. But don't blame me if the culprit disappears into the night with your brooch, never to be seen again.'

The next morning, Emma invited Fredrick to meet her at Brew a Bean, the quaint village café. They sat by the window, looking out at the snow, covered pine trees and sparkling bobbles.

'There's no place on earth that makes lattes the way they do here,' Fredrick said, sniffing the steam rising from his mug.

Emma smacked her lips tasting the freshly brewed coffee before taking a bite of her warm, buttery muffin. She slid the mysterious Christmas card across the table. 'Have a look at this and tell me what you think. I'm trying to solve the puzzle of Sarah's missing brooch. Do you want to help?'

Fredrick leaned forward, his expression thoughtful, as he studied the Christmas card. 'I think the note is referring to Agnes Thompson,' he said. 'She knows everyone's business and notices everything. I bet she saw who put this on your mantlepiece.'

After finishing their hot drinks, they bundled up and headed outside. Fredrick's car, dusted with a fine layer of snow, roared to life. He drove through the winding, frosty roads to Agnes Thomson's small, homely bungalow. Their winter boots crunched over the icy path that led them to her front porch.

The scent of wood smoke greeted them as Agnes opened the door. 'Emma, Fredrick – what a lovely surprise. Please, come in,' she said, with a kind smile. She ushered them into her living room, where a crackling fire added a comforting glow to the poorly lit room. 'Let me fetch some tea,' she said, delighted with the chance to show off her expensive porcelain cups.

'Did you see anyone acting strangely at the party?' Emma asked, as Agnes returned with a tray.

Agnes reminisced about the party, her eyes blinking with the thrill of village gossip. 'You know,' she mused, stirring her tea slowly with a silver spoon. 'I did notice Arthur Brown lingering near the mantlepiece. He seemed rather fidgety, almost as if he was hiding something.'

Emma and Fredrick exchanged glances, waiting for Agnes to catch her breath, having recounted several other village incidents. When she eventually paused, Fredrick swooped in, his words coming thick and fast. 'Thank you for sharing all this news with us,' he said, keeping his patience intact. 'It's good to know we have such an alert and sharp-eyed neighbour looking out for us all.'

Agnes escorted them to the end of her garden path, pulling her shawl tight around her shoulders. 'Good luck,' she called after them, watching until they became a spec in the distance.

They rattled the letterbox on the weathered door of the red-bricked house a few times before Arthur appeared. He greeted them with a guarded smile. 'Emma, Fredrick . . . how nice to see you. What brings you here?'

Emma couldn't help but wonder what secrets he kept behind his polite façade as she had never taken time to get to know him. 'Mr Brown,' she began, her tone firm. 'Do you happen to know anything about this?' she asked, handing him the mysterious card. 'It was left on my mantlepiece at the party after Sarah's brooch went missing.'

He looked down through the small-rimmed spectacles perched on his face, absorbing the cryptic message. 'Please, come in for a minute. I have something you need to see.'

With haste, he led them to his study, heading towards an antique writing desk. He pulled open a stubborn drawer with a soft screech, retrieving a second card. 'I received one too,' he said, handing it to Emma. 'I thought it was a prank at first and was going to bin it. I'm glad I kept hold of it now.'

Emma's fingers traced the words written in the same slightly faded ink. 'Where the bells chime, seek the lime,' she murmured. Suddenly, it clicked into place like a missing piece of a jigsaw. 'The village church,' she exclaimed with certainty. 'There's a lime tree on the garden green right at the entrance.'

'That's where we should head now,' Fredrick said, shaking Arthur's hand in a firm grip. 'Thank you for your help.'

Arthur patted Emily heartily on the back. 'You've got this,' he said with a knowing smile and a wink. 'Let me know how you get on.'

Emma and Fredrick arrived at the village church, its stone walls battered by time. The bells chimed softly as they approached the lime tree, its branches swaying in the wintery breeze. Nestled at the base of its trunk, sat another envelope. The message sent a shiver down Emma's spine as she read out the clue to Fredrick. 'In the place of books, you'll find the crooks.'

She glanced up at Fredrick. 'This implies there is more than one thief. How many people does it take to steal a brooch?'

Fredrick's brow knitted in concentration as he pondered the meaning of this new riddle. 'The library is just around the corner. Let's go,' he said, taking Emma by the arm and guiding her over the icy pavement.

The library was a charming building, its frontage adorned with intricate architectural details. Inside, the polish from the wood floor mingled with the faint hint of pine needles from the festive decorations. Shelves lined with books stood tall and orderly, like soldiers standing to attention. Prudence Hawthorn, the librarian, a tall, elderly lady with silver hair pinned neatly in a bun, sat at her mahogany desk.

'Good afternoon, Miss Hawthorne,' Emma said. 'We're looking for something rather specific today.'

Prudence's eyes narrowed slightly. 'And what might that be?' she asked. 'I hope it's not something from our special collections stored in the archives. I need more time to gather anything like that. You should know that Fredrick, considering your line of work.'

Fredrick held out the latest cryptic Christmas card they had found. 'No, it's nothing to do with books or research. Have you received one of these?' he asked, handing the Christmas card over.

Prudence pondered the message in the card, her face stern with concentration. After a moment, she looked up. 'No, I can't say I have. What does it mean?'

'We have three Christmas cards, each offering a different message,' Emma said. 'We believe they are clues relating to finding Sarah's brooch, and ultimately – who stole it.'

Fredrick handed Prudence his business card. 'Can you call us if one happens to turn up?'

'I'll be sure to do so,' Prudence said, nodding primly. 'And by the way, I'd love you to take out a library membership, Emma. It would be good to have you read our books. We have a wonderful section on botany. Might even give you so tips for your lovely shop.'

'Thank you. I'll think about it,' Emily said, wondering why she had never joined when she first arrived. Perhaps she should have made more of an effort but had never gotten the urge to do so.

The winter evening wrapped around Emma and Fredrick like a soft blanket of snowflakes as they stepped outside. The fading daylight brought to life the blinking Christmas bulbs dotted around the village, and the distant sound of children's laughter rumbled from the frozen pond nearby.

'Don't you just love the atmosphere, here in Jinglebell?' Fredrick said. 'It's such a wonderful place, especially at this time of year.'

Emma hardly heard what Fredrick had said, her interest solely on Sarah's stolen brooch. 'What do we do now?' she asked, disappointed their efforts had hit a dead end.

Fredrick didn't get the chance to reply as Prudence flung open a window, leaning out halfway and screaming as loud as her lungs would allow. 'Come back . . . I found it.'

They hurried back towards the library, anticipation mounting as they darted inside to find her holding a dusty old book. 'I saw this lying on one of the reading tables. When I picked it up, it fluttered to the floor.' She handed the envelope to Emma, who opened it immediately.

Once again, Emma read the clue aloud. 'Where the old clock is stuck on twelve, seek the message on the highest shelf.'

'Who was the last person to borrow this book?' Fredrick asked.

'Follow me,' Miss Hawthorn replied, marching to her desk. She tapped the keyboard on her computer. 'According to our logs, this book hasn't been checked out in over twenty years,' she said, looking up with a baffled expression. 'Someone must have slipped in, placed the card inside and left it on the reading desk when I wasn't looking.'

'Do you have security cameras?' Fredrick asked, his eyes scanning the library's interior.

'No, we never felt the need. Nothing exciting ever happens in Jinglebell,' Prudence said, her lips forming a frown. 'Well, not until Sarah's brooch went missing.'

'We should take a trip over to the town hall before it closes for the evening,' Emma said, tugging at Fredrick's elbow. 'The clock above the entrance is stuck on twelve, it hasn't worked since it was struck by lightning last autumn. That must be where we'll find the next clue. There are several shelves inside the main hall holding all sorts of odds and ends.'

Prudence sighed as she picked up her mobile phone. 'I'm sorry I couldn't have helped more. Let me call ahead to the town hall to make sure Mr Jenkins waits on your arrival.'

'Thank you, you're so kind,' Fredrick said, as they rushed towards the exit.

'Have fun,' Miss Hawthorn called after them. 'And remember to call by for a library card, Emma.'

The janitor, Billy Jenkins, a stout man with a twinkle in his eye and a ring of keys jangling at his waist greeted the duo on the front steps. His ruddy face broke into a warm smile as he led them down the corridor into the main hall. 'The highest shelf is just up ahead,' he said, grabbing a ladder from a store cupboard on the way past. 'We haven't touched it in years; it might be dusty.'

Fredrick climbed the sturdy ladder as Billy stood with his feet planted wide and his hands gripping the sides for support. Fredrick's fingers searched the wide lofty shelf until he spotted it – nestled among the clutter of bric-a-brac, hidden from view.

'Got it,' Fredrick called down, his voice echoing softly in the spacious hall. He placed the envelope in his pocket as his footfall brought him back to the ground where Emma waited with baited breath. She took the envelope from Fredrick's outstretched hand.

Emma held the Christmas card carefully between her fingers. The words danced before her eyes as she announced the latest clue. 'Where the shadows grow tall, seek the room with the scribbly painted wall.'

Fredrick tapped his chin, deep in thought. 'It has to be somewhere with graffiti or murals if it's scribbly,' he mused aloud.

Emma nodded, her mind racing to find the possible setting where the next clue awaited them.

'Perhaps I can help you with that one,' Billy said, rubbing the back of his neck. 'The youth centre down by the park has artwork on its back wall. The latest masterpiece is called Long Shadows; it's by one of the village's promising young artists. I stop by and admire it every morning, making sure there are no frozen pipes in the building.'

'You've been a great help, Mr Jenkins. Thank you so much,' Emma said.

'It's a pleasure, and I hope you find what you're looking for, Emma.'

'It's Sarah's brooch,' Emma said.

'Yes, that too,' he said, waving Emma and Fredrick off.

Emma and Fredrick mulled over the clues they had gathered as they returned to his car. They found it particularly strange that no one had witnessed the cards being placed in their hiding spots. Amidst the bustling activity and constant presence of villagers, the mysterious appearance of the cards was inexplicable. This added a chilling layer to their investigation as they grappled with the enigmatic puzzle surrounding the stolen brooch.

Fredrick unlocked the car with the click of his key fob, and they settled into its cosy interior. He turned the engine on and adjusted the heating to combat the winter chill seeping into their bones. The dashboard lights cast a warm glow as they sat in comfortable silence. Fredrick glanced at Emma, a small smile playing on his lips, before shifting the car into gear.

The youth centre buzzed with activity. Groups of teenagers huddled around tables, some playing cards while others were engrossed in video games; their faces illuminated by the flickering blue screens. The faint scent of popcorn wafted from the small kitchen area, and plastic bowls filled with crips were scattered across every table.

Ethan Chalmers, one of the youth leaders, approached Emma and Fredrick, hesitating slightly before extending a tentative high-five. His uncertainty stemmed from the gap between his age and theirs. 'Hey,' he said, his voice laced with enthusiasm. 'Are you guys here for the mural?'

Fredrick returned the high-five with a chuckle. 'Yes, we'd love to see it.'

'Wait, how did you know that's what we came to see?' Emma asked, unable to hide her suspicion. 'Have you put something there for our arrival?'

Ethan shrugged, his expression innocent and relaxed. 'There's no other reason why anyone your age would come to the youth centre. The whole village has been to see it in the last few days apart from you, Emma. It is a masterpiece,' he remarked, his voice filled with pride.

'Sorry,' she said, feeling guilty at her false accusation. 'Sarah's stolen brooch has made me a little cranky.'

They followed Ethan towards the rear exit into the manicured gardens. 'You've got to see this,' he said with a grin, guiding them to a painted wall illuminated by a large spotlight. The abstract colours, dazzling in their brightness, were a sight to behold against the brick backdrop.

'You won't get better talent anywhere in the world than what we have right here in Jinglebell,' Ethan said, raising an eyebrow at Emma.

She approached the mural, her fingers brushing the cold stone. As she reached the base of the artwork, she found the concealed envelope wedged inside a small crack. 'I've found it,' she said, tearing it open. 'To find the sparkle that you seek, look where music fills the week.'

'That could be a number of places,' Fredrick said, rubbing his chin. 'There's the village radio station, the community hall - they do a variety of dance lessons every night. Or Perry Duncan's homemade bar where he brews terrible-tasting beer. There's always a heavy beat coming from his place.'

Emma nodded, considering their options. 'Let's start with Perry's pub,' she suggested. 'It's the most likely place where music is always playing. Sometimes too loud, may I add.'

'Try his root beer while you're there,' Ethan said, licking his lips. 'There's not another brewery on this planet that can make it as good as he does.'

'I don't think root beer will help us on our quest but thank you for the recommend,' Emma said, then turned to Fredrick. 'Is he not too young to drink?'

Fredrick snorted before offering a reply. 'He's older than he looks.'

Emma settled herself into the passenger seat beside Fredrick. 'Don't you think there's something fishy about all this?' she asked. 'I feel like the culprit is playing games with us. Why go to the trouble of stealing Sarah's brooch and then leave clues about where to find it?'

'Whoever it is, they are extremely organised,' Fredrick replied. 'This crime must have been planned months in advance, with the cards placed long before Sarah's brooch was stolen. Do you think she could be playing a prank?'

Emma's eyes widened. 'A prank? Are you serious?' she exclaimed. 'Sarah would never do such a thing. She was devastated – the brooch is a family heirloom. Besides, she doesn't have time or the inclination to set up something so elaborate. No, this is something more sinister, Fredrick. Someone's playing a game with us, but it's not Sarah.'

Fredrick checked the rearview mirror before pulling the car out of its parking spot. 'Since the first clue was found at your party, one of the guests must have planted it.'

Emma adjusted her seatbelt, then turned to Fredrick with a thoughtful look. 'Rather than follow the clues on the Christmas cards, we should investigate each guest to see if anyone had a motive. We might have better luck.'

Fredrick drew in a deep breath. 'Let's stop by Perry's first since it's on the way. You never know, it might prove fruitful. How many guests were at your party?'

'Almost the whole village,' Emma said, smacking her forehead in despair. 'We could be investigating forever at this rate.'

'We'll get to the bottom of it,' Fredrick said, locking eyes with her briefly.

Caught off guard by his confident gaze that held something she couldn't quite place, Emma felt her cheeks flush. She had hidden her feelings for him all this time and couldn't afford to reveal them now. He might think her silly, imagining that a humble flower arranger like herself could dream of being with a handsome and successful journalist. Their relationship could never progress beyond mere friendship.

As they stepped inside Perry's garage-turned-pub, Emma and Fredrick were immediately hit by a cloud of stale cigarette smoke, mingling with the sharp tang of spilt beer. The heavy metal door creaked shut behind them, muffling the roar of rock music blaring from the speaker, its baseline vibrating through the concrete walls to the outside world.

The room was dimly lit, filled with mismatched furniture and a bar cobbled together from old pallets. Conversations competed with the music, blending into a cacophony of laughter, shouted orders, and the occasional smash of a glass on the concrete floor. Sam Taylor and Jack Pollock leaned on the bar, their elbows resting in pools of alcohol, while the scent of homemade moonshine, spicy and slightly medicinal, drifted from behind the counter.

Fredrick worked his way through the haze, past a group of locals huddled around a battered dartboard. Emma's nose wrinkled at an overflowing mountain of cigarette butts, each stubbed out like a tiny tombstone in a circle of dead smokes. The floor felt sticky underfoot, as they headed towards Perry behind the bar.

'Welcome, Fredrick,' Perry said, flashing his brightest smile. 'And hello to you too, Emma. I don't believe you've been here before, so your drink is on the house – or in my case, the garage. What can I get you?'

Fredrick answered before Emma had a chance to refuse. 'If you still do your Christmas cocktail special, she'll have one of those.'

Perry's grin widened, 'Coming right up,' he said, reaching for a dusty bottle from a shelf lined with an assortment of jars and bottles.

Emma's eyes darted around the smoky room. 'We don't have time for drinks, Fredrick,' she said, tugging his coat sleeve. 'We need to find the next clue.'

Ignoring her irritation, Fredrick nudged Emma towards a small table for two in the corner draped with festive cloth. It seemed out of place amid the cluttered chaos of Perry's garage pub. He pulled out a wobbly chair, the wood groaning under her light weight. Fredrick sat across from her, sliding the raspberry-coloured cocktail in front of her. 'You deserve a drink, after all your running about. Even at your party, you never stopped to enjoy yourself. Sarah said you hosted the party this year because you think it will be your last Christmas in Jinglebell. She said you've been headhunted to manage a garden centre abroad and will be leaving us soon.'

Emma's finger trailed the rim of the glass. 'Sarah told you that?' she asked, her voice barely above a whisper. 'It was supposed to be a secret. I guess that sums Jinglebell up. Everybody knows your business even though nothing exciting ever happens.'

Fredrick gave her a gentle smile. He leaned in closer, his expression turning more serious. 'Do you think life will be any better in the sunshine? Everyone will miss you.'

Emma's mouth opened and closed as she tried to find the right words. 'I . . . I didn't want to make a big deal of it. The opportunity I've been given is incredible. It's too good to turn down.'

She glanced away from his intense gaze, her eyes landing on a table made from a beer barrel, set apart from the bustle of the room. On its top, sat a solitary envelope. Jumping up, she weaved her way through the dancers, snatched the envelope and waved it so Fredrick could see.

'In a spot that's warm and bright, you'll find another clue in the soft moonlight. Amidst the ferns with leafy bower, grows the mystic Jade Vine flower,' Emma shouted, above the music and loud chatter.

Fredrick took the card from Emma and read it again to himself. 'Flowers are your speciality. What do you think it means?'

Emma bit her bottom lip. 'It's describing flowers growing in my greenhouse at the bottom of my garden. But why would the clues take us back to where we started?'

'Finish your drink before we head off,' Fredrick said with a chuckle. 'It's not every day Perry gives drinks away free.'

The last voice calling behind them when they stepped out into the frosty night was Perry's, calling out a cheerful, 'Come back soon.'

'You know what Perry does is illegal,' Emma said, as they drove towards her cottage. 'I don't know why Inspector Smyth allows it.'

Fredrick shook his head. 'Perry's got a licence and has registered his bar. It might not be conventional, but believe me, it's all above board. Perhaps if you had visited before, you'd have known that. Even Sarah pops by now and again.'

'Really?'

'Sure. Sarah told me she asked you out for drinks a few times but you refused. She thought it was something to do with Perry, you not liking him. He's a very nice guy.'

Emma realised she had judged Perry unfairly. 'Perhaps,' she said, feeling a cosy heat spread through her. 'It's a shame I never

THE CHRISTMAS CARD CONUNDRUM

took the time to get to know him. The Christmas cocktail he made was delicious. How much alcohol was in it?'

They passed through Emma's garden gate, into a white wonderland. Glistening snow blanketed the ground and draped the fir trees in shimmering veils. Twinkling lights blinked from the hedgerow, casting soft patterns of coloured light all around. They treaded towards the greenhouse where a hot lamp bathed the plants in a beautiful, warm orange glow.

'I can't understand why you would want to give all of this up,' Fredrick said, holding the greenhouse door open to let Emma enter. 'Everyone loves you in Jinglebell.'

Emma sighed. 'It's not a decision I made lightly.' She ambled over to the clay pots holding her Jasmine plants. Reaching into one of them, she pulled out an envelope. 'Do you want to do the honours, or shall I?'

'Go on, you read it,' Fredrick said, watching Emma tear it open with keen eyes.

'Way up high and under tonight's starry sky,' Emma stopped, screwing up her face. 'That's all it says. What kind of clue is this?'

'I think I've got it,' Fredrick exclaimed. 'It must be Holly-bush Ridge. Do you think whoever took the brooch wants us to climb it?'

Emma's breath caught in her throat. 'What . . . at this time of night? Wouldn't that be dangerous?'

'Where's your sense of adventure?' Fredrick teased, giving her a playful punch on the shoulder. 'Go inside, put on proper winter boots and grab a torch. There's a footpath that takes you up quite far. Don't worry about it being too cold. I'll keep you warm.'

Emma's heart raced, and she couldn't meet his gaze as she moved past him. 'Okay, I'll be back in two minutes,' she murmured, feeling nervous excitement flutter in the pit of her stomach.

As they climbed Hollybush Ridge, the town shrank below to a mere cluster of tiny lights. Their breaths formed a white mist in the cold night air, illuminated by the torch beam Fredrick carried. The icy wind nipped at their faces, while the crunch of snow underfoot broke the stillness. As they ascended higher, the torchlight cast eerie shadows among the trees, disturbing wildlife with a rustle or hoot.

'Have you ever climbed Hollybush Ridge before?' Fredrick asked.

'No, this is my first time,' Emma admitted, finding talking and climbing a demanding task. 'I wish it was done in daylight and the weather a bit warmer.'

'Nonsense,' Fredrick scolded. 'This is the best time of year to do it. We're nearly at the end of the footpath.' Slowing down, he linked his arm through hers. 'Look, down at the village. It's the most breathtaking sight?'

Emma paused to catch her breath, glancing down at Jingle-bell below. It resembled a miniature snow globe, while above, a vast expanse of velvet sky dotted with countless stars shimmered like diamonds. A sense of peace washed over her. 'It's beautiful.'

'I bet we'll find the clue in Edmonds Cave,' Fredrick said, pulling Emma along. 'Legend had it that Edmond lived up here, hence the name of the cave and the footpath to it. There are many different chambers filled with stalagmites that look like frozen fangs of ancient dragons. It's a magical setting for something special.'

'Pity it has been wasted by a petty thief stringing us along with a bundle of silly clues. Honestly, you'd think they'd steal the gem and run.' Emma stopped suddenly. 'What was that?'

'What was what?'

'I thought I heard someone,' she whispered. 'I don't think we're alone.'

Fredrick's laugh echoed around them. 'It's your imagination. Our gem stealer will be long gone. Come on, we're nearly there.'

They rounded a bend, and the mouth of the cave emerged with a soft, inviting light. Stepping inside, they found the cavern brimming with hundreds of candles, their tiny flames casting a golden glow across the walls, their scent of vanilla and wax infusing the air. A small red cushion rested on a boulder, a small box wrapped in Christmas paper placed on its centre.

Emma's stomach churned. 'I don't like this,' she said, feeling a shiver of unease. 'This has been staged. What does the thief want with us?'

'Let's find out,' Fredrick urged, picking up the box and holding it out to her. 'You've gotten us this far. We should see it to its end.'

Emma gulped, hesitating for a second. Her fingers trembled as she tore the paper and opened the lid. Sarah's brooch dazzled from a plush purple cushion. A neatly written note at its side.

Dear Emma, I hope we gave you at least one night of excitement before you leave us for new pastures. We hope you'll return to our village soon. Love from us all, Jinglebell.

Muffled footsteps vibrated from a deeper recess in the cavern. Before Emma could ask what was happening, the teenagers from the youth centre burst from their hiding places shouting, 'Surprise.' Smiles beamed from their faces as they brandished trays of festive nibbles and flasks of piping hot coffee.

Sarah appeared from among them, a sheepish grin on her face. 'I hope you can forgive us, but we wanted to give you some excitement since you complained Jinglebell was boring.'

Emma's heart swelled with relief as she embraced Sarah, feeling the weight of the brooch in her hand. 'Here,' she whispered, pressing the heirloom back into Sarah's palm. 'There's nothing to forgive.'

Tears welled in Sarah's eyes. 'I'm going to miss you. You've not been with us that long but I feel you're part of who we are.'

'Come on,' Fredrick said, pushing himself between them for a group hug. 'We need to head back down. The whole village is at the community centre preparing food and drinks. We're all in on it.'

The village lights twinkled below like a constellation brought to life. Fredrick took Emma's hand gently in his as if it had always belonged there. The crisp winter air closed in around them, carrying with it a bittersweet sense of farewell. 'I'll miss you too,' Fredrick admitted, his gaze lingering on Emma's face. 'And I hope you'll come back soon.'

Emma squeezed his hand. 'I won't stay away too long,' she promised.

'I'll be waiting,' he said, his words carrying a quiet certainty.

At that moment, Emma knew Fredrick, and the spirit of Jinglebell Village, was truly something special.

BIO

Having had a passion for reading and writing since an early age, this passion has only grown over the years. Marti M. McNair has been writing since she could pick up a pen and after her children flew the nest she turned to writing seriously. Her main focus is writing for a YA audience, and her books feature dystopian settings, dark political undercurrents and places her characters in precarious situations which tests them to the limit. She was the winner of the prestigious Scottish Association of Writers, Barbara Hammond Prize. She is also a partner in Auscot Publishing and retreats and a graphic designer for Writers' narrative eMagazine.

https://www.martimcnair.com

Chapter Seven

DECK THE HALLS WITH DEADLY DRAMA

Alex Greyson

Retired investigative journalist Lena Loxley had planned for a peaceful Christmas in her sleepy English village – until the star of the local drama group's *A Christmas Carol* is killed in a suspicious hit-and-run. Now, the festive production is in shambles, and Lena's instincts are screaming that this was no accident. Reluctantly dusting off her sleuthing skills, Lena dives into the mystery, only to find herself working alongside an old flame, Detective Mark Jenkins. Together, they uncover a tangled web of jealous cast members, long-buried grudges, and suspicious alibis. With old tensions rising and the pressure to maintain the village's treasured Christmas tradition mounting, Lena must race against time to uncover the killer – before the holiday season is ruined for everyone. This festive, short read is packed with cozy village charm, suspense, and a touch of deadly drama perfect for mystery lovers.

The morning mist enveloped the narrow streets of Hampton-on-Avon as Lena Loxley stepped out of her thatched cottage, her shoulder-length dark blonde hair catching the light, framing her friendly, open face. The old stone buildings, adorned with festive decorations couldn't rival the Christmas lights of Regent Street, but the village had become Lena's sanctuary after leaving behind the chaos of London and her career as an investigative journalist.

The Red Lion pub doubled as a coffee shop and stood at the heart of the Gloucestershire village, its inviting glow drawing Lena in. Pushing open the heavy wooden door, she was greeted by the familiar aroma of freshly brewed coffee and cheerful chatter of the locals.

'Morning, Lena!' called Tom, the landlord, from behind the bar. 'The usual?'

Lena nodded with a smile, taking a seat by the window.

'Still glad you left that 9 to 5 behind?' Tom joked as he placed the China teapot and cup on the table.

'Too right I am. It was more like 8 until 10 and I don't miss it one little bit!'

Lena's thoughts turned to the tasks that awaited her that day. She was due for her volunteer shift at the food bank at 11 and, if the rain held off, she would go for a long walk in the early afternoon. It wasn't just the natural beauty of Hampton-on-Avon that had drawn Lena to the place. Its sense of community, the warmth of its people, and the promise of a fresh start had captured her heart from the moment she arrived.

Lena barely noticed when Roz, the village gossip, sidled up to her table with a spiteful glint in her eye. Well, the warmth of most of its people, Lena groaned inwardly.

'Lena, my dear, have you heard the news?' Roz gushed.

'What news is that, Roz?'

Roz leaned in. 'After all that business with Robert Jones, there's a vacancy on the village drama group's committee. They're looking for someone to be part of the audition panel for their upcoming Christmas production as well as someone to write the programme. And a little birdie tells me they're going to ask you.'

Lena had tried to ignore the gossip about Robert Jones, but her interest was piqued. The posters advertising 'A Christmas Carol' were plastered all over the village and this could be a great opportunity to meet more people.

Saying farewell to Tom, Lena stepped back out into the chilly morning air admiring the quirky houses as she ambled back up Watergate Lane and paused for a minute to admire the honey stone and neatly trimmed garden of her own cottage. What was missing?

'You need a wreath Ms Loxley!' the strident voice of Dorothy Noble, retired professional actress and leading light of the Hampton-on-Avon Players, seemed to assault Lena's own thoughts.

'Here! Toby asked me to pass this on to you,' the tall woman marched towards Lena brandishing an envelope, her eyes shielded from the milky winter sun by a pair of oversized designer sunglasses. Before Lena had the chance to thank her, the older woman was halfway down the lane, the tails of her cashmere coat flapping behind her.

Inside Pear Tree Cottage, Lena examined the invitation to be part of the audition panel from the Chair of the drama group. Despite Dorothy Noble's brusqueness, excitement bubbled.

The next day, the village hall was buzzing with anticipation as Lena settled into a seat at the front, exchanging nods and greetings with her fellow panellists. Lena was impressed with the number and range of auditionees. She hadn't really known what to expect, but villagers of all ages tried out for parts in 'A Christmas Carol', and, at times, the talent was surprisingly impressive.

Roz flitted about the room, her sharp tongue wagging as she whispered scandalous titbits into eager ears and handed out teas and coffees. Lena sighed, rolling her eyes at Roz's antics.

Amidst the laughter and applause, there were moments that

were, frankly, dreadful. However, everyone was doing their best, and Lena applauded each performer with genuine encouragement. It was after one of the less impressive auditions that Dorothy Noble took the stage. A distinct air of arrogance surrounded the retired actress as she stepped into the spotlight.

'She's quite the character, isn't she?' Lena murmured to the woman beside her.

The woman nodded in agreement her eyes fixed on Dorothy's performance. 'Absolutely. Dorothy has always known how to command attention.' Dorothy delivered her lines with a flourish; Lena couldn't deny the woman's talent and was genuinely captivated by her presence. The applause that followed Dorothy's final line was polite but surprisingly subdued, a testament to the mixed reactions Dorothy's performance had elicited.

As Lena and the rest of the panel discussed the performances and finalised their casting decisions for the upcoming production, she overheard whispers about a fierce backstage argument between Dorothy and Jeremy, a seasoned actor who was vying with the older woman for the role of Scrooge. The dispute, centred around previous roles and bruised egos, had escalated into a heated exchange that left the drama group divided. Beneath the surface, this unresolved tension cast a shadow over the usually cheerful atmosphere, making the final decisions all the more fraught.

It wasn't until later that evening, as Lena was preparing to retire for the night back at Pear Tree Cottage, that she received news that would send shockwaves through the village. Dorothy Noble had been killed in a hit-and-run accident on her way home from the auditions. Lena stared out of the window; the glimmering lights of the village seemed to dim in the wake of the tragedy.

As she closed her eyes and let the darkness swallow her whole, Lena Loxley felt a familiar tug at her journalistic instincts, might the events of that fateful evening be the beginning of a mystery that would unravel the fabric of Hampton-on-Avon's idyllic existence?

The news of Dorothy Noble's death reverberated through the cobbled streets of Hampton-on-Avon like a thunderclap, casting a pall of disbelief over the community.

Despite the lack of suspicion from the police, Lena wondered if there was more to Dorothy's death than met the eye. The circumstances seemed too convenient, too neatly tied up. It wasn't just about uncovering a story; it was about seeking justice. Lena sensed that Dorothy's death was more than just an accident. Driven by the need to seek justice, Lena began discreetly approaching some of the villagers, trying to piece together the truth. But as she probed for answers, she was met with cold stares and curt replies. Mrs. Hargrave, the local grocer, clammed up the moment Dorothy's name was mentioned. Even the normally chatty Tom at the Red Lion seemed uneasy, deflecting her questions with nervous laughter. The more resistance Lena faced, the more determined she became to uncover the truth that the village seemed so eager to keep buried.

Dorothy had always been a polarising figure in Hampton-on-Avon. Her ostentatious displays of wealth, like insisting the village hall showcase her donated chandelier, were hard to miss. Lena learned this from Mrs. Templeton, the local florist, who reluctantly shared how Dorothy's demand had rubbed people the wrong way. Others were tight-lipped, but Mrs. Templeton hinted at deeper tensions. Dorothy's condescending remarks, such as calling the village fair 'charmingly provincial,' had turned friendly smiles into stiff nods. These slights built up, creating an undercurrent of resentment, leading Lena to suspect that Dorothy's haughtiness had made her more than just silent enemies.

Among Dorothy's adversaries was Robert Jones, the

disgraced former chair of the drama group. Once a pillar of the community, Robert's fall from grace had been swift and brutal. Dorothy had been the one to expose his embezzlement of funds from the drama group, which had rocked the foundations of the village. Whether her motive had been a relentless pursuit of justice, or power, it had earned her both admirers and enemies in equal measure.

Might it be possible that Robert had played a role in Dorothy's death? Lena couldn't discount the possibility.

Armed with her notepad and pen, Lena felt the familiar rush of adrenaline as her journalistic instincts stirred. What did she know so far? With the precision of a seasoned investigator, Lena tried to piece together clues, her mind a well-oiled machine processing information with the speed and efficiency born of years of relentless pursuit.

Lena had previously considered the close-knit nature of Hampton-on-Avon and its residents to be a blessing, but now it seemed to serve as a barrier to the truth as she encountered unexpected obstacles at every turn.

Lena sat at a corner table in The Red Lion, ready to jot down any leads or insights that might come her way. She observed the villagers bustling about. Tom, the pub owner, approached her with a thin smile, his demeanour more guarded than usual.

'Morning, Lena. Earl Grey?' Tom asked, his tone polite but lacking its usual warmth.

Lena nodded, sensing Tom's unease. 'Yes, please, Tom. And, if you don't mind me asking, is everything alright?' she inquired.

Tom hesitated for a moment before responding, his eyes darting around the room. 'It's just been a bit of a rough morning, you know how it is,' he replied cryptically.

While Lena sipped her tea, she noticed Roz hovering nearby.

'Had you heard about Dorothy Noble's recent situation?' Roz asked, in a low voice her curiosity evident.

Lena raised an eyebrow, 'No, what's that?'

Roz continued, 'It appears Dorothy was involved in a close relationship with Dr. Coleman before her passing.'

Lena's expression remained neutral, though inwardly, she was already formulating her next line of inquiry. 'Dr. Coleman? The GP?' she clarified, her mind already racing with the implications of such a scandal.

Roz nodded eagerly. "Yes, that's the one. It's quite surprising, isn't it? He's significantly younger than she was. I can't imagine why he'd leave his poor wife at home to gallivant around with Dorothy. Perhaps his head was turned by her fame and sophistication,' she added.

Lena nodded, maintaining her composure despite the tumult of thoughts in her mind. As Roz spoke, Lena recalled that last time she'd seen Emily Coleman, a friendly woman she'd encountered during volunteer shifts at the food bank. She remembered Emily's approachable manner and untroubled countenance, contemplating how this revelation might impact her and her family. Lena made a mental note to investigate further into Dorothy's relationship with Dr. Coleman and the potential repercussions it might have on the tight-knit community.

But before she could delve deeper into the matter, Roz continued, her voice dropping to a whisper. 'And did you hear about the massive row Dorothy had with Tom the other night? Some say it was about money. No-one knows for sure, but they were raging at each other!'

Lena frowned slightly, but Roz ploughed on obliviously.

'Of course, Dorothy could pick a row with anyone. She had a bust-up with someone at the end of the auditions too. I was so busy with refreshments that I'm not sure who it was. But it definitely wasn't with Robert, he left the hall before the first audition. And Jeremy disappeared in a flood of tears when he heard Dorothy had been cast as Scrooge.'

As Lena listened to Roz's prattle, she recalled the tension in the air yesterday. Could the argument Roz mentioned have been with Jeremy, Lena wondered? It was true that Jeremy had been furious about the casting decision for 'A Christmas Carol.' He had assumed he would be cast as Scrooge, but to his astonishment, the role had been given to a female actress.

Surely not being cast in the lead role wasn't a motive for murder, Lena reasoned. As she mulled over Roz's gossip, she decided to speak to both Jeremy and Tom, in the meantime, she needed to silence Roz.

'Let's not jump to any conclusions,' she cautioned, her tone firm but gentle. 'We don't have all the facts yet. It's important not to spread unfounded rumors.'

Lena ignored Roz's scowl as she got up from her seat. Pulling her hat firmly over her ears, Lena let the heavy door shut behind her. To her left, just behind the pub wall, Lena's keen eyes caught sight of a discreet exchange between two younger villagers. Lena pondered the significance of their hushed tones and furtive glances. A clandestine affair perhaps, or maybe something more sinister?

'I'm as bad as Roz!', Lena scolded herself for the wild supposition.

As she turned the corner, Lena's thoughts fixed on the pressing need for assistance in unravelling the mystery surrounding Dorothy Noble's death. Who could she call upon for help? The memory of Mark Jenkins surfaced in her thoughts. Despite their past, Lena couldn't deny the expertise and the comfort of the detective's presence. She remembered his warm smile and the way his eyes had sparkled as he talked about the future. Caught in the whirlwind of her career, Lena had pushed him away, fearing the complications that a romantic entanglement would bring. But now, faced with the perplexing mystery, Lena realised she needed his assistance once again. With a determined nod, Lena hastened her steps, her decision made.

Back in Pear Tree Cottage, Lena sank into her favourite armchair, her mind drifting back to the last time she had seen Mark Jenkins in London. They had parted on good terms, but Mark had swiftly transferred out of the Metropolitan Police and they had not been in touch for well over a year. Perhaps she had been too quick to dismiss the possibility of a relationship with Mark. Lena had recently discovered that the detective had joined the force in Gloucestershire. Although it was a total fluke that Lena had only discovered this after her own relocation to the area, the irony wasn't lost on her.

With a flicker of uncertainty, she dialled Mark's number, her heart beating a little faster with each ring.

Mark, it's Lena,' she said, trying to keep her tone casual despite the flutter of nerves in her stomach.

'Well, well, well, Lena Loxley,' Mark replied, his voice tinged with amusement. 'To what do I owe the pleasure of this unexpected call?'

His voice was warm and familiar, sending a shiver down Lena's spine. 'I was hoping we could catch up,' she said, her words coming out in a rush. 'It's been too long.'

'Indeed it has,' Mark agreed. 'I'd love to, but I'm not in London anymore. I'm down in Gloucestershire now.'

Lena felt a surge of excitement at his response. 'That's quite the coincidence,' she remarked, a hint of flirtation in her voice. 'I've recently made the move to Gloucestershire myself.'

There was a moment of silence on the other end of the line, and Lena's heart skipped a beat.

But then, to her relief, Mark spoke again. 'Gloucestershire, you say? Wow, that is a coincidence. How about we find a halfway point?'

'That sounds perfect,' she replied, unable to hide the smile in her voice.

The pub Mark had suggested had low ceilings and a warm, inviting atmosphere. Lena spotted him sitting at a table near the back.

Their eyes met, and Lena felt a jolt of electricity shoot through her.

'Mark,' she greeted, crossing the room to join him. 'It's good to see you.'

'You too, Lena,' Mark replied, rising from his seat to greet her with a burly hug.

As they settled, Lena found herself drawn to Mark's easy charm and effortless confidence.

So, what brought you to Gloucestershire?' Lena asked, trying to steer the conversation toward more serious matters.

Mark looked down for a moment before responding. 'I transferred to the detective team here a two years ago. It's tiny compared to the Met, but I like the change of pace.'

Lena nodded, filing away the information for later, only briefly wandering if Mark's relocation might have been because of her. 'And have you heard about the Dorothy Noble case?' she asked.

Mark's expression grew serious. 'I have,' he replied. 'It's been all over the news. Tragic business.'

Lena nodded, her mind racing with questions. 'Do you know anything about the investigation?' she continued.

'It's still early days, Lena,' he said carefully. 'We're treating it as a hit-and-run at the moment, but there are a few... complicating factors that we're looking into.'

'Off the record,' Mark continued, dropping his voice, 'there were tensions between Dorothy and several members of the drama group. Reports suggest she had clashes with Robert over the group's finances and she'd also been particularly harsh towards Jeremy, who felt she was undermining his chances for Scrooge. We're investigating whether these disputes could have played a part in her death.'

Lena's brows furrowed slightly. 'I heard about the argument,' she replied, 'do you have any idea who it might have been with?'

Mark hesitated, then shook his head. 'Nothing concrete yet,' he admitted. 'But we're following up on a few leads. It's a small community, Lena. Secrets are hard to keep hidden for long.'

Lena nodded, masking her disappointment. 'And what about the hit-and-run?' she pressed,

'Has there been any progress on that front?'

Mark sighed, his expression grim. 'It's going to take time to track them down. There's no evidence suggesting premeditation at this stage. We've questioned Dr. Coleman thoroughly, given his involvement with Dorothy, but he's been completely cleared. There's no indication he had any part in the accident.'

A sense of frustration gnawed at Lena. She had hoped Mark would have more information to offer, but it seemed they were both grappling with the same lack of substantial leads. She leaned back in her chair, stealing a glance at Mark, admiring the way the dim light cast shadows across his chiselled features. Memories of their past flitted through her mind, igniting a flicker of longing that she quickly suppressed.

As Mark finished speaking, Lena's mind raced with the thrill of the chase, the unsolved crime lingered like a dark cloud over Hampton-on-Avon. Their conversation left her hungry for answers, eager to uncover the truth hidden within the shadows.

The next morning, Lena still couldn't shake the nagging feeling that Dorothy's death was more than an accident. Social media sleuthing had cleared Jeremy from suspicion - he'd left for the airport directly after the auditions, and photos of his Spanish music festival visit were timestamped. With that lead exhausted, Lena was left with four main suspects, each with a plausible motive.

First on the list was Tom Whiteman, the publican at the Red Lion. Overheard making threats to Dorothy, Tom had a reputation for a fiery temper. Lena decided to pay him a visit.

When Lena walked into the pub, she spotted Tom behind

the bar, his face a mask of irritation as he polished glasses. She approached, trying to remain casual.

'Hello, Tom,' Lena greeted with a friendly smile. 'I'd like to ask you a few questions about Dorothy Noble.'

Tom's eyes narrowed. 'Look, I don't see why you're poking around,' he snapped. 'Dorothy was a pain, but I never wanted anything bad to happen to her. Just had a spat about some unpaid tabs. Now, if you don't mind, I'm busy.'

Before Lena could respond, Roz appeared, casting a disapproving glare. 'Lena, dear,' Roz said loudly enough for everyone to hear, 'some of the villagers think you're getting a bit too nosy. Might want to be careful not to step on too many toes.'

Lena ignored Roz's barb but was taken aback by the tension in Tom's reaction. Her visit had clearly ruffled feathers. Lena noted Tom's explanation but sensed that there was more to the story.

Next, Lena decided to approach Robert Jones indirectly. From her informal inquiries around the village, she'd learned that Robert was particularly touchy about the embezzlement scandal and his fallout with Dorothy. To avoid direct confrontation, Lena posed as a writer researching local history and the drama group's past.

At Robert's bungalow on the outskirts, she engaged him in conversation about the village's history and its drama group. Robert, visibly nervous but polite, eventually mentioned past events.

'Dorothy knew about the embezzlement,' Robert admitted reluctantly during their conversation. 'It was a tough time for me. But that's all in the past.' Lena noted Robert's nervousness and avoided pressing too hard, recognising that his discomfort might be linked to the sensitive nature of the topic. While she sensed his desperation, could she really trust his words?

For Emily Coleman, Lena approached the visit with genuine compassion. Having met Emily through their work at the food bank, Lena had a sincere concern for her well-being. She decided to check in on Emily, offering her support during a difficult time. When Lena arrived at Emily's home, she was greeted by the sight of a cosy living room adorned with Christmas decorations. Emily's eyes were red from recent distress, and she welcomed Lena with a tired but grateful smile.

'I'm so sorry to intrude,' Lena said softly, 'but I've been thinking about you. How are you holding up?'

Emily's voice trembled as she sat down. 'It's been so hard. Dorothy's involvement with my husband... it's been devastating. I felt like my whole world was crumbling.'

Lena listened with empathy as Emily poured out her heart. 'I thought we had a perfect life,' Emily continued, her voice breaking. 'But now everything feels like a lie.'

Lena offered Emily a comforting presence, avoiding any direct probing about the incident. 'I'm here if you need anything,' Lena said gently. 'Just know that you're not alone in this.'

Lena pondered her next move. Dr. Coleman had already been cleared by the police, so she knew he wasn't a suspect in Dorothy's death. But could there still be more to Emily's story than met the eye? For now, she would have to tread carefully, lest she risk alienating a grieving wife in her own quest for the truth.

With each suspect's alibi checked and their motives explored, Lena was no closer to solving the mystery of Dorothy's death. The answer felt out of reach, waiting to be uncovered amidst the festive cheer of Christmas. By the time she left Emily's home, the sky had darkened, and the village streets were illuminated by the soft glow of streetlights.

As Lena walked back to her cottage through the quiet, chilly streets, her thoughts swirled with the unresolved questions. Passing the village hall, she noticed the door ajar. Drawn by curiosity, Lena peered inside, her heart racing with the hope of finding something overlooked. Lena made her way to the small dressing room where the actors had prepared for the auditions. In the empty dressing room, Lena rifled through the scattered costumes and props. Amidst the clutter, her fingers brushed against a crumpled note partially hidden under a costume. Unfolding it, Lena read a few hastily written lines: a threat against Dorothy for 'ruining lives.', signed 'R'.

Lena's heart raced. The note suggested someone's anger was more than a mere dispute. With the incriminating evidence in hand, she left the hall, her thoughts spinning about who might be involved and the danger that loomed.

Clutching the note tightly, Lena continued her walk back through the village, her mind racing. She dialled Mark's number but the call went straight to voicemail. She left a message: 'Mark, I found a note in the village hall. It might be crucial for our investigation. Call me back as soon as possible.'

At the next corner, a car sped by, its engine roaring loudly. The vehicle came alarmingly close to her, and Lena felt a cold rush of fear. The driver's face was hidden, and the car vanished into the night.

With a shiver running down her spine, Lena realised the stakes had just got higher. Determined to uncover the truth, she knew she was getting closer to unravelling the mystery of Dorothy's death, even if it meant risking her own safety.

The crisp bite of winter air nipped at Lena's cheeks as she made her way to Roz's cottage. Her mind buzzed with the weight of what she was about to do - confront Roz about the malicious rumours that had swirled through the village, and perhaps ascertain if Roz might be the 'R' in the note.

Roz greeted Lena with a tight-lipped smile, her eyes betraying a mix of curiosity and apprehension. Lena wasted no time diving into the heart of the matter.

'Roz, I need to talk to you,' Lena began, her voice steady despite the tension in the air.

Roz's expression shifted warily, but she gestured for Lena to take a seat nonetheless.

'What's on your mind, Lena?' she asked, her tone guarded.

Taking a deep breath, Lena plunged ahead. 'Roz, I've heard some troubling things lately. I think you know I'm someone who values truth; you really must understand the importance of facts and how damaging spreading rumours can be.'

Roz's facade remained intact, her expression a mixture of defiance and irritation. 'I see you're trying to be the village hero,' she said with a scoff. 'But don't think for a second that your prying will make you any friends around here. People don't take kindly to outsiders sticking their noses where they don't belong.'

Lena looked at Roz, her gaze steady. 'I'm just trying to find the truth,' she said, keeping her voice calm despite Roz's hostility.

Roz's lips curled into a bitter smile. 'Truth, huh? Maybe you should be careful. Some of us remember the kind of trouble that curiosity can stir up. If you're not careful, you might find yourself in the middle of something you're better off avoiding.'

With that, Roz turned away, leaving Lena to digest her words. Roz's hostility was tangible, but Lena believed that Roz's aggressive deflection was more about protecting her own secrets than about any crime. Roz's known penchant for gossip and her tendency to stir trouble in the village didn't align with the specific anger and motive described in the note. The 'R' on the note, was far more likely to point to someone else entirely.

Lena stopped at the edge of the pavement, only now taking the time to listen to her pounding heart. She took a shaky breath and quickened her pace. The near miss was a stark reminder of the danger Lena was in. Could it be a warning? Was someone trying to scare her off, or was it just a coincidence? She let out a long breath at the sight of Mark's parked car outside Pear Tree Cottage. Rushing inside, Lena's fingers tapped impatiently as she handed Mark the note with the mysterious 'R.' Mark's eyes widened as he examined the note.

This is significant,' Mark said, his voice serious. 'If this note is genuine, then whoever 'R' is has a serious motive to harm Dorothy.'

Lena nodded. 'I've been thinking, and I believe Robert Jones might be our person. Roz was initially a concern, but given her behavior and interactions, it's clear her hostility was more about gossip than direct involvement. This note, however, points to someone with a more personal motive.'

Mark agreed. 'We need to speak to him immediately. If he's involved, we need to confront him.'

Lena nodded, her heart pounding in her chest. 'I found it hidden away in the dressing room at the village hall,' she explained. 'It seems Robert might well have had a motive for wanting Dorothy dead.'

Mark frowned, his mind spinning with possibilities. 'We need to bring Robert in for questioning,' he said, his voice firm. 'And we need to do it now.'

Lena and Mark made their way to the modern bungalow on the outskirts of the village. Lena's pulse quickened with anticipation. Would Robert confess to his crimes, or would he deny everything and try to cover his tracks?

Mark knocked on the door, his knuckles rapping against the wood decisively.

The door creaked open, revealing Robert standing on the threshold, his expression one of surprise and confusion. 'What's this all about?' he asked, his voice tinged with suspicion.

Mark stepped forward, his gaze steady as he met Robert's eyes. 'We need to ask you some questions about the death of Dorothy Noble,' he said, his tone grave.

Robert's eyes widened in shock, his hands trembling at his sides. 'I don't know anything about Dorothy's death,' he insisted, his voice shaking with emotion.

But Lena could see the fear in Robert's eyes. She knew they were close to uncovering the truth.

'Robert, we found a note signed with an 'R' in the dressing

rooms at the village hall,' Mark said, his voice steady. 'It was clear that the writer was deeply upset with Dorothy. Can you explain this?'

Robert's eyes darted nervously, and he fumbled for words. 'I... I don't know what you're talking about,' he stammered, his voice barely above a whisper.

Mark pressed on. 'Robert, we know about your past with Dorothy. You had a serious dispute with her, didn't you? If you have anything to say, now's the time.'

Robert's shoulders slumped, and he sighed heavily. 'Alright, yes, I was angry with Dorothy. But I didn't mean for things to end like this. I didn't think it would go this far. I just wanted her to leave me alone.'

Robert's face paled, his eyes darting between Lena and Mark as he struggled to find the right words. 'I... I didn't mean for any of this to happen,' he stammered, his voice barely above a whisper. 'I was angry, yes, but I would never hurt anyone.'

But Lena knew better than to believe Robert's lies. She had seen the truth written in his own words, felt the weight of his guilt pressing down on her shoulders. And now, it was time for Robert to face the consequences of his actions. As if reading her mind, Mark stepped forward 'Robert, you may as well tell us everything,' he urged, his voice firm.

Robert's shoulders slumped as he let out a heavy sigh. Slowly, he began to recount the chilling details of how he had meticulously orchestrated the hit-and-run that tragically claimed Dorothy's life. Each word was laden with guilt as he described his desperate attempt to frame the incident as a mere accident. Falteringly, he revealed the intricacies of his plan, from the initial conception to the moments of hesitation and fear that troubled his conscience ever since.

With a sense of finality, Mark placed Robert under arrest, his hands bound behind his back as he was escorted to the waiting police car.

As the mystery of Dorothy Noble's death found closure, Christmas Eve wrapped Hampton-on-Avon in a cosy embrace.

Lena and Mark were tucked away in a corner of the Red Lion, the warmth of the crackling fireplace and the holiday cheer surrounding them.

'Lena,' Mark began, his voice serious, 'Robert's been charged with Dorothy's murder. His confession sealed it.'

Lena nodded, a mix of relief and sadness washing over her. 'It's a tragic end, but at least we found the truth.'

Mark gave a reassuring smile. 'You've been crucial in this, Lena. I'm glad you're here.'

As their conversation shifted to lighter topics, Lena noticed Roz across the room. Their eyes met, and Roz offered a small, seemingly genuine smile. Lena returned it, feeling a sense of peace. Perhaps, despite everything, there was room for understanding.

Lena turned back to Mark, her eyes meeting his in a way that made her heart skip. 'I'm glad I'm here too, Mark,' she said softly, warmth spreading through her.

Lena smiled, her heart light with possibilities—not just in the village she loved, but maybe with Mark as well.

As the carols played softly in the background, Lena let out a contented sigh, knowing she had found her true home in Hampton-on-Avon, where mysteries were solved, hearts healed, and the future was as bright as the Christmas lights twinkling in the square.

BIO

Alex Greyson is an exciting new voice in crime fiction, currently writing a gripping British police thriller. Born in Liverpool, before being raised in the ocean city of Plymouth, Alex's fascination for criminal justice was sparked during a decade spent teaching inmates to read in various prisons and young offender institutions. This first-hand experience immersed Alex in the intricacies of the human psyche and the complex dynamics of law enforcement. Drawing upon this unique background, Alex weaves atmospheric narratives that delve deep into the shadows of the genre. *Deck the Halls with Deadly Drama* is Alex's first cozy mystery.

https://www.alexgreyson.com

Chapter Eight

THE TIME BEFANA SAVED CHRISTMAS

Julia Fancelli Clifford

In a picturesque Italian village that turns into a winter wonderland each December, eighteen-year-old Anna steps up to lead the Christmas festivities when her mother falls ill. As she dives into the holiday preparations, the village's beloved Christmas stocking disappears. Anna's determination to retrieve it leads her to uncover a devious scheme by local shop owner Claudia involving a secret cellar and a cunning plot to boost sales.

With her tech-savvy friend Alex, Anna exposes Claudia's plot and clears the name of the young actor playing the Grinch, whom Anna secretly fancies. Yet, as the mystery unwinds, Anna ponders a haunting question: was it indeed her cleverness that uncovered the truth, or did Befana, the benevolent witch of the Italian Epiphany, subtly guide her hand?

Anna loved Christmas, even at eighteen.

Each December, she and her mother, Paola, explored the festivities around Rome and their village of Viterbo, which transformed each year into mesmerising versions of the North Pole.

Paola's infectious enthusiasm for the season painted Anna's childhood Christmases in vivid, bittersweet colours. It wasn't merely the twinkling lights, ornate decorations, or wrapped gifts; it was a precious time that drew her closer to her mother.

Paola had always been central in organising the Christmas festivities within the village. But this year, ill health had held her back.

Stepping into Paola's shoes, Anna took charge. 'It's time I helped keep our tradition alive.'

Her mother managed a faint smile before her usually bright chestnut eyes clouded under the influence of morphine.

'Don't worry, *Mamma*. I'll take pictures, especially of the stocking.'

Leaving Belcolle Hospital, Anna walked home, excited to start work the next day.

Of all the Christmas traditions, Paola cherished the legend of Befana, a generous witch who flies across Italy on Epiphany's Eve, 5th January, filling children's stockings with sweets—or coal for the naughty—as she searches for baby Jesus.

Inspired by this enchanting story, Paola championed the introduction of the special stocking when the village was first founded. It was a unique piece—the villagers had handcrafted it many years ago, each adding to it, making it a patchwork of the community's spirit and love for Christmas.

Anna knew the mere sight of it would lift her mother's spirits.

The following morning, Anna's heart brimmed with anticipation as she approached the village. Clad in a cosy coat, her auburn hair tucked under her elf hat, she walked through Viterbo's snow-covered streets, excited at the thought of unveiling Paola's cherished stocking.

While assembling Father Christmas's sleigh in the main square, Anna contemplated sneaking an early peek at the stocking, which was spending the week in the Grinch's backroom.

Seizing the moment, she announced, 'I'll take the spare costume to the Grinch's house!'

'Ho, ho, ho, don't get too caught up with the boy who plays that green gremlin!' her dad, Franco, dressed perfectly as Babbo Natale, teased from behind.

Anna smiled. After capturing the stocking, she planned to photograph him for her mother, who had always said he'd make a great Babbo Natale. The grandeur of Alessandri's Palace's upstairs hall, being transformed into Father Christmas's house, accentuated his costume.

However, her dad's teasing words made her blush. '*Papà*! It's not like that!'

Perhaps it was, but she wouldn't confess—not to her teasing dad, whose twinkling eyes displayed his amusement.

'Sure, my dear.'

'Will you leave her alone, poor darling?' Claudia, the owner of Viterbo's most famous sweet shop, interjected in her overly sweet tone, wiping the smile from Anna's face.

For as long as Anna could remember, she had found Claudia unsettling. Their interactions had been limited to brief visits to her shop, but working together at the Christmas Village this year meant they would meet more often. Claudia's sugary words, especially how she lingered on *darling*, reminded Anna uncomfortably of the witch from Hansel and Gretel.

Tearing Anna from her thoughts, her dad's words were more severe than his tone. 'That boy, Carlo, is very handsome, Claudia. Anna's too young and innocent—'

'That's why you should keep your big, fat nose out of it, Franco. Let kids be kids,' Claudia quipped, patting Anna's shoulders with cold hands.

'I'm eighteen, *Papà*!' Anna sighed, desperate to leave and take a picture of the stocking to show her mother that evening.

The fact that Carlo the Grinch was indeed handsome wasn't the problem.

With a determined stride, Anna headed for Scacciaricci Tower, currently reimagined as the Grinch's House. From the window, she saw Carlo remove his Grinch mask to reveal a mop of brown curls. She felt her breathing falter as he ran his fingers through his hair and flashed a playful smile.

'Hey. How's it going?' His blue eyes sparkled.

An involuntary smile escaped her lips. 'Hey, it's been some time.'

'I didn't think you'd remember me.'

How could she forget? They attended the same class for a few months after he transferred mid-year to her high school. All the girls—and some of the boys—gossiped about him. But since they'd finished school, she hadn't heard from him.

'I thought you'd be in Hollywood by now.' That's what he wanted to do. Be an actor, and he had the looks—and the talent —for it.

'I stayed for *Nonno* after *Mamma* passed.' He sighed. 'Me leaving would've broken him. That's why I'm here playing the Grinch.'

Anna's heart jolted. 'I'm sorry to hear that. Can I see the stocking, please? It's for my *mamma*.'

Carlo didn't question why her mother wanted to see the stocking. He just opened the door and gestured for Anna to enter.

'She's in hospital,' Anna muttered as she looked around, her cheeks strangely warm.

The interior of the Grinch's house was a whimsical collection of Christmas decorations, resembling the Grinch's lair from the classic Christmas story.

Carlo led Anna through the maze of festive clutter. 'I under-stand,' he said, sidestepping a box of decorations, his smile warming the chilly room. 'My *nonno* is also ill but prefers being home rather than in hospital. I spend my evenings with him.'

'Maybe you could visit *Mamma* with me sometime?' Anna suggested as they neared the room where the stocking was stored.

Carlo opened the door, stepped inside, and paused abruptly.

'What the?' he blurted.

'Where's the stocking?'

'I don't know.' Carlo panicked. 'It was here yesterday.'

Picking a piece of paper from the floor, he began reading.

'What does it say?' Anna moved closer.

'Giovanni's been naughty and won't get sweets.'

'Giovanni... Borrelli? Could it be a prank? I mean, he's the village director. He's too upstanding to be naughty.'

Carlo agreed.

The hours sped by. Anna contacted her dad, and together, they approached the Director, who enlisted Constable Rossi, a trusted police officer friend, to investigate the theft discreetly. Having searched the Grinch's house to no avail, Rossi and Borrelli assembled everyone with access to the room for questioning. The tense atmosphere contrasted with the cheerful decorations. Carlo, Anna, her dad, Claudia, and Stefania, who was playing Befana's part, were all suspects.

After a rigorous interrogation, Anna slumped beside her dad, who had already been questioned. He was absorbed in the local newspaper, reading about a local toy shop's closure and devastating job losses.

'This is ridiculous; you can't keep me here!' Claudia stormed past Borrelli while he interrogated his suspects, stomping her feet and sulking into the seat next to Anna's dad.

Borrelli scowled. 'You'll stay here like everyone else. I don't care what your excuse is, Claudia. We need to find the stocking!'

'Of course, you don't care.' Claudia snarled. 'You never do. Like when I asked to be Befana to advertise my shop, and you refused.'

'You're too young,' Borrelli said. 'Stefania is much more suited to the role. And you can't monopolise the stocking filling.

It's meant to be a collaborative effort to strengthen community spirit.'

'Bullshit!' This time, it was Stefania who crossed her arms and glared at Borrelli, her fiery brown eyes flashing daggers towards him. 'I agree with Claudia. You don't care about our community. You only care about bringing in tourists and filling your pockets. All this tourism is taking away the authenticity of our village.' Her anger accentuated her wrinkles.

Anna agreed with Borrelli. Stefania had been the village's unanimous choice, bar one vote, and she made a far better Befana than Claudia could. Claudia's was the only vote against Stefania. Anna couldn't help but wonder why anyone would be upset at not being ugly or old enough for a role.

Borrelli decided they would all keep the theft quiet for the time being to avoid panic and preserve the festive spirit but insisted they act quickly to retrieve the stocking. The Christmas Village would soon open its doors, and the children would expect to see the stocking. It was tradition, after all!

'This is a catastrophe,' Borrelli exclaimed, his hands in his hair and his face pale, frowning at Carlo. 'Something's off. Nothing else is missing; they've only taken the stocking.'

That's right, Anna thought. And this was serious—the stocking was irreplaceable.

'I assure you, Mr. Borrelli, I had nothing to do with this.' Carlo's voice was steady despite the accusation in the director's gaze. 'I was at home attending my *nonno*. He's bedridden and needs help at night.'

The director appeared less convinced by Carlo's statement when Constable Rossi whispered in his ear.

'Rossi's found evidence that you're lying, Carlo.'

Carlo looked shocked. 'What evidence?'

Constable Rossi held up a flash drive. 'CCTV footage. Someone wearing the Grinch costume entered the stocking's room around midnight.'

'It makes sense,' Claudia declared. 'He's taken his role far too seriously. He intended to steal Christmas all along!'

The room fell silent, except for the soft hum of the Christmas lights. Everyone appeared to agree with Claudia. Anna's heart sank.

'I-, I wasn't here.' Carlo's Adam's apple bobbed. 'I told you; I was with *Nonno*.'

Anna believed him. With a determined chin lift, she stepped forward. 'There must be some mistake. Anyone could have worn the costume. Carlo, can you verify your alibi?'

Carlo nodded. 'Yes, I took over from the carer at around nine, and *Nonno*, I'm sure he woke up around midnight; I helped him to the toilet. I sleep in the room with him.'

Borrelli turned to Rossi. 'Check his alibi. And verify the time stamps on that footage.'

As Rossi left, Anna turned to her dad. '*Papà*, we must do something. We can't let Carlo take the blame for something he didn't do.'

'My dear, are you thinking with your heart rather than your brain?'

Glancing at Carlo, Anna was thankful he hadn't heard. 'Shush, *Papà*. It's not that. I don't want an innocent to get the blame.'

Anna was torn. She worried for Carlo; she felt that he was being framed. But she also knew the loss of the stocking would break her mother's heart.

'We need to find it before January 6th,' her dad said. 'The stocking is the highlight of the Epiphany celebration. Without it, the festival-.'

'Will lose its heart,' Anna finished.

Anna spent hours searching the Grinch's house but found nothing. Carlo was scared and pale, and Anna could understand why. Even Stefania agreed he was in a worrying situation, especially after Constable Rossi showed everyone the CCTV footage.

Alone in the room where the stocking had hung, Anna paced the floor. Her phone rang.

'Hey, Anna, it's Alex checking in. How's Paola?' Alex's voice was a welcome distraction. He was an old friend of hers, a real geek who loved playing video games and was a genius at coding. Her father had often pulled her leg, saying that a programmer wouldn't be a bad idea for a son-in-law, but Anna had always given him an eye roll. She didn't like him that way, and besides, she had often suspected he was gay.

'Thanks, Alex. *Mamma*'s holding on. Chemo isn't making her any stronger, but the anticipation of Christmas is lifting her spirit. I'm working at the Village now, and... well, there's a situation here,' Anna hesitated, as the theft was supposed to be confidential. But this was Alex—she trusted him, and she needed a friend. Besides, his technical knowledge may come in handy. Before she knew it, she had told him everything.

'Anna, I know you want to prove the innocence of your boyfrien—'

'Alex! He's not my boyfriend!' Anna hissed.

'Yes, you can imagine my tongue in cheek, right?' He chuckled. 'You have taste anyway. If I recall correctly from school, he was quite a catch.'

As Anna's gaze wandered around the cluttered room, she noticed a slither of grey poking out from beneath a pile of colourful Christmas garlands.

'Hold on, Alex, I've found something.' She bent down to pick it up.

'What?'

'I'm not sure. It looks like some old, square piece of plastic with a metal slide. I'm sending you a photo.'

Seconds later, Alex chuckled. 'Anna, that's a floppy disk! It's an old storage device. It should almost be in a museum.'

'A flossy what?' Anna couldn't hide her confusion. A museum?

'A *floppy* disk. It looks tatty. Probably doesn't work anymore. Who knows how long it's been there?'

'But—' Anna protested, whispering into her phone. 'It was in the room where the stocking was stolen. What if there's important data on it?'

Alex sighed. 'I doubt one and a half megabytes of data could be relevant, but okay. I have the hardware to read it. Can you bring it over?'

'Sure, I'll drop by before visiting *Mamma* at the hospital. This could be a lead, right?' Anna's spirits lifted at the prospect of finding a clue.

'As I said, I don't think so, but for the sake of your boyfriend, I'll give it a go.'

Anna glared into her phone, but Alex hung up before she could protest. After securing the disc in her bag, she went to leave the room, but Rossi appeared, blocking her path.

He folded his arms. 'You're not going anywhere, kid. Nobody leaves the hall.'

Anna panicked. 'Please, Constable Rossi. My mother's in hospital; she's expecting me.'

Carlo, who also appeared to be panicking, interjected. 'I need to go too. *Nonno* needs supervision. I have the doctor's report in my emails to prove it.'

'*Papà*, please, tell Mr Borrelli I'm not lying.'

After a lengthy discussion, Borrelli had been convinced to allow Anna and Carlo to leave. But not before he warned them, 'You can go, but no funny business. Rossi will escort you home and keep watch outside for the night, Carlo. We can't take any risks. And you, Anna, make sure to return here first thing tomorrow morning!'

Anna promised and left the room, determined to deliver the floppy disk to Alex.

By the time she arrived, Alex had set up the old computer.

'This is a rare find in today's tech landscape,' he whispered.

'It's never gonna work,' Anna replied, inserting the disc into the drive.

But the LED light lit up, and a weird noise escaped the computer.

'And yet...' Alex gasped as the disk contents appeared on screen, including SQL databases labelled 'Miele_Vaniglia_-Clients' and 'La_Giraffa_Stock.'

'That's Claudia's sweet shop,' Anna exclaimed.

'And La Giraffa is the toy shop next to Claudia's, right, Massimo Trozzi's shop?'

'Yes,' Anna nodded, 'but what is it?'

'And why would it have been in the Grinch's house?' he replied, pursing his lips.

Alex skimmed through the other files on the disk. 'There's more,' he said, clicking on a folder that opened to reveal a series of low-resolution photographs. Among them was a picture that caught Anna's attention—a map of the Viterbo Sotterranea, the ancient underground pathways beneath the village. One room on the map was circled in red, marked 'TS.'

'This has to mean something,' Anna's excitement and apprehension were evident in her tone.

Alex dashed from the old computer they were working on to his ultra-modern PC. 'TS? If it's top secret, Claudia might be up to no good.' His fingers rattled across the keyboard, breaking the room's silence.

'Uh-huh!' he exclaimed.

'Did you find something?'

Alex slammed his hand on his desk, showing Anna the Italian Land Registry database, the *Catasto*, and the cellar's registration during the *condono*, the building amnesty. 'The room was registered four months ago; not under Claudia's name, but Trozzi's. There's something fishy going on.'

Anna was impressed; this was highly confidential information —Alex's hacking skills were better than she thought.

'If they registered it during the *condono*, it's now legal, right?'

'If it weren't Trozzi who built the cellar, then that would imply that something fraudulent has gone on. You know, misrepresentation of ownership, fees-avoidance, compliance issues. I'm not a lawyer, but that's my understanding. We should check it out.'

'It could be a lead, maybe?'

'Or it could be nothing, but it's worth checking.' He zoomed in on the map, trying to pinpoint the exact location of the room. 'Whether it's related to the stocking or not, it could put Claudia in trouble with the law.'

Determined to uncover the truth, Anna and Alex devised a plan. The next day, armed with the map and their wits, they would venture into the Viterbo Catacombs, searching for the mysterious 'top secret' room. But first, Anna needed to go to the hospital.

As she sat beside her mother's bed, gently holding her hand, the quiet hospital room was bathed in the soft glow of the evening sun. Despite the frailty the illness had brought, Paola's eyes still sparkled with the same warmth and wit Anna cherished.

'So, how's our Christmas Village doing? Is the stocking getting all plumped up for the Epiphany?' Paola asked with a gentle smile, her voice a soft echo of its usual vigour due to her weakened state. 'How's our North Pole doing without me, its head elf?'

'It's chaos, *Mamma*.' Anna chuckled. 'You've always been the one to make everything run smoothly. And-.' She hesitated, her expression clouding over as she contemplated how to break the troubling news.

'And what, sweetie?'

'It's the stocking, *Mamma*. It's gone missing,' Anna confessed, the words spilling out in a rush as she filled her mother in on the latest events. She watched her mother's face fall, the joy fading into a worried frown.

'Oh no!' her mother's voice broke. 'That stocking isn't just fabric and threads. It's a tapestry of our community's spirit and love. This is a tragedy, Anna.'

Nodding, Anna felt the weight of her mother's words. 'And *Mamma*, you won't believe who might be involved—Claudia.'

'Claudia?' Her mother's eyebrows arched. 'I can't believe it. She loves providing sweets to fill the stocking. Why would she do that?'

'I've never truly trusted her, *Mamma*. There's something about her that's, I don't know, two-faced?'

Her mother sighed, a shadow of a smile crossing her lips despite the grim topic. 'I know what you mean. Franco always joked that her 'darling' reminded him of Patsy from Absolutely Fabulous. *Darling, darling,* always with a glass in hand.'

'Exactly. The way she speaks sounds fake. And I'm serious about getting to the bottom of this. I will find that stocking and prove Carlo's innocence.'

'Carlo, the handsome Grinch? Am I detecting signs of a crush?'

Anna's cheeks flushed as she averted her gaze, focusing instead on a loose thread on her sweater. 'No, *Mamma*. I just don't think he's to blame. It's unfair! Alex has been helping me and thinks Carlo's innocent, too.'

'Alex, your hacker friend? He's your partner in solving this crime?'

Anna nodded.

'Your *papà* told me there was a spark between you and Carlo, and he mentioned Alex a few times. Is there something you're not telling us?' her mother prodded gently, the twinkle in her eye as clear as daylight.

'*Mamma*!' Anna protested. 'Alex is just a friend. I've told you many times. I don't even think he's interested in girls. And Carlo... He's *just Carlo* right now.'

Her mother's lilting laughter filled the room. 'Just Carlo, hmm.'

Anna groaned, though the warmth in her chest at her mother's teasing was a welcome sensation. 'You're impossible, you know that? This is serious. We found a floppy disk that might have clues, and Alex is helping me figure it out.'

'Ah, a floppy disk! Now, that brings back memories. Believe it or not, Claudia used to store all her data on floppy disks. Did Alex manage to read the disk you found?'

'Yes, he did.' She sighed. 'We think the floppy belongs to Claudia. At least, it contains databases about her clients, stock for a toy shop, and more.'

'I knew it,' her mother replied with satisfaction, a sudden yawn betraying her tiredness. 'What else did you find out?'

Anna knew her mother was getting worse. But given she kept asking, Anna went on to tell her about the mysterious room and the cryptic note implying Giovanni's involvement.

Her mother appeared lost in thought. Her gaze was sharp despite her weakened state. 'I wonder,' she mumbled, her index finger tapping distractingly on her jaw.

'What?'

'I was just thinking that the note sounded weird, that's all. As if Befana is involved in some way.'

'Yeah, I know.' Anna laughed. 'The thief must have a sense of humour.'

'You know,' her mother chuckled, 'Claudia isn't a saint. I've known her for years, and I've often suspected she's had an affair.'

'Really?' Anna gasped.

'Yeah,' her mother replied. 'She was way too involved with Massimo Trozzi, the owner of the shop next to hers.'

'You mean the toy shop? The one that has gone bankrupt?'

Anna spotted a copy of today's paper resting on her mother's bedside table. Picking it up, she skimmed the cover page. 'The floppy contained a database of Massimo Trozzi's shop stock, too.'

'Claudia mentioned a cellar a few times,' her mother managed, 'hidden beneath her shop.' Her voice lowered to a whisper. 'She built it illegally as she needed more storage space, but that was many years ago. She mentioned it was accessible through the old catacombs. Sometimes, she would joke that she could use it as a *garçonnière*, her private little romantic hideout.' Her mother chuckled again, her voice returning to its usual tone. 'Probably, she kept it quiet because she didn't want her husband to find it. But, Anna,' her gaze becoming serious. 'The room might not be in *Catasto's* records. You'll have to prove ownership. This is more serious than just the theft of a stocking. Claudia could go to jail.' She started coughing as if the effort of her words had drained her.

'Alex noticed the cellar was registered during the latest *condono* but not in Claudia's name. In Trozzi's. How can I find out the truth?'

'Contracts, utility bills, builder's receipts,' her mother managed between coughs. 'If someone owns a property, there will be a paper trail somewhere. Nowadays, it's probably kept in the cloud.' She winked at Anna. 'And no cloud is entirely secure from hackers.'

'*Mamma*! You're amazing, you know that?' Anna gave Paola a gentle hug.

'Be careful, sweetie. It might not be worth gaining enemies for the sake of a crush.'

'But *mamma*, you taught me to hold people accountable. I want the truth,' Anna complained.

'I'm proud of you, sweetie.' Her mother beamed. Her frail hands gently moved Annas's auburn locks from her forehead, and a teasing sparkle returned to her eyes. 'If you can gain a boyfriend in the process, even better.'

Anna could only laugh. Her mother knew her well.

Early the next morning, Anna and Alex disguised themselves as tourists and made their way to the grocery shop that served as an entrance to the catacombs. After paying the fee and gaining directions, Anna received a text.

'Hi Anna, it's Carlo. Sorry for the txt—kept ur # from school. U coming back? Borrelli's freaking, thinks u r to blame.' The message ended with a little red heart. Anna gasped, her eyes widening. Alex peeked over her shoulder.

'He kept your number from school? Hmmm, and the heart emoji.' Alex sighed. 'I wish a cute boy sent me messages with hearts.'

Anna gave Alex's shoulder a playful slap, causing him to chuckle. She didn't need him to add hope to her wandering mind. The more she looked at that message, the more she pictured a rosy-tinted future, with her discovering the truth and Carlo falling in love with her, her fantasy ending in marriage with a pretty home, two kids, and maybe a pet.

She blinked and shook her head to clear her mind. *Damn, Alex, for giving me ideas!*

'Be right back, promise. Tell Borrelli 2 chill. Will explain everything when back.'

'KK!' followed by a heart and a kiss emoji.

'Told ya.' Alex poked her in the ribs.

She poked him back and pursed her lips before hurrying down the stairs that led to the catacombs.

Guided by the map, they navigated the dimly lit passages. After what felt like an eternity, they arrived at a wall that matched the location marked on the map. A careful examination revealed a cleverly concealed door leading them to the hidden cellar.

Using their smartphones as flashlights, they entered the darkened room.

Anna squealed, breaking the eerie silence.

'The missing Christmas stocking!' She gasped.

It was draped over a chair, surrounded by boxes bearing the unmistakable branding of Claudia's sweets factory and other wrapped parcels that looked like presents.

'What are these presents doing here?' Alex picked up a few, and Anna tore a piece of wrapping paper from one to check its content. When she couldn't determine what it was, she groaned and ripped the paper off, revealing a doll house.

Anna surveyed her surroundings. The cellar felt clammy, intensifying her claustrophobia and adding to the already creepy atmosphere. She tore the wrapping from the other boxes, revealing toys for all ages.

Anna's heart raced as the pieces of the puzzle began falling into place: the floppy disk, the cellar, Claudia's sweets, the gifts. But she needed evidence.

'Alex, I'll take pictures here and return to the Village. Would you do me a favour before joining me at Alessandri's Palace?'

'Yes, of course; what?'

Anna felt herself lean closer as she whispered her instructions. A bit silly since no one was around, but given the walls might have ears, it seemed appropriate.

Returning to the surface, they went in separate directions, with Anna ready to confront Claudia and expose the truth.

'*Papà*, got news. Plz get everyone @ Alessandri's? OMW .' As she wrote this message, a gust of fresh air hit her face—a welcoming feeling after the claustrophobic thickness of the atmosphere in the cellar.

'On it!' her dad replied. 'Bout time. Been tough keeping Gio chill. He thought u ran off & blamed u.'

'Nearly there. I'll explain everything when I c u.'

As she entered the room, it fell silent. All eyes were on her, including Carlo's.

'Thank you all for being here,' Anna began, her voice echoing in the room's vastness. Her fingers felt like ice, and not simply because of the cold. She wasn't used to talking publicly, and although it was only a handful of people, she knew that Carlo's future lay in her frozen hands. She gulped, pausing for a moment to steady her nerves.

'I've found the missing Christmas stocking,' she announced. 'It was hidden in a cellar beneath Claudia's sweet shop, surrounded by boxes of toys and gifts.'

'Oh, please, Anna,' Claudia scoffed, her voice thick with sarcasm. 'Is this some grand scheme? Maybe Stefania, fed up with our village's sell-out to tourists, decided to make a statement. Or maybe you want us to believe it's the real Befana's magic at work? Please...' She cast a doubtful glance at Stefania, who frowned back.

Continuing defensively, Claudia added, 'And a secret room under my shop? I had no idea about any such thing!' Her voice climbed as she threw her arms up in exasperation.

Although Claudia's denial surprised her, Anna quickly regained her composure.

'The evidence speaks for itself, Claudia,' Anna replied, holding her phone to the audience. She displayed photos of the cellar, with the stocking visible among the toys and bags of sweets with Claudia's factory branding.

Alex arrived, stopping at her side. She shot him a warm smile. He was just in time.

Claudia's face flushed red as murmurs began circulating in the hall. Her eyes darted back and forth as if looking for support but finding none.

Aware of the shifting mood, Anna continued. 'The entrance to this cellar was concealed behind a wall in the catacombs, directly beneath your shop, Claudia.'

Anna let the information sink in before continuing. Her gaze swept briefly to her dad, who was looking on with pride. Then to Carlo. Her heart skipped a beat when she noticed how emotional he had become and how attentively he was waiting for her to continue. Then there was Claudia, who was standing near the back, ashen-faced.

'But this isn't just about the stocking. I think Claudia orchestrated this ploy to fool us all.' Whispers turned to gasps. Anna continued, 'The toys we found had come from Massimo Trozzi's shop. Stefania wasn't involved. It was you, Claudia. You and Trozzi. This wasn't just to boost your shop's sales. It was to help fuel your lover's as well.'

Claudia's expression crumbled, her earlier composure giving way to panic. 'How dare you. I'm a married woman!'

Anna held her gaze. 'I might be eighteen, Claudia, but I'm not stupid.'

The murmurs in the room grew louder as the atmosphere turned from suspicion to disbelief. Before Claudia could respond, Alex rested his hand on Anna's shoulder.

'It's amusing that Claudia claims to know nothing about this room,' he teased, waving a stack of papers towards her. 'Trozzi may have declared it as his in the latest *condono*, but I've discovered that the electricity contract for the cellar has been in Claudia's name since the 1990s. Her name also appears on the building plan and construction records. It wasn't Massimo Trozzi who built the cellar. It was Claudia.'

Gasps echoed around the room as Alex continued, 'And there's more. I've also found records of hotel rooms booked under their names and a significant order for toys that mysteriously never reached Trozzi's shop.'

Whispers turned into audible speculation, particularly from Anna's dad, who recalled the headline in the local paper about Trozzi's toy shop going into bankruptcy.

Anna shot Alex a thankful glance. 'This confirms my suspicions. Thank you, Alex. I suspect she used the *condono* as an opportunity to register the cellar under Trozzi's name, planning to craft a myth about his factory being Befana's secret workshop. This strategy likely aimed to boost sales and attract tourists to her and Massimo's shops.'

Claudia, now visibly shaken, attempted to interject. 'That's not true! It's all circumstantial-.'

But Borrelli, who had been listening intently, interrupted her. 'Enough, Claudia! This isn't just about a missing stocking.' Taking the papers from Alex with a brief thank you, he quickly scanned their contents before pulling his phone from his pocket. 'We have evidence of misinterpretation and fraud, possibly with criminal charges. I'll let Constable Rossi handle this. Franco, come with me. We need to check on that stocking.' With his phone pressed to his ear, the Director fled, pulling Anna's dad along.

The room filled with palpable shock as Claudia slumped defeatedly into her chair. Carlo's joy and relief made her heart jolt.

'How did you find out about the cellar?' Claudia asked, taking Anna's attention away from Carlo's gaze.

'I found a floppy disk on the floor in the Grinch's house.' Anna held up the disk for Claudia to see. 'It contained a database of your shop's clients and Trozzi's stock, along with a map of the catacombs pointing to the cellar.'

'That's impossible,' Claudia shot back, her voice pitching. 'The disk was locked in my safe.'

Constable Rossi stepped forward, his expression stern yet sympathetic. 'Claudia, it's time for you to come with me.' Then, turning to Anna and Alex. 'Thank you, kids. You've done well today. Not just in finding the stocking, but clearing an innocent lad of suspicion.' He nodded at Alex. 'I need a statement from you, young man. Can you come with me to the station?'

As Rossi escorted Claudia away, followed by Alex, who waved Anna a quick goodbye, a gust of wind howled outside, its sound eerily reminiscent of an old witch's laughter. Anna paused. Could it be? Could Befana be real? Has she somehow helped unravel the mystery?

Before she could reason further, Carlo approached. His gaze held gratitude and maybe a hint of tenderness. Anna felt her cheeks warm.

'Thank you, Anna, for everything,' Carlo began. 'You believed in me when it would have been easier not to.'

Lost in his gaze, Anna managed a small smile. 'Maybe you shouldn't just thank me,' she replied, half-joking. 'Maybe Befana helped, too.'

Carlo's laughed. 'If that's the case, I must have been exceptionally good this year to deserve such a wonderful gift.' His eyes twinkled with amusement and something she couldn't quite decipher.

As the festive lights from the village cast a gentle glow around them, he took a slight step closer. 'Speaking of presents,' he continued, 'I was wondering, um, if you're not doing anything on New Year's Eve, maybe you'd like to... join me at *Nonno*'s? We could watch the fireworks together.'

Anna's heart raced. It was a simple question, but its implications were life-changing. Her earlier daydreams surging forward, she envisioned a future with Carlo filled with laughter, love, two kids, and a pet. Could this be Befana's doing? Had Anna been so good this year that she, too, deserved such a beautiful twist of fate?

'It sounds perfect.' She beamed.

Carlo's smile widened as he reached for his phone. 'I also took this,' he showed her a photo from earlier, Anna and Alex facing Claudia proudly. 'I thought we could take it to your *mamma*, along with the photos of the stocking you took in the cellar.'

Anna blushed, but her eyes lit up. 'Thank you, she'll be thrilled!'

Slipping back into his Grinch costume, Carlo lowered his voice to mimic the Grinch's gruff, teasing tone. 'Then what are we waiting for.'

The pair left the building giggling. As dusk fell, the village was sparkling with Christmas lights, and the echo of the mysterious wind's laughter blended spookily with the festive atmosphere.

Leaning into Carlo, Anna couldn't help but feel that Befana was watching over them. Giving them a chance at happiness and a future that looked as bright and promising as the Christmas lights.

BIO

An Italian native who spent half her life between the UK and Ireland, Julia juggles the challenges of raising an autistic son, a spirited neurotypical son, and a cat that adopted her rather than the other way around —oh, and a husband who thinks he's just as high-maintenance. With a background in Creative Writing, she writes engaging stories in English and Italian, inspired by her love for genres ranging from crime fiction to sci-fi and romance. This anthology presents her first published original work, a milestone in her creative journey.

https://www.facebook.com/giulia.fancelli

Chapter Nine

DEATH OF THE FOOD SELLER

Stella Oni

The bustling streets of Lagos hold more than just the aroma of street food and the hum of daily life. When Mama Kola, a beloved street food seller, is killed in a hit-and-run, rumours swirl that her death was no accident. Her son, Kola, hires private detective, Lara Ayodele to uncover the truth. Facing warnings from the police detective assigned to the case, the contempt of a local restaurant owner who looks down on street vendors, and secretive meetings with informants in remote bushes, Lara and Edith, her assistant, gradually piece together a pattern that leads them to the killer.

Christmas always gave Lara Ayodele anxiety. Her parents had died at Christmas in a mysterious car accident when she was ten and Lara who had been in the car had escaped with only a scar on her face. She spent the holiday with her sister, Remi, who used the ten-year gap between then to boss Lara around and always prepared for the holiday with manic fervour. It was as if Remi was trying to make up for what happened in the past. She would have the huge trees that lined the drive to her mansion festooned in twinkling lights. Trees would tower over visitors in the hallway, lounge and different nooks and crannies of her home. Then she would prepare a feast - jollof rice, stewed meat, spicy grilled fish, pepper soup, fried chicken, moin moin - of all of Lara's favourites - and abundant drinks. Lara appreciated Remi's effort, but it never completely took away the sadness that always enveloped her.

Today, for the sake of trying to look festive, Lara reluctantly dragged a Christmas tree out of storage and placed it in the corner of her detective agency's visitors' lounge, a converted garage at the front of her home. She lived in a large four-bedroom house in the government-reserved area of Ikeja, Lagos, with a tiny bungalow at the back for Moses, her house help. Her agency that she set up a year ago had expanded beyond the office space in her living room to the converted garage. She was grateful for the increase in business, but it had gone quiet in the week leading to Christmas meaning she and Edith her assistant could do a bit of housekeeping in readiness for the new year.

The lounge was large, with beige wood flooring, spare modernist chairs, and a centre table. The cream wall was dominated by some of Lara's father's art collection, which she cherished. She gazed sadly at the striking painting of a hawker balancing a large basket full of dried fish. Her father, an anthropologist, loved street food and passed his love on to Lara. She had inherited his curiosity, so started the detective agency after working with the National Intelligence Agency.

She pulled strands of white lights and tinsel from a large

carrier bag, added them to the tree, then stood back and frowned at her finished work. The fake leaves on the Christmas tree poked out like accusing fingers, mocking the spindly trunk beneath. This wouldn't impress Remi one bit. She was done. Edith, her assistant, or Moses could finish it. Her phone rang.

'Edith, where are you?' she hissed, checking the time. They had agreed to use the slow week leading up to Christmas to catch up on their admin.

'Boss, Mama Kola is gone!'

Lara was not in the mood for Edith's penchant for drama.

'What do you mean gone?'

'That hit and run yesterday, boss. That was her.'

Lara recalled hearing Moses say someone had been hit by a car on Leyland Road, the main road beyond her cul-de-sac.

Lara bit her lip as she absorbed the news. Mama Kola's food was as familiar as her mother's cooking. The food seller had been running her small street stall for 30 years. Lara's favourite was her fluffy white rice wrapped in banana leaf and accompanied by Ayamase stew with pieces of beef, tripe, and succulent cow skin.

'I'll be there soon, boss.'

Lara sat down to look at the cases they had successfully completed. Their cases in the year that she began the agency had been interesting and varied. She was glad that they resolved the case of the missing body for Imade's funeral home. That was a twisted case. And here was the black widow of Oshogbo case. That was from her former boss in intelligence, Mr Okoye. He was still trying to cajole her to come back. What about the wedding that ended up with a murdered guest. She and Edith would remove all paper references and digitise everything this week. But none of it could remove her sadness that one of her favourite food sellers had been killed.

Edith arrived without her usual buzz of energy and laden with bags of food. Lara towered over her assistant's 5'2" frame. The contrast was striking. Where Lara was tall, almost gaunt, with dark skin evocative of the Sudanese, close-cropped hair, and a thin scar that ran down one side of her face, an injury from the accident that killed her parents. Edith, of Nigerian and Chinese mix, was small, light, and curvy.

Lara peered into the food bags. 'Tell me exactly what happened. And why did you buy so much food?'

'This is free food from Mama Kola's Buka. They did not want the previous day's ingredients to go to waste. They're shutting it down to start the days of mourning. Boss, this might be the last time we will eat food from Mama Kola's buka.'

It was sobering, and they started their work in pensive silence.

Lara was in her office, a few days later, when she heard her gate bell ring. She twitched the blinds aside and watched Moses run out to open the side gate.

At last, Moses came to rap on her door.

'Who is it?'

Lara had rescued Moses, a former mercenary, from the streets of Lagos, where he had been begging for a living. She had never said that to Remi, her sister who imagined everyone on the roads was out to rob or kill you.

Moses, a francophone, spoke pidgin English that he had picked up on the streets. He had shown his gardening skills by untangling the bushes behind her house and revealing the garden that used to be her mother's pride and joy. She also discovered that his knowledge of the streets of Lagos made him a mine of information.

'It is Kola, the son of Mama Kola, Aunty.'

'Oh?' said Lara.

'He wan talk to you.'

'Take him to the lounge. I'll be there in a few minutes.'

Lara recalled Kola in her teenage years as a studious young boy who always had a book in his hands, even as he sat beside his mother's large pots of bubbling stews. Mama Kola had proudly told her he had gone to study accounting in England.

She entered the visitor's lounge quietly, but Kola saw her and jumped to his feet. He was about 5'9" with a mild face marred by acne scars. He wore neat, pressed, good-quality trousers topped with a buttoned-up shirt.

'Good afternoon, Miss Lara. I hope you remember me. I am Kola, mama Kola's son.'

'Good day, yes, I do,' said Lara. 'Please sit down. I'm really sorry for your loss. We will all miss your mother. How can I help you?'

He drew back his crisp trousers, sat down and cleared his throat.

It's about my mother. As we are Muslims, my mother was buried a day after she died. But I don't believe that her death was an accident. I told the police this.'

'How so?'

'Miss Lara, my mother is the head of the market women's association and was returning from a meeting with her neighbour the owner of Toyin's Delicious Grill who sells next to ours. Toyin said that the car swerved deliberately in their direction. She was lucky to have landed in hospital with just fractures.'

'As far as I know, the police ruled this as an accident, but I can try to find out more for you,' said Lara.

He looked relieved. 'Thank you so much. I look after our books, and since a recent YouTuber's visit, we have doubled our income. My mother might be a threat to many jealous people.'

He hid his brimming eyes by wiping his face with a large handkerchief.

Lara understood how he felt. The person that caused her parents' car accident was never found.

'Help me, Miss Lara. If you say it was an accident, then I will rest and not pursue this any further.'

'Did you tell the police?'

'I told them, but they said that witnesses only saw a hit and run. I do not trust the police, Miss Lara.'

Lara thought of her friend, Detective Inspector Bibi Adamu, who worked hard each day with limited resources to solve the overwhelming crime in her division. She would arrange to meet Bibi and find out more.

'I will look into it for you,' she said. She had started the detective agency when she tried to unravel the mystery of her parent's deaths. Now she was helping others to do the same.

'Thank you so much! Please let me know how you charge, and I will transfer the full money to your account.

As he disappeared through the gate, Edith clattered in laden with more bags of food.

'Wow! Where did you buy these?'

Edith looked guilty. 'Roli's Spicy Food now has more variety.'

'That's another interesting one. Roli has become busy with Mama Kola and Toyin out of the way,' mused Lara.

"Boss, who was that man?'

'Kola. He says the hit and run was no accident. He's hired us to investigate it.'

Edith went into the kitchen and dumped the bags onto the counter.

'How do we find a hit and run driver in this mad city? And close to Christmas as well!'

Lara opened a food bag to reveal moin moin wrapped in a leaf. She closed her eyes and inhaled the aroma of ground bean paste mixed with peppers, spices, and dried crayfish steamed in banana leaves.

'That smells nice.,' she said as she took a mouthful. The savoury richness of the moin moin bloomed on her palate as it melted away. 'Gosh! I had no idea Roli is this good.'

Edith looked smug.' I try to sample everything on the street.'

They walked to the office.

'I am going to visit Inspector Bibi to see if she has made any progress.'

Edith smiled. 'Good luck with her boss. That one is like the sun and the moon. Wonder which one you'll get.'

Bibi, Lara's main contact with the police after she helped her with a complex case, was mercurial.

'I might get her to meet me at the Majestic restaurant.' Lara grinned at Edith's look of horror.

'Boss, that is being disloyal to the street. The sellers have been complaining about how the owner and his chef tries to bully them. He only just arrived!'

'That is why I want to check them out.'

'Let's make a list of who benefits from Mama Kola's death,' said Lara as they settled at their desks.

Edith grinned, revealing a gold tooth.' That's easy. Kola and Dotun, her sons. Roli and Toyin her neighbours and the Majestic restaurant. Dotun is now running the buka'

Lara looked thoughtful. 'Our list of suspects is growing but why a hit and run? It's so violent and public.'

'Boss, it is the easiest way in Lagos.'

Lara called Moses, who appeared from the backyard glistening with sweat, in his scruffy gardening clothes.

'Ah, Moses,' said Lara. 'Have you heard anything on the streets about Mama Kola's death?'

Moses twisted and untwisted his hands as they waited. 'They say it is not an accident, Aunty.' He wiped the sweat from his face and dashed unshed tears from his eyes.

'Mama Kola feed me when I was hungry.'

Lara stood up. 'I'll go see Detective Bibi. Edith stay and dig for every scrap of information you can on our list of suspects.'

Moses ran to open the gate as Lara jumped on her powerful Yamaha motorcycle.

Niagra police station was a battered, faded building, low to the ground and scruffy. Bellicose police officers sat outside on the benches and eyed Lara as she parked her bike. One or two nodded, and others were openly hostile. Lara had solved many crimes that some of the officers thought should have been solved by them.

The police reception was a large room with cracked ceiling and peeling paint of multiple faded colours. A full-bodied woman sat on the floor and bawled openly as she begged for the police to release her son. A man, with his face scoured by tribal marks and seemingly oblivious to the wailing woman, stood before a table with two police officers listening to his entreaty to follow him to the spot where his daughter had been kidnapped. Lara went to a tall officer watching the scene with a bored look. The whole place reeked of fear and sweat.

'Good morning, Sergeant. I'm here to see Detective Inspector Bibi.'

His large, lazy eyes rolled over her scar as he unfolded his arms. Lara could see his resistance and was prepared to fight her way in. But his eyes suddenly snapped to attention as he stood up straighter and looked beyond her.

'Good afternoon ma!'

Lara turned to see Bibi surveying the scene with sharp, assessing eyes. Her long-lashed brown eyes filled with amusement.

'Welcome to hell in Niagra.'

'Hello, Bibi,' greeted Lara, glad her friend was in a good mood. Bibi's job was hampered by bureaucracy and the corruption of some of her bosses.

'Ok, follow me,' said Bibi as she strode past. Her trouser suit clung to her full figure, which she lamented made her job harder as male bosses and even colleagues propositioned her daily. They walked to Bibi's cramped office, which consisted of a desk chair and two opposite chairs. A cabinet slunk in a corner and a window across the room provided a little light.

'Right, how can I help you?'

'I'm investigating Mama Kola's death.'

Bibi's smile left. '

It was a hit and run. We talked to all the witnesses. Even the state governor is now on my back about it. I heard that her Ayamase and Rice reminded him of his long dead grandma's. You'll save me work if you find the driver.'

Lara stood up. 'I'll get back to you if I find anything. All the son wants is to prove that his mother was not murdered.'

'Good luck. But I warn you. Don't get in my way.'

Lara gave her a slight smile and left. She knew how to handle Bibi.

Lara decided to visit Toyin, the proprietor of Toyin's Delicious Grill, while she was still a patient at Mopelola Hospital, just a few miles from her house. Hopefully her injuries were not serious, and she could shed some light on what happened. Whipping through the crazy Lagos traffic on her motorbike gave her joy, as it was madness to try to drive a car through the tangle of cars that lined the roads.

Toyin with her smooth dark skin and short braids covered in hairnet laid in her hospital bed with eyes closed as relatives and friends clustered around her. Lara loved her grilled fish, which was spicy and delicious. Unlike Mama Kola, who was always serious, Toyin used to exude cheerfulness. Now, she looked exhausted as she lay on the bed with a cast covering her whole arm and right leg.

Lara asked to speak to her privately and was relieved when the room emptied.

Tears tracked down the woman's face as she recounted her ordeal

'We were on our way home from the street food seller's association. That road is a bad one with plenty of pot holes, but that car came straight for me and Mama Kola. I told the police this.'

'Did you see the person driving it?'

Toyin wiped her tears with the sleeve of her hospital gown.

'I did not, Aunty. It was a man, and he had a cap pulled down low. '

Lara asked more questions but could get nothing else from the food seller.

Lara decided to visit the other food sellers to see if she could get anything from them. Obi Street was lined with stalls under the burning sun. Heat pulsed on her skin as she started at the beginning of the street. The wide street was festooned with large bright umbrellas that offered shade to the busy food sellers.

Lara looked across the road. Mama Kola and Toyin's buka each looked eerily silent as people crowded around the food vendors. On their side of the street was the Majestic Restaurant. Lara saw nothing remarkable about the silent, squat building except the signage that promised "an eating experience beyond your dreams".

Business was already underway for the food sellers as hungry workers swamped the vendors. Lara was famished as the smell of food tantalised her senses. People sat on plastic chairs dotted across the sidewalk and ate with zeal.

She was strolling to Majestic restaurant when its front door opened. A bald man wearing traditional baggy trousers and a top came out. He shaded his eyes and started inspecting the building.

'Good day, sir,' she greeted.

He turned and examined her, his eyes large and myopic behind thick, dark frames.

'How can I help you, lady?'

'Is this your restaurant?'

He nodded with pride. 'Yes, I opened it a nearly a year ago. We want people like you to be our customer.'

Lara looked at the line-up of busy food sellers. 'You don't look busy. Do you only open in the evenings?'

He glared at the row of sellers.

'My food is of the greatest quality. I owned a restaurant in

England. You cannot compare that to the dirt they're serving here on the streets and I will make sure of that.'

Lara was amazed at how his affable manner had changed.

'You're aware that one of the food sellers was killed a few days ago by a hit and run driver?'

He eyed Lara with suspicion.

'Who are you? Why are you asking me all these questions, eh? What has a hit-and-run got to do with me, eh? '

'I'm a private detective, sir. I am helping the police to track the driver.' Lara was glad Inspector Bibi was not standing behind her to hear her lie.

'And why are you asking me about it, then? ' he flapped his hands at the street. 'Go out there and find this person. You are a private detective, eh? Maybe you will tell me who has been coming to dump mess in front of my restaurant every morning. My name is Adam Dafe.'

'And I am Lara Ayodele.'

His hands was soft, as they shook hands.

'I know it is one of these sellers. They know we are planning to ensure that only the Majestic Restaurant sells authentic food around here.'

'What kind of mess?'

He examined her again. 'Come, follow me.'

He led her to through a side gate to an open space with concrete ground swept clean except for a pile of rubbish made up of paper, leaves, and food leftovers.

'Someone or some people have been leaving this heap every morning at the front of my restaurant. I was examining my building to install a camera. The police will not take me seriously. You're a detective. Perhaps you can find the person. I don't understand what it's about. My chef said it might be some kind of juju.'

'May I speak to your chef?'

'Of course. Can I offer you a cold drink?'

'No, thanks.'

Lara took a bottle of water out of her small rucksack and drank from it.

They walked into the cool building. She heard the clattering of pots and pans as her nose filled with the smell of cooking from a stainless-steel kitchen with industrial-sized cookers. A middle-aged man issued orders to what looked like an army of kitchen staff. He walked to a cooker with a small bubbling pan of sauce, dipped in a spoon, tasted it and began to yell at a kitchen staff who looked terrified.

'Chef Bami,' called Mr Dafe. 'Come, please. Let me introduce you to this lady.'

The chef stopped and strode to them. He was still bristling and tried to smile at Lara.

'This is Detective Lara Ayodele. I want her to help us find the culprit that is leaving the dirt in front of our building.'

'I thought you're installing a camera.' The cook's voice was high, almost falsetto.

Mr Dafe smiled with despair. 'I will do it but who knows how long it will take? Everything takes forever in this country.'

'Chef Bami, did you hear about the street seller that got killed a few days ago?'

The cook shrugged. 'I heard. It is a sad thing to happen.'

'Do you know her?'

He frowned at her as his eyes darted to his busy staff. 'I don't know anything about these foodsellers. Why are you asking all these questions? Are you a reporter? I must go back to work. Good day!'

They left the kitchen, and Mr Dafe led her into a cool large, room with empty chairs and tables. He sat down, looking despondent.

'I inherited this building from my late mother. I thought she would be proud of me opening a restaurant. But where are the customers eh? Let me get us some cold water.'

He went to the empty bar and brought back two bottles of water.

'This is cold and will refresh you.'

'No, thank you. I am fine.'

'Now, tell me where you buy your food. Do you cook, Miss Lara or is it Mrs?'

'Just call me Lara. I'm not much of a cook and eat street food. Especially the ones around here.'

'I see.'

Lara stood up. 'It was nice meeting you, Mr Dafe.'

'Will you help us to get to the bottom of this and find out who is the culprit?'

'Give me a day or two. I need to finish another case and will contact you.'

Back in the office, Lara filled Edith in.

'Boss, I checked Mr Dafe's social media. He only has Face-book, and it's full of his photos and a few political posts.'

'I didn't like the way that he and his chef look down on the food sellers. The chef was also hostile.'

'What about Mama Kola's household?'

'Her staff work in shifts including Dotun, the younger son.'

The front doorbell rang, and Lara went. It was Moses. He grinned at her, and Lara realised he might have information.

'Go on, spill it,' she said.

'You said mek I check to see if there is job for hire on the street, Aunty.'

'And?'

' Someone hire a hit and run killing.'

Lara went still. 'For real?'

' The driver is gone, Aunty. It was someone from the North that they use.'

'And you think this was for Mama Kola.'

'The person has instruction to hit a woman and run.'

'But how would they know where?'

'Boss, it has to be someone that knows Mama Kola's move-ments. It is an inside job.'

'Without the car or the driver, we have no proof of who killed her. We need something more,' she mused.

'Will this informant speak to me?'

Moses frowned. 'I will ask.'

'Moses, you know you can arrange it for us,' said Edith, grinning.

'Boss, I have arranged for Mama Kola's manager and Dotun through Mr Kola to talk to us after lunch.'

'Lunch is past, let us go.'

Mama Kola's buka the front shop of a multi-storey building popular in the 1970s, was small, with wooden flooring and bamboo tables and chairs. Lara remember how busy it always was at lunch time.

The manager was a tiny, spare woman who reminded Lara of a chicken with her long neck and fidgety body.

'My name is Tayo. Mr Kola said you want to speak to me and Mr Dotun, ma. I will take you inside.'

She led them to a cool sitting room with stuffy brown chairs, heavy cream curtains and a thick expensive carpet.

'Who inherits all this?' asked Lara, looking around.

The manager set her lips primly.

'Mama left the business and her properties to be divided equally between her two sons. Mr Dotun wants to continue to run the business.'

She sat at the edge of her seat and tapped her fingers together as she continued.

'This land has become very valuable. Many developers have approached Mama Kola and offered her a lot of money. But she is very committed to selling our food.'

'Do you have any more questions, ma?'

'I have,' said Edith

The woman stiffened.

'We hear that Mama Kola's death is not an accident. What do you say to that?'

The woman flinched and pressed her lips together.

'It was an accident, ma. Who would want to kill a kind woman like Mama? People say wicked things. They need to let her rest in peace. Have you anymore questions, ma.'

'No, thank you,' said Lara

'Let me bring you drinks while you wait for Mr Dotun. He will soon come.'

They refused her offer as a tall man entered.

His voice was low and deep as he introduced himself.

'My brother said that he is looking into the death of our mother. I told him it is a waste of time. Lagos streets can be dangerous. It was unfortunate for our Mama.'

Lara examined him. 'We will do our best. I was told that people wanted to buy your business and property.'

'A lot of developers say it is now prime land. But no one would kill our mother for it? What would they gain?'

'Will you sell?' asked Lara.

He jerked as he glared at her. 'Me and my brother have argued about this. He wants to sell.'

He wiped his wet eyes and his voice became gruff. 'I don't want to sell our inheritance. I told him I will run the business. But he is ready to move on.'

Lara did not think they got much out of him after that.

Back in the office, they went through the brief interview.

'Not much here, boss. But why is Kola in such a hurry to sell up? His mother has only been dead a few days.'

'Dig up everything you can about him, Dotun and the manager.'

Edith looked thoughtful.

'You're right, boss. The sons have strong motives and the manager was acting suspiciously.'

'She might just be nervous,' said Lara.

'Are you still planning to speak to Moses' informant?'

Lara nodded. 'It might be a waste of time, but I'll go.'

That evening, Lara changed into a scruffy top and jeans, pulling a peaked hat low over her face. They rode on Moses' motorbike. He sped up and veered off the main road, leading toward the inner Oshodi area and into the bushes to a dirt road. The motorbike, not as powerful as hers, hurtled down the road, lighting a lonely path until it came to an abrupt stop half an hour later. Lara clambered off and stretched. Moses had brought out a powerful torchlight that illuminated their path. Low-lying scrub, parched and brown, flanked it, offering no cover. On either side, hulking trees cast long shadows over them.

Lara chuckled. 'Are you sure we're safe doing this, Moses?'

'Aunty, this person is very careful, but I trust him. We must pay him for what he will give us tonight.'

Lara had brought some cash and also ensured she had her gun and a knife strapped to her ankle. She was taking no chances.

A shadow materialised out of the bushes and walked towards them. It was a man dressed in black. Lara tensed in readiness as Moses took him to the side, and they exchanged brusque whispers. They walked back to Lara, who could see nothing except that the man towered over her and had bushy hair which sprouted below the balaclava he was wearing.

'Good evening. My friend said you have information on the hit and run that killed the food seller. '

'Madam, I hope you bring my money. I have a photo, that is all.'

Lara tried not to search his face, but she could see by the definition of his muscles that he spent a lot of time working out.

'How do I know that your information is real?'

'Ask Mr M. He knows I give him good info.'

Lara tried not to smile. *Mr M?* Moses was full of caution and dramatics.

'Can I at least see what I'm paying for?'

'I'm sorry ma. You pay. I give. You have to trust me it is good information.'

'Ok, let's do it this way. I give you half. If it is what I'm looking for. I give you the rest. If it is not, then I give you the photo back.'

He abruptly rummaged through a satchel that he carried across his shoulder and brought out a print photo. 'I developed this myself. I cannot use my phone to send it. Please give me the money.'

Lara carefully split the cash in her pocket and gave half to him. He took it and handed her the photo.

She took it and walked to Mose's torchlight to get a good look. The hair on her arms stood on end as she saw a photo of the owner of Majestic restaurant, Mr Dafe, and Kola, chatting to a stocky wide chested man. Whoever took the picture was close enough to capture their serious expression. The man they were in conversation with was dressed in army fatigues, but the angle of the image meant they couldn't see his face.

'Dat man did the job. His boss gave him the order. He has gone, and you cannot catch him. Those men ordered for him to do it.' He pointed to Kola and Mr Dafe.

She could hardly believe it. Kola, the man who had hired her, was implicated in his mother's murder. But she would need more evidence if she was to prove it.

'If you tell me where to find the man they hired, I will pay you double.'

He shook his head. 'I tell you, I die.'

'Thank you. You did well.'

She gave him the rest of the money.

He turned to Moses. 'Mr M. I see you another time.' He slid back into the bushes and disappeared.

They returned to the house in silence, and Lara jumped off as soon as they got back home.

'This photo shows that Kola knows Mr Dafe. But we still have to prove they ordered his mother's killing. I need more to take to Bibi. Thank you, though.'

'Aunty, I wish I have more. But I beg dat guy before he agree to share this photo.'

Lara yawned. 'We will find more tomorrow.'

Lara messaged Edith to come in early the next day and collapsed into a dream full of men wearing dark clothing and asking for Mr M.

The next morning, she updated Edith on their night's adventure.

'Boss, I found out more about Kola. I had to do some creative searches.'

Lara did not bother asking her assistant how she did it. Like her, Edith was brilliant on computers.

'He likes to invest in start-ups but over extended himself and owes a lot of money. That is why he wanted to sell quickly. Mr Dafe is keen to take over the streets and build a hotel.'

Lara shook her head. 'Was it worth killing his own mother in such a brutal manner?'

'What do you plan to do, boss?'

'I'm going to Bibi. See if she can put some kind of pressure on both of them.'

Lara called Bibi, who sounded disgruntled but agreed to meet her at a cafe near the police station.

Lara arrived early, ordered a cold drink and meat pie then waited. Bibi entered with a cloudy expression and dropped into the seat opposite.

'This had better be good. '

Lara brought out the photo and showed it to her. 'Hi to you as well, Bibi.'

Bibi grunted and squinted at the images. 'Who are these?'

'Kola meeting with Mr Dafe, the owner of Majestic hotel and speaking to a man we believe was the hit and run driver.'

Bibi gave the photo back to Lara, disappointed.

'Doesn't prove anything.'

'It shows motive and means.'

'You think that Kola got someone to mow down his mother, so he could sell her property to Mr Dafe?'

'Yes. You know people have done more for less.'

Bibi stood up. 'I'm not convinced. Get me something more.'

Lara watched her retreating back and sighed. This may be as far as it could get with the case. After all, her suspect was the person that hired her.

She was halfway home when her phone rang. It was Bibi.

'You must be under some lucky star. We found the hit and run driver. He is someone we've been hunting for a long time.'

Lara ran to join her at the station.

Bibi was grinning with triumph, her dimples making sweet grooves in her cheeks.

'He was on a robbery job when one of our other teams arrested him. They found a photo of Mama Kola on his phone. I still have to tie him to those two, but I can bring them in for questioning now.'

'Thank you,' said Lara.

Bibi watched her with a quizzical look.' So, your client ordered his mother's killing. Why did he hire you?'

'That is what I want to know. Can I watch when you question him?'

Bibi paused and then shrugged. 'We have a two-way mirror that still works. But try and be quiet. My people hate you.'

Lara grinned and shrugged. 'Tell them to try to be as good as you and not feel threatened.'

Edith jumped up and clapped when Lara gave her the update.

'You caught Inspector Bibi in a good mood.'

She became serious. 'I know this case means a lot to you, boss.'

Lara stared at her fingernails. Finding who killed Mama Kola helps her inability to solve her parents' mysterious car accident.

The next day, she went to the police station to hear Bibi and her team question Kola.

He was facing the one-way mirror but could not see Lara. He was dishevelled, with wrinkled shirt and trousers and uncombed hair.

He caved in pressing his hands to his face.

'I wanted to scare my mother to sell her property. She was a superstitious woman. An Imam had told her to sell the property as there was danger around it, she refused to listen. She had other properties and a clothing business. I arranged for her to sell to Mr Dafe. The driver was supposed to make it look like a near accident. Just be near enough to seem she just missed being killed. Not to kill her! Then he ran away. I did not know much about him, so I wanted Detective Lara to trace him for me.'

Lara heard shouts coming from the reception area and ran out. Dotun was being held back by the officers as he yelled to be allowed to go to his brother.

'Kola! You killed our mother. You will die today. Bastard!'

He burst into tears. 'She was a kind woman. She loved us. Got you good education and this is how you repay her.'

And like that, it was over.

Lara hoped Mama Kola would rest in peace.

It was finally Christmas day and Lara sat back replete in Remi's magnificent living room shining with Christmas decorations, and allowed the murmur of her sister's guests to wash over her. Each year she suffered through her sister's dinners, but this year felt different. She watched as Bayo, Remi's husband, held his wife's waist and how her sister happy that her get together was successful threw back her braided head in a deep laugh. Lara silently thanked Remi for never giving up on her. Perhaps she would finally start to enjoy Christmas.

BIO

Stella Oni's debut police procedural, "Deadly Sacrifice," featuring detective British Nigerian Toks Ade, the first black female police detective in UK fiction, was shortlisted for the SI Leeds Literary Prize and was an Audible Crime and Thriller pick. She has contributed to various anthologies, including "Midnight Hour", published by Crooked Lane. Stella is an ITW judge, a Novel London Literary Prize judge, was an adjudicator for the Scottish Association of Writers Crime Fiction Pitlochry Prize 2023 and a 2024 Jhalak Prize judge. She is a popular speaker and delivers crime fiction workshops. She is currently writing book two of the Toks Ade Mystery series and the first of her contemporary crime cosy, The London House Mystery series.

https://stellaonithewriter.com/

Chapter Ten

THE GIFTS GRAB

Dianne Ascroft

S et within the Century Cottage Cozy Mysteries series, 'The Gifts Grab' steps into December 1984 in Fenwater, a fictional Canadian town. The Community Christmas Charity Evening is in full swing at the local market, and middle-aged librarian Lois Stone is enjoying the sights, sounds and scents of Christmas until she hears her best friend Marge's wail of frustration. Despite her friend's diligent care, a 1914 silver-plated slipper-shaped pin cushion and a pair of 1941 women's crystal heeled pumps have gone missing from the museum's "80 years of gifts bought from Christmas mail order catalogues" exhibit. Silver lanes, candy canes and holly on the door will have to wait as it won't look much like Christmas for Marge until Lois helps her find the thief and retrieve the museum's treasures.

Lois Stone pulled her dusty rose wool coat tighter around herself, shivering in the breeze that blew in the entrance to the old market building. The cold air nipped at her ears, which were barely covered by her short, grey hair.

She turned to Connie, the volunteer helping her at the library's discarded books sale table. 'Ugh, it's chilly in here, but I wouldn't miss the Community Christmas Charity Evening. There's such a great atmosphere.'

Above the women, the wooden beams criss-crossing the building were decked with holly garlands, Christmas ornaments, and twinkling lights. The PA system serenaded the steady throng of customers wandering through the market with Christmas songs.

Lois glanced at her best friend, Marge Kirkwood, who was standing at the museum's exhibition table next to her own. 'Great turnout, isn't it? Even though it's my second Christmas here, I still can't get over how many faces are familiar to me. Not like when I went to markets or craft shows in Toronto. And I love how all the stallholders are donating a percentage of their profits today to local charities, the library and the museum.'

Marge patted her dyed-blonde hair and stood straighter, pushing out her ample bust. 'Yeah, our donation box is filling up fast. Folks can't resist me or this great display my team and I put together. Isn't that right, Greg?'

The thin, grey-haired man beside her grinned and winked. 'That must be it, Marge. As a lowly museum volunteer, I bow to the archivist's learned assessment.'

'Don't let her take all the credit, Greg. She should be glad of the work you've put into this.' Lois turned to Marge. 'What a marvellous idea to feature gifts bought from mail-order catalogues. When I was a kid, I was so excited the day the catalogue arrived. I spent hours picking what I wanted Santa to bring me.'

The large white sign hanging on the divider wall behind the museum's table read BEFORE THE MARKET THERE WAS MAIL-ORDER in red letters and below that, in forest green,

1904 – 1984: EIGHTY YEARS OF GIFTS FROM EATON'S AND SIMPSON'S CATALOGUES. A selection of gifts was arranged on a red tablecloth spread over a long wooden table, grouped by the eras they were from: dainty lace collars for women's dresses, gold pocket watches, a wooden toy kayak and oars, *The Roosevelt Bears Abroad* children's book, and a silverplated comb, brush, and mirror set from the early 1900s; and a mechanical toy car, a multicoloured tin ball filled with chocolates, a mechanical walking man and barrow, an Old Spice shaving lotion bottle and shaving mug set, a Kodak Starlet camera, and a brass captain's wheel wall barometer from the middle of the century. More recent years were represented by a pink Remington Princess women's shaver and case, a rayon and wool combined hat and scarf head warmer, several mood rings, a selection of GI Joe action figures, pet rocks, and a drink-and-wet Baby Tender doll.

'Don't you have *Schindler's Ark*? That one by Thomas Keneally?'

The insistent voice drew Lois's attention back to her table. She looked at the thin woman wrapped in a shabby brown wool coat. 'I'm afraid not. The library is selling older books we've discarded. *Schindler's Ark* was only published a couple of years ago. We do have quite a few historical fiction titles, though. Let's see what I can find.'

Lois rummaged through the books piled on the table and pulled out a couple as the woman gazed into the distance, unwrapping a butterscotch candy and popping it into her mouth.

Talking around the candy, the woman said, 'No, it's *Schindler's Ark* I want. I saw it in a bookshop in Toronto, but it was too expensive.'

Lois took a deep breath and tried to be patient. 'That's because they don't reduce the price of new books.'

Shifting her green cotton shopping bag from one hand to the other, the woman frowned at Lois then darted to the museum's table. Lois tried to shrug off her abrupt departure, telling herself,

'*You can't please everyone.*' Beside the disgruntled woman, Lois noticed two young teens studying the array of diverse gifts displayed on the museum's table.

'Heather, remember I got a Snoopy charm for my birthday in grade eight?' the sandy-haired girl said to the brunette, pointing to a red velvet cushion where several charms rested, including a golden horse, Snoopy, a maple leaf, and a pair of silver skates.

'My grandma has one of those fancy comb and brush sets. The design in the silver bits is gorgeous but it weighs a ton.' Heather lowered her voice. 'What I'd really like is one of those gold heart lockets.'

'But they're old.'

'I don't care, Bonnie. I'd cut Keith's face out of our class photo and put it in it.'

Lois shifted her gaze away from the giggling girls, not wanting to be caught eavesdropping and embarrass them. Standing beside the girls was a short woman wearing a purple ski jacket and a matching long-handled purse slung over her shoulder. She scanned the objects on the table, pausing to stare at several items.

The arrival of four customers, who each bought multiple books from the library table, turned Lois's attention back to her work. When the last shopper left, she ducked under the table, pulled out another box of books, and emptied its contents onto the tabletop. As she glanced up from her work, the woman in the purple ski jacket picked up one of the books she had set out.

'Is there anything in particular you're looking for?' Lois asked.

'Not really. I'm just having a look around.'

'Take your time. Enjoy the evening,' Lois replied. 'I'm glad the market runs this event every year. It supports such good causes and adds to the market's festive atmosphere.'

'Yeah, but some of it is a bit tacky. Have you seen the decorations on the Christmas tree? Why would anyone put a miniature Dutch windmill on it?'

Lois peered towards the far end of the aisle where the twelve-foot Christmas tree stood, decorated by the townsfolk. She had studied it earlier, trying to guess who had brought each ornament.

'The mayor invited residents of the town to bring ornaments that are special to them for the tree. The Dutch windmill probably belongs to my neighbour, Blanche. She's from Holland and she told me it reminds her of her homeland.'

The woman grunted and shrugged. 'Umm, that may be, but what's with the miniature red and blue high-heeled shoes with the fake gems on them? They just look cheap.'

Lois gave the woman a conciliatory smile. 'They must hold special memories for someone.'

From outside the market's double doors, Lois heard the faint sounds of 'Jingle Bells'. The volume quickly rose as three pipers in smart blue tartan kilts, white shirts, and black jackets marched into the building and formed a semicircle inside the door. They continued playing, moving seamlessly to 'Oh, Come All Ye Faithful' and then 'Silent Night'. A crowd quickly formed in front of them. Lois's fingers twitched as she listened to the trio. Christmas songs were so much fun to play, and the audience always loved them.

A complaining voice in her ear made Lois jump.

'Well, it drowns out that Perry Como. I don't know how many more chestnuts roasting I could stand.'

Lois laughed. 'Don't be such a Scrooge, Marge. You don't really hate the market's festiveness.'

'I got some eggnog from the refreshments table earlier. Needs some rum, but it's alright.' Marge inclined her head to the pipers. 'Don't you wish you were out there with your bandmates?'

'I don't mind tonight. I volunteered for this and I'm enjoying chatting to people who come to our table.'

Lois and Marge stood listening for several minutes as the pipers continued to play. As the last notes of 'We Wish You a

Merry Christmas' sounded, the women clapped enthusiastically; then Marge sidled back to her table.

Lois gave her own table a cursory glance to be sure it was still well-stocked. As the crowd around the pipers dispersed, several people drifted to the library's table and rifled through the books piled on it. Lois forgot about everything else as she took payments from customers and gave them change.

A few minutes later, Lois heard Marge's growl of frustration. 'It can't be. Not again!'

Lois turned to her friend. 'What's wrong?'

'I don't believe it! A couple of my exhibition items are missing.'

Lois raised her eyebrows. 'You sure? You've got lots of stuff there.'

'I'm sure. I've checked my list. How could I be so careless? Especially after that antique watch was stolen during the sesquicentenary celebration last summer.'

'You and Greg have been here all the time, though.'

'But we weren't keeping an eye on things while the pipers were playing. Greg was right beside me at your table.'

'Oh. Well, at least that narrows it down a bit. Someone who was here within the last little while must have taken them. Who was around your table before the music started?'

Marge screwed up her face, thinking. 'There were a couple of teens, Heather and Bonnie. They live a few blocks from here, off St David's Street. Who else?'

Lois noticed a candy wrapper lying at the edge of Marge's table. 'There was a rather unfriendly woman that stopped at my table then moved on to yours. Brown coat. Eating butterscotch candies.'

Marge nodded. 'Yeah, I noticed Phyllis Weller, but she's harmless. Just a bit odd.'

'That may be, but she hung around your table longer than mine. We can't discount her. There was also a woman in a purple ski jacket who was really staring at some of the items on your table.'

'Purple ski jacket – yeah, I saw Joan White here.'

'Anyone else?'

Marge shook her head. 'Those were the ones I saw. Other people just glanced at the table and walked past or stopped for a second.' She drew herself up to her full height. 'Right, that's where we start then. We need to have a word with all of them. I saw PJ Ross patrolling the building earlier. If we bump into her, we can report the theft too.'

'Shouldn't we report it to *Constable* Ross first?' Lois asked.

'We can't waste time looking for PJ. Whoever took the stuff may still be in the building. We need to catch them red-handed.'

Lois motioned to their two tables. 'We can't just take off from here.'

'Connie and Greg can hold the fort for a while.'

After a brief conversation with her co-worker, Lois stepped out from behind her table and moved to stand in front of the museum's one, surveying the items on it.

'What exactly was taken?' she asked.

'A silverplated pin cushion shaped like a Victorian women's ankle boot. It was bought from the 1914 Eaton's catalogue. It's about six inches long and almost three inches high. The etching detail on it is beautiful. Also, a pair of women's size five black leather pumps with crystal heels and clear vinylite bows. They're from Simpson's 1941 catalogue.'

Lois stared at the floor, thinking. 'So, the shoes might be small enough to fit a teenager, but each item is relatively large. You couldn't easily fit them in your pockets.'

'I doubt it. Come on, let's go.'

Marge crossed in front of the table, heading towards the aisle nearest the door. As Lois turned to follow her, she noticed a small flyer lying under the table and bent to pick it up.

'Emilio Pelle, renowned artisan shoe designer, appearing at Toronto's One of a Kind Christmas Craft Show, stall 594,' Lois read. She thrust the flyer in front of her friend. 'Marge, look at this.'

Marge stopped and glanced at it, then shrugged. 'Someone from town's been to the big craft fair. Dump it in the bin.'

'Think, Marge. Whoever dropped this might really like shoes. And what's missing from your table?'

'A pair of shoes and a pin cushion.'

'A pin cushion shaped like what?'

Marge groaned. 'Of course. Maybe they were both taken because they were shoes.'

'Do you know if anyone who stopped at your table collects shoes or shoe ornaments?'

Marge shook her head. 'No, but that's something we'll ask when we find them. Let's go. Keep an eye out for any of them.'

Quickly scanning the shoppers browsing at the first few stalls, Lois followed Marge down the first aisle. She tried to keep the faces of the women they were looking for in her mind. She didn't see any of them as they moved down the aisle.

Lois glanced into a knick-knacks and second-hand books stall near the end of the aisle. The woman in the brown coat stood hunched over a bookshelf, reading the titles on the shelf. Lois nudged Marge and inclined her head towards the woman.

Like a cat ready to pounce, Marge strode into the stall. 'Hi, Phyllis. Found anything interesting?'

Lois stepped up beside Marge and spoke gently to Phyllis, motioning towards the bookshelf. 'Do they have historical novels?'

'Some. Not *Schindler's Ark,* though.'

Phyllis shifted her shopping bag from one hand to the other. It looked fuller and heavier than when Lois had spoken to her a short while earlier.

'That's a shame. Have you found anything else you wanted at any of the stalls?' Lois asked.

Phyllis reached into her pocket and pulled out a butterscotch candy. Not meeting the women's gazes nor offering any candies to Lois and Marge, she unwrapped it and popped it into her mouth.

Phyllis shrugged. 'Just this and that.'

Marge smiled tightly at her. 'We'd like to see what you got.'

Phyllis shrugged again, reached into her bag, and pulled out a Blue Mountain Pottery trinket dish in the shape of a swan.

'Oh, isn't that pretty. I love Blue Mountain's ornaments. Do you collect them?' Lois asked.

'No, I got it to keep safety pins in.'

'What *do* you collect?' Marge asked.

Phyllis shook her head, her gaze straying to the bookshelf. 'Nothing.'

Marge fixed the woman with a hard stare. 'So, you don't collect shoes?'

Phyllis gave Marge a confused look.

'A couple things went missing from the museum's table this evening. Do you know anything about that?' Marge continued.

Lois gave Phyllis an apologetic smile. 'We noticed you at the table and we're talking to everyone who was there around the time we noticed them missing.'

Phyllis's eyes widened. 'Well, I never took them!'

'We aren't accusing you of anything,' Lois said mildly.

Marge continued to stare at the woman as Lois attempted to placate her.

'You better not be!'

Phyllis grasped the sides of her cotton shopping bag and pulled it open wide. Lois and Marge peered into it. Several loose apples and tomatoes, and a bunch of bananas filled the bottom half of the bag. No wonder it was bulging. Phyllis must have stopped at the fruit and vegetable stall after she left the museum's table. Phyllis shifted the bag back and forth so that the women could see there was nothing else in it.

Lois smiled warmly at Phyllis. 'Thanks for showing us. Did you notice anything unusual when you were at the museum's table?'

Phyllis pursed her lips tightly before she spoke. 'Wasn't much use stopping there. I couldn't look at anything properly. A couple silly girls were giggling and hogging all the space. I could hardly get near it.'

'Maybe if you head round to the museum's table later it will be quieter and you can have a better look,' Lois said.

'I've done my shopping. I'm heading home soon.'

Marge smiled at Phyllis. 'We appreciate your help. We didn't mean to upset you, but we need to get those things back.'

Without a word, Phyllis turned her attention back to the bookshelf. The women said goodbye to Phyllis, and Lois caught Marge's eye and inclined her head towards the aisle. They stepped out of the stall, walked to the end of the aisle, and turned the corner.

'Not exactly cooperative, but it's not her,' Marge said.

'She wasn't really difficult. She did show us what was in her bag. She didn't have to do that. We're not the police or security.'

Marge sighed. 'True. I'm just frustrated. We need to get those things back.'

A voice several feet away from the women drew their attention. 'You ladies here to replenish your coffee or hot apple cider levels? Or maybe another eggnog, Marge?'

Stall-holder Dave Stewart, dressed in his trademark red Stewart tartan kilt with a matching red Santa hat, stood behind the refreshments table with several other volunteers.

'Hi, Dave. I'd love a hot apple cider, but we'll have to take a rain check. We're in the middle of something,' Lois said.

'It's not like you to turn down cider. Must be serious,' Dave replied, laughing.

Marge quickly filled their friend in on the theft from the museum's exhibit.

'Constable Ross was here a few minutes ago. She headed up aisle two. You should let her know what happened,' Dave said.

'We will, but we're also keeping an eye out for some people who were around the table when my stuff disappeared. Have you seen Joan White or two young teenagers, Heather and Bonnie, recently?' Marge asked.

'Not the girls, but Joan walked by a couple of minutes ago. Our profits tonight are going to charity, but I couldn't tempt her to buy a coffee, even after I serenaded her with 'White Christmas' and changed the words to 'I'm dreaming of a Joan White Christmas'.'

'Yeah, I bet she gets razzed about her surname every year. Where did she go?' Marge asked.

'Up aisle two, not long after Constable Ross.'

Calling goodbye to the market trader, the women walked past the two long tables put together to serve refreshments. Lois couldn't help eying the assortment of cakes and cookies laid out beside the tea, coffee, and cider urns. She would love to sample the peanut butter cookies and maybe a thin slice of walnut cake, too, but she just didn't have time right now.

Rounding the corner into aisle two, Lois peered into a clothing stall on the outer wall of the building. It was crowded with young people rummaging through the garments on the clothes rails. At the back of the stall, two teenage girls, with heads bent together, were browsing through a railing of colourful sweaters.

Lois nudged Marge and pointed. 'That's the girls, isn't it?'

Lois shrank back as Marge nodded curtly and marched into the stall. She hoped her friend wouldn't storm up to the girls and make a scene.

Stopping behind the girls, Marge said in a low voice, 'I want a word with you two. Come out here now.'

The girls looked startled as they turned around, but seeing Marge's no-nonsense expression, they meekly followed her out of the stall. She led them to a corner of the back aisle, out of earshot of the staff working at the refreshments table a few yards away.

Standing in front of the two girls, Marge glared at them. 'You know stealing is wrong, don't you?'

The girls exchanged confused looks and then nodded.

'Why did you do it then?'

'Do what?' Heather asked. 'We haven't done anything wrong. We're just shopping.'

Marge glanced at the girls' feet. 'What are your shoe sizes?'

'Four,' Bonnie said.

'Five,' Heather said. 'Why?'

'I bet you like sparkly things. A pair of black shoes with crystal heels and a silver pin cushion went missing from the museum's table around the time you two were hanging around it.'

'We didn't take them! I saw the shoes. They're pretty, but they're like something my mom would wear,' Bonnie said.

Marge continued to give the girls a hard stare. 'Don't make things worse by lying. We will find out if you did it.'

Lois glanced at Marge, then said softly to the girls, 'The best thing to do is just tell the truth. If you did take them, it would be better to say so now.'

'But we didn't!' Heather insisted.

Marge glared at the girls. 'Are you willing to prove it?'

'How?' Bonnie asked.

'Open your backpacks. I want them emptied out,' Marge commanded.

Reluctantly, the girls swung their packs off their shoulders and started pulling out the contents. After a minute or two, they had a pile of their belongings that included hats and mittens, *Sixteen* and *Tiger Beat* magazines, Wrigley's chewing gum packets, powder blush compacts, cherry lip gloss, and a roll of Rockets Love Hearts candy.

Marge nodded. 'Okay. Anything in your pockets?'

Heather patted her flat pockets and shook her head, her face flaming.

Bonnie reached into her coat pocket and pulled out a pink change purse. 'Just this.'

As Lois surveyed the contents of the girls' backpacks spread out on the bench, she felt sorry for the teenagers. They were obviously embarrassed and upset by Marge's accusation.

Making a sound of irritation, Marge shook her head. 'Alright, girls. I'm sorry I had to check your packs, but I can't let whoever took my exhibition pieces get away.'

'Did you girls see anything suspicious when you were at the museum's table?' Lois asked.

The girls looked at each other and shook their heads. Bonnie replied, 'We looked at the stuff on the table, then we listened to the pipers.'

'You didn't notice what other customers were doing?' Lois asked.

'No, not really. A woman in a brown coat seemed to want to crowd us out. She kept pushing in like she was trying to shove us away, but I didn't see her take anything,' Heather said.

Marge looked at Lois. 'Phyllis.' She turned back to the girls. 'Thanks, we've already spoken to that woman. Nothing else you can remember?'

Both girls shook their heads.

'Okay, thanks for cooperating with us. Off you go. Enjoy the rest of the community festival evening.'

The girls shoved everything back into their backpacks and hurried away. Lois noticed that they headed straight back to the clothing stall. She hoped some retail therapy would help them forget Marge's interrogation.

Lois knew there was no point chastising her friend for her bullish questioning technique right now so she inclined her head towards aisle two. 'Let's head up there and look for that woman in the purple jacket. She's the last one on our list.'

'Yeah, okay. But what if she didn't take them either?' Marge huffed.

'Come on, Marge. Don't give up. That's not like you.'

Lois led them into aisle two, scanning the area as she weaved through the throng of shoppers. That purple jacket should be easy enough to spot. She made slow progress through the crowd towards the front of the building, but she didn't see the woman they were looking for. As they neared the last stall in the aisle, a flash of purple caught her eye.

Still one stall away, she craned her neck sideways for a better look into the jewellery stall. She spotted the jacket and pointed. 'Look, Marge – she's there.'

As Lois spoke, the woman glanced into the aisle and met her gaze. The woman's expression froze, and she dashed out of the stall. Trying to dodge between the people in front of her, Lois gave chase, but a group chatting in the middle of the aisle held her back, and the woman was gone before she could reach the end of the aisle.

Behind her, Marge shouted, 'Keep going. Don't let her get out of the building.'

Lois wriggled between shoppers, pushing forward to the front aisle. She darted glances around her but didn't spot a purple coat. A moment later, Marge caught up with her and pulled her down the aisle to the double doors at the far end and out of the building. Lois wrapped her arms around herself as they dashed out into the cold darkness. Light from the building spilled a short distance outside the doors but didn't reveal the woman.

Marge huffed. 'I don't think she came this way. Let's check inside again.'

The women returned to the building, puffing slightly at their unaccustomed exercise.

'You ladies taking a break from your tables?' a woman's voice said.

Ignoring the friendly question, Marge said, 'Am I glad to see you, PJ.'

Lois nudged her friend. 'Hi, *Constable* Ross.'

'What was that sprint I just saw you two do?' the police officer asked.

"We need your help, PJ." Marge explained about the missing

museum artifacts and gave the officer a detailed description of both items.

'So, you saw her enter the front aisle, but there's no sign of her outside the building?' Constable Ross said.

'Yeah, she must still be in here somewhere,' Marge replied.

'Okay, I'll go out to the cruiser and radio it in. Officers in this area can keep a lookout for her. If they spot her, they can stop her to ask a few questions. Then I'll come in and help you look for her.'

'You take aisle one. Lois and I will go back to aisle two. We'll meet at the back aisle,' Marge said.

Lois tensed, hoping that Marge's commanding manner didn't irritate the police officer, but Constable Ross didn't seem to mind. She gave them a cheerful smile as she headed out to her cruiser. Lois glanced down the front aisle to the end furthest from the door. A flash of purple slipped from behind the large Christmas tree in the corner and disappeared into aisle two.

Lois pointed to where she had spotted Joan. 'Marge, she was there all the time! She's going back down that aisle.'

The women hurried back to aisle two, and Lois almost knocked over a woman balancing on a cane as they skidded around the corner. She put her hands on the woman's shoulders to steady her, apologising profusely as the woman berated her carelessness. A couple of minutes later, feeling like her face was on fire and still apologising, Lois carefully edged around the woman.

Without acknowledging the accident they had almost caused, Marge commanded, 'You take the left side.'

Lois raised her eyebrows but said nothing as she headed down the left side of the aisle and peered into each stall, frequently darting glances ahead to be sure she didn't bump into anyone else. A couple of stalls from her, she spotted the purple jacket leaving Stewart's Antiques stall.

Lois grabbed Marge's arm and hissed. 'There!'

Joan crossed the aisle from Dave Stewart's stall to the hand-knit garments stall opposite it. Marge dashed the few yards to the stall, and Lois almost bumped into her when she stopped at the entrance.

'What are you waiting for?' Lois whispered. She mentally prepared herself for the strident attack Marge would launch on her target but her friend didn't move.

'Just watching her for a minute.'

Joan wandered from one table to another, lifting a sweater at one and several hats at another. She appeared to be casually shopping, yet she gripped her purse so tightly that her knuckles were white. After a second circuit of the tables in the small area, she abruptly turned and left the stall, hurrying towards the back of the building.

Before Joan could take more than a few steps, Marge caught up with her. 'Find what you were looking for?'

Joan started at Marge's voice and gripped her purse tighter. 'Uh, not really.'

'Have you heard that we had a couple things go missing from the museum's table?' Marge continued.

'Uh, no, I didn't.'

Without explaining further, Marge changed tack. 'I noticed you at Stewart's Antiques. Did you go to the shoe repair and second-hand shoes stall next door, too?'

Joan screwed up her face. 'I don't like scruffy shoes. My collection is—'

'You collect shoes?' Marge asked.

'Uh, I collect, ah, some things.'

Lois felt a flutter of excitement. This line of questioning seemed to be heading towards a confession. She glanced across the aisle to the antiques stall and waited for Marge's next question. Something clear and sparkly glistened on a table near the front of the stall. Squinting, she realised it looked like a shoe's heel.

'No, it can't be,' she thought. She glanced at Marge and Joan, then darted across the aisle.

On a small wooden table, behind a wooden jewellery case, sat a pair of shiny black vintage pumps with crystal heels.

Lois turned to the plump woman perched on a high stool against the wall. 'Have you had those shoes in stock long, Laurie?'

Laurie Stewart, the stall owner's wife, came to the table and lifted one of the shoes. Frowning, she twisted it back and forth to get a better look. 'I don't think it's ours. We don't stock clothes or shoes. I wonder where it came from?'

Lois drew in a deep breath. 'I think I know – back in a second.' She darted across the aisle to rejoin Marge and Joan.

Joan was glaring at her friend. 'I don't like your accusations, but I've nothing to hide.'

Joan jerked her purse off her shoulder and yanked the zipper open. Lois leaned forward to peer into the purse. It was crammed with odds and ends, but she didn't see the items they sought.

'I hope you don't expect me to take everything out of it,' Joan spat.

'Oh, no, not at all,' Lois said before Marge could speak. She carefully schooled her voice to be upbeat. 'Thanks for being so understanding. Now that we've sorted that out, come and see what I've found.'

Lois ignored Marge's confused look as she led the trio across the aisle. She lifted one of the black pumps by the toe and twisted it to show them the gleaming heel.

'Isn't this beautiful? I have to buy it,' Lois said.

'B-b-but, you can't,' Joan stammered.

Marge's eyes narrowed. 'Why not?'

'Um, well, you just can't.'

'But I really like it.' Lois turned to Laurie and winked discreetly. 'Can I give you ten dollars for the shoes?'

'Ah, I guess so,' Laurie replied.

'Great,' Lois opened her purse and rooted inside it.

'Y-y-you don't want those old shoes,' Joan stammered.

Marge fixed her with a hard stare. 'Is that because *you* want them?'

'W-w-why would I want them?' Joan asked.

'For your shoe collection,' Lois said gently. 'You know, these shoes don't even belong in this stall. So, how did they get here?'

Joan's face flamed. 'I-I-I don't know.'

'Yes, you do. You took them from the museum's table and ditched them here when you realised we were looking for you,' Marge said sternly.

'I didn't ditch them!'

'But you took them from the museum's table?' Lois prompted.

Joan slumped and nodded miserably. 'I was gonna come back and get them later.'

'I can see why you wanted them. They are beautiful,' Lois said.

'I would have won the Canuck Club's Festive Collections Photo Contest with these.'

'You swiped them to take a photo?' Marge asked.

'Not just a photo. For my collection. The judges would want to see them if I won.'

'But they're not yours,' Marge said.

Constable Ross appeared beside Marge. 'There you are, ladies. How's the search going?'

Lois motioned to the pair of shoes on the table, and Marge explained what had happened. As Marge talked, Lois checked the contents of nearby tables and display cabinets in the stall. She spotted the Victorian shoe pin cushion perched on the middle shelf in a walnut cabinet at the rear of the stall.

She lifted it and brought it to the police officer. 'I think we've now accounted for both missing items.'

'Good. I'll take Mrs White to the station to get a formal statement. I won't drag you and Marge away from your tables here tonight. Drop into the station tomorrow to give your statements. Will the museum press charges?'

'I'll ask the director in the morning,' Marge said.

Constable Ross nodded and took Joan's arm as she led her out of the market.

Lois watched them until they rounded the corner of the aisle. 'We better get back to our tables before Connie and Greg think we've left town.'

'We will, but first, we hit the refreshment table. All this activity has emptied my caffeine reserve, and I know you need hot apple cider.'

Lois smiled. 'You're right, and I could do with some walnut cake. I guess we could spare a few more minutes to celebrate our success.'

With a frown, Marge glanced up at the speakers blaring Christmas music. 'Ugh, candy canes and silver lanes – it's more than beginning to look like Christmas around here.'

'I know. Isn't it wonderful?'

'I definitely need that coffee. Let's go.'

Humming the tune of the song and ignoring Marge's feigned grumpiness, Lois squeezed her friend's arm and allowed her to pull her towards the refreshment table.

BIO

Dianne Ascroft writes the Century Cottage Cozy Mysteries series, set in a small town in 1980s Canada. Writing cozy mysteries allows her to explore the characters and the place, as well as the mystery, at the heart of each story. She shares a small farm in Northern Ireland with her husband and some elusive wild creatures.

https://www.dianneascroft.com

Chapter Eleven

THE SCENT OF CHRISTMAS COFFEE

Linda Mather

M eet Naomi Chalk, museum curator, who is helping to prepare her beloved Verney Hall for Christmas. Every year, she has helped the volunteers dress the tree to make sure the Hall looks its traditional best; she has set out the dining table and sung carols with the team the night before opening. But this year is different. She is not sure who she can trust in her team anymore. Even worse, she is not sure if she can trust herself. And why? Because Naomi has a terrible secret and, now that it is nearly Christmas, she knows it will be revealed. She has good reason to be afraid: revelations can sometimes have deadly repercussions.

The snow spattered onto her cheeks as she watched the drift and sway of white flakes against the beloved red brick of the Hall. It was already settling in a thin line on the roof of the portico and making delicate white traces in the curlicues of the stone engraving of the date over the door. Lifting her chin, she could see over the stately chimneys to the stand of pines on the hilltop, which were hazy with the threat of more snow. It wasn't until tiny clusters formed on the lenses of her glasses that Naomi finally shifted her feet. Although she was already late, she delayed again at the staff entrance to settle her shoulders and inhale a long, cold breath. As soon as she lifted the latch, the old place enveloped her in its damp, fuggy embrace; the thrum of the heating pipes was like a heartbeat. Even the slightly oily smell was familiar and reassuring.

Voices cascaded down the narrow wooden staircase, one voice rising above the others: Dena. The harsh sound made her hesitate on the bottom step. Naomi used to love coming to work at the Hall. But that was before the horrible virus had seeped away her strength and fogged her ability to think. And before Dena.

'And finally we have Naomi Chalk, Museum Curator,' Dena announced when Naomi tried to slip into the staff room unnoticed. 'So you've turned up. I half-expected you to phone in sick again because of the snow.'

'Oh the lanes are not so bad. I just had to take it slowly,' Naomi plumped down on the nearest chair, hoping to stay below Dena's sharp blue eyeline.

'Well, the rest of us have made it.' The manager's smile was all teeth and no heart as she regarded the four staff members grouped uneasily in front of her. 'Even Kevin in his ancient bus –'

'It's not ancient, nor a bus,' Kevin bridled. 'It's a classic VW campervan and worth a small fortune if you don't mind.' Arms folded, legs wide, he stood across the room from Naomi, hogging the heat from the corner fireplace.

Their staff room had once been the Hall's estate office. The

table, against which Simon was leaning his long body, was actually a large Victorian plan chest and a sink had been plumbed
incongruously between two sets of oak bookshelves. Their
kettle, coffee, mugs and microwave oven were lined up on an
aged, pockmarked dresser behind Dena, who was now scowling
at her clipboard.

'Dena, when are you going to let us know the new shift rota
you've been threatening? Some of us have a life outside this
place,' Kevin went on. He was clearly feeling cantankerous this
morning, Naomi noted. Maybe it was the snow.

'There's no time now. I'll issue the new rota before you go
home this evening. I need to go through today's targets,' Dena
consulted her notes. Fitzy, who was enthroned in the only
armchair, with a rug over her lap, threw an exaggerated eyeroll at
Naomi, like a rebellious teenager in class. It was all the funnier
because it must be at least 60 years since Fitzy had been in a
schoolroom, and Naomi ducked her head to hide her smile.

'Simon, I need you to finish the deep clean in the dining
room this morning so you can help tidy up after the volunteers
have finished decorating the entrance hall,' Dena went on,
ticking her list. 'The trouble with real trees is they make a
hideous mess.'

'There's a lot still to do,' Simon said mildly. It was hard to
discern his expression as he was clothed from head to foot in his
white cleaning suit, including a hood and a face mask dangling
from one ear.

'Talk about over the top,' Fitzy had said the first time she had
seen him in this uniform. 'You're only going to be doing the
cleaning for goodness sake. My old godmother used to spit on
the china and rub it with her hanky. It brought up a lovely shine.'
Fitzy was fond of mentioning her godmother. She was the only
one of the staff with a connection to the Mount family, who had
once owned the Hall. Her godmother, Dora Fitzgerald, had been
their last housekeeper and Fitzy remembered visiting the Hall as
a young girl.

'Dora was treated as family and so was I,' Fitzy liked to say. 'She used to let me play hopscotch in the servants' hall.'

One quiet autumn afternoon, not that long ago, Fitzy had given a demonstration for Naomi and Simon, who had never heard of hopscotch. She had marked out the game in chalk on the tiles 'to show you young uns what I'm on about,' she'd said and had then kept up a disparaging commentary as Naomi and Simon hopped back and forth. That was before Dena, of course.

'There can be no missing these targets,' Dena glared at her staff, as if she expected only the worst from them. 'Because, as you know, we will be open to visitors from tomorrow until Christmas Eve. Now, Fitzy, your job is to check that the kitchens and café are ready for the catering team and to prepare hot drinks for the volunteers.'

Fitzy brought her bushy white eyebrows together fiercely. 'I don't do catering. I need to oversee the decorating of the tree. There is a particular way that the lights must be strung and I must ensure the volunteers handle the old glass baubles with proper care.'

While the older woman was speaking, Dena turned away to refill her coffee mug from the small pink cafetiere, which she kept for her sole use. The spicy scent of Christmas coffee wafted over to Naomi and allowed her thoughts to drift away from this tense staff meeting to previous Christmases when they had ended the day with a sherry and carols around the tree.

'No need,' Dena's voice, addressing Fitzy, broke into Naomi's reminiscences. 'I've ordered new lights, which were delivered yesterday. As soon as the volunteers arrive, Kevin, you can put them to work. I want the tree complete by lunchtime.'

Fitzy's distinctive eyebrows shot up. 'Hold on a minute. What new lights? You haven't bought those horrible flashing blue things? What with him in his CSI suit, the place will look like a crime scene.' She prodded an arthritic finger towards Simon and Naomi stifled another giggle.

'Will they get sherry and carols at the end?' Naomi almost

surprised herself when the question came out of her mouth. 'The volunteers, we always used to give them...'

When her voice trailed off under Dena's hard stare, Fitzy chimed in to fill the gap. 'It's a family tradition that we thank the volunteers with sherry and carols.'

'Well that is not going to happen,' the colour was high in Dena's cheeks. 'You claim that everything you like doing is down to tradition, but I am not dishing out alcohol to people driving home in snow and there won't be time for any singing.' She turned to face Naomi. 'Today I want you to bring out the English bone china dinner service from the storeroom. You know exactly what to select. As the Curator, you shouldn't need me to tell you. Afterwards, you can help sweep up. If it's not beneath you.'

At the mention of the storeroom, Naomi's stomach gave a nasty twist. Since returning from her illness, she had noticed that certain artefacts, which the family had long ago bequeathed to the charity which now ran the Hall, were missing. She would have mentioned it straight away but her last stocktake sheet was also absent. She felt sure she had logged it onto the system before going off sick but she had been feeling so rough those last few days at work, she couldn't be certain.

She had promised herself that while the house was closed for winter, she would list all the missing items to establish the extent of the problem before raising it. Now, it was nearly Christmas and she could no longer avoid the terrible holes in the collection coming to light. For one thing, when she had to set the delicate dinner service in its rightful place on the mahogany dining table, it would be obvious to everyone that the 18th century Worcestershire porcelain basket was not the centrepiece, where it famously belonged.

'I won't be able...' she began and felt Simon glance across at her.

'Or can't you use a broom? I know there are certain physical things you still can't do,' Dena interrupted.

'No that's fine, I can sweep up,' Naomi said hastily. When she looked in Simon's direction, he had donned his mask so only his brown eyes were visible beneath the mop of dark hair that showed under his hood.

A shrill bell echoed up the grand staircase from the front door and Dena brightened. 'Right, the volunteers are here at last. We need to go down and make sure they know what they are doing.' She broke off abruptly and brought a hand to her face. A small moustache of sweat had formed on her lip and she wiped it off. 'Remember, I want this house to absolutely shout Christmas from 10am tomorrow.'

She downed the last of her coffee and led the way out of the wide door, opposite the staff door, which led directly onto the main landing with its corridor flanked by family portraits and the grand staircase spread out below.

As Naomi trooped out behind them all, Simon caught her eye, 'Don't worry, I've found the sherry. Maybe we can still give out a splash if Fitzy can bring the plastic cups from the kitchen.'

She gave him a wan smile, filled with dread at the prospect of revealing to her old friends – especially Fitzy - that the family's showpiece porcelain had been lost on her watch. 'Maybe.'

Downstairs, the six volunteers were spilling through the main door into the large entrance hall below, shaking snow off their shoulders and craning their necks to admire the enormous tree. Their amiable chat drifted up the stairwell and, mingled with the scent of cold pinewood, lifted Naomi's spirits a notch as it reminded her of earlier, happier Christmases at the Hall.

Descending the stairs in front of her, Dena suddenly wobbled on her high heels and Naomi snapped back to the present. 'Are you all right?' she asked quietly, putting out a hand to steady her boss. 'The carpet is a bit worn here.'

Dena shook off her hand and grabbed at the polished wooden banister. She flashed her toothy smile at the group of volunteers gathered below and announced that they would be decorating the tree in the entrance hall 'under Kevin's supervision.' She was about to say more when she suddenly seemed to choke. She swivelled towards Naomi, who was closest. Her face, which had been flushed, was now emulsion white.

'You take over,' she muttered over her shoulder and staggered down towards the door behind the staircase, which led to the toilets.

'I'll go and see what's wrong,' Fitzy gathered her stick and hobbled after her.

'There's nothing to worry about,' Naomi spoke up, seeing the flurry of concerned glances from the little group at the foot of the staircase. She recognised a few people, who responded with friendly smiles, and realised that they had not seen her since her illness. This was because she had been spending her days in the storeroom counting and recounting artefacts. Now, she showed them where the greenery lay in wooden trugs and the battered packing crates of tree decorations, including the new lights still in their delivery boxes.

'Kevin will be around if you need him,' she said, although when she looked up, she saw he had also disappeared. She could hear that Simon had already started up the mini vacuum cleaner in the dining room so she gave a cheerful shrug. 'Or it might just be me.'

One of the older gentlemen asked her how to tie the evergreen branches. She remembered the method from previous years and showed him. 'Nice to see you back,' he smiled.

Kevin emerged from the back corridor and jerked his head at her. 'Dena's not feeling too well,' he muttered in her ear. 'She's going to drive home before the snow gets any worse. I said I'd fetch her coat and bag from the staff room and walk her to her car.'

Having established there was nothing she could do to help, Naomi watched him run upstairs, surprisingly light on his feet for a stocky man, and then pitched in to lift a heavy yew branch as two of the volunteers fastened it over the dining room door. She was still happily absorbed in weaving holly into the yew when Kevin returned from his errand, grumbling about the worsening snow.

Once he was back, she had no excuse but to repair to her storeroom, where she spent more fruitless minutes searching for objects that she knew in her heart were not there. Perching on the wooden step ladder, she faced the day she had dreaded since returning to work after her illness. She had been over and over in her mind what would happen next: how she would be rightly sacked for her appallingly incompetent record-keeping and for failing to take care of the precious items entrusted to her and for letting down the standards of her profession. It was not so much Dena's harsh judgement that she dreaded but the look of horror and disappointment, which she could imagine dawning on Fitzy's face. She would never be able to face her or Simon again.

And yet, it had to be done. She was still trying to convince herself that she had the courage for it when, deep in the pocket of her denim dress, her phone rang, cutting into her bleak thoughts.

'Is that Mount Vernon Hall? I have been given this number and told to contact Naomi Chalk.' It was a woman's voice, official but not cold.

'Yes that's me.'

'This is Mount Vernon Police Station. I understand you are the curator at the Hall? And your manager is Dena Watkinson? I'm afraid I have some bad news. Miss Watkinson was taken to hospital earlier following a car accident,' the woman spoke slowly and with care, 'Paramedics were called to the scene but I am very sorry to tell you that Miss Watkinson died in the ambulance.'

It took Naomi a full minute to find her voice and then it came out as if from a distance, 'Dena? She's been in an - an accident - was it the snow?'

'There were no other vehicles involved but no, we don't believe it was due to the snow. She was in anaphylactic shock when the paramedics found her, which is almost certainly what caused her to drive off the road. They tried to administer adrenalin but it was too late. Of course, there will be a coroner's inquiry.' The woman paused. 'She was driving on the lane leading away from the Hall. You are her deputy there?'

'Yes, I suppose I am.'

'You saw her this morning?'

'Yes, she fell ill. That's why she left early,' the shock was gradually crystallising into cold truth as hard as the phone in Naomi's hand. 'Someone should have gone with her,' she whispered. 'I didn't realise.'

'You knew she had an allergy? She carried the details on a card.'

'Yes, we all know she is allergic to nuts. We keep everything separate in the staff room and in – ' Naomi broke off, interrupting herself. 'Where was her EpiPen? She carries it in her handbag. She told us how to use it but she can inject herself too.'

'It hasn't yet been traced.' There was a long pause in which Naomi blinked at the shelves of neatly stacked objects in her tiny storeroom. She experienced a stab of guilt: if something else was missing, maybe it was her fault? The calm voice in her ear continued. 'Officers will be with you as soon as the weather permits. Who have you got there?'

'There is just me plus three other staff members and six volunteers.'

'Don't let anybody leave. We will need to speak to you all.'

Naomi sat on the ladder after the call ended, her heart racing while the rest of her remained very still. After a few minutes, she felt she knew what she had to do and got stiffly to her feet. She went to Simon first, who was on his hands and knees, cleaning the bottom of the display shelves. 'Don't ask me anything,' she said. 'Just come to the storeroom.' She was grateful when he nodded, pushed off his hood and mask and followed.

Fitzy was setting out chairs in the café, eager to tell her what a mess the catering staff had made of the kitchen, but she soon fell silent when she saw Naomi's grave face. Kevin, however, who she found surrounded by empty packing crates under the tree, was full of questions. 'Is this about the rotas? Do you know Dena wants to change them again? We should all object this time because if we all...' he came to a halt. 'Hold on, is this about Dena?'

'Wait until we're all together,' Naomi led the way to her storeroom and closed the door. They were cramped tightly into the small space but at least it was private and she felt the staff should know before the volunteers. After she had broken the news, she had to hold onto the step ladder because her legs were shaking so badly.

'The nut allergy,' Fitzy was the first to recover. 'I mean, I knew it was serious but I didn't think it could actually – kill her.'

'She was always so careful to keep her food and stuff separate,' Simon said.

'But why not use her EpiPen as soon as she felt it coming on?' Fitzy said, pulling her long cardigan around her. 'She must have known.'

'It's only for an emergency,' Kevin said. 'And she told me she didn't feel that bad.' He rubbed his bristly chin. 'I should never have let her drive off.'

'That's what I feel too,' Naomi said. 'The police are on their way to interview us. Meanwhile we mustn't disturb anything they may want to see, which means not using the staff room.' She had a sudden vivid image of the small pink cafetiere on the wooden dresser and the haunting scent of Christmas coffee.

'We'll have to tell the volunteers,' Fitzy said. 'It will be all round the village by the time they get home anyway.'

Kevin offered to tell them but Naomi felt she should do it. 'Then we may as well go back to work until the police arrive,' she said. 'After all the visitors will still be arriving tomorrow.'

'Will they?' Fitzy barked. 'The family may want to close the house now. They still have a say in opening times and they need to know this news. I'll talk to them.'

Naomi agreed as Fitzy was the one who had contact with the

family and, without Dena, the obvious person to tell them. 'In the meantime, we'd better assume the Hall will be open,' she said.

Fitzy paused grandly on her way out of the storeroom. 'I won't be a hypocrite,' she announced, surveying them all. 'I didn't like the woman and I don't believe she was a force for good and I'm not going to say different now she's dead.'

Into the silence once she had left, Simon said, 'Why don't you send the volunteers to the café once you've told them? Give them an early tea break. I'll go and man the urns.'

Kevin stuck like glue to Naomi on her way back to the entrance hall. 'There's one thing I don't understand,' he muttered. 'Why did the police call you? I thought Dena had made me her official deputy while you were sick. So it should be my name on their contact list.'

'I really don't know,' Naomi said honestly. 'Right now I just want to get this next horrible job over with.' In fact, the volunteers took the grim news in their stride and she realised as she answered their questions that they had probably not seen very much of Dena. As soon as she had sent them off for tea, she hurried back up to the staff room. She couldn't get the image of the pink cafetiere out of her head and wanted to make sure it was under lock and key.

The old, panelled door near the top of the grand staircase took a bit of heft to open and she virtually tripped into the room. Facing her was the much narrower door, leading to the staff entrance and the wooden dresser that ran along the same wall, lined with the familiar mug stand and floral storage jars, kettle and microwave. But no pink cafetiere. Instead, it sat inverted on the draining board next to the sink, washed and rinsed. Nearby on one of the hard chairs, Simon sat very still and almost ghostly in his white suit.

'What are you doing here?' her voice was strained, unbelieving.

'I might ask you the same thing,' Simon didn't turn his head.

She pointed uncertainly to the washed cafetiere. 'Who did that?'

'It was like that when I came in.'

'But, but you shouldn't be here,' she said miserably. 'We should leave things for the police to – to investigate.'

'Maybe I thought the same as you,' Simon pushed off his hood and turned to look at her fully.

'What? That someone – doctored her coffee?' She felt her eyes drawn to a plain white jar with a clear label: Dena. 'It wouldn't be too difficult, would it?'

'No, it wouldn't,' his eyes challenged her and with one move he was at the dresser. Still wearing his cleaning suit and gloves, he picked up the jar, unscrewed it and held it out to her. She dipped her head, expecting the waft of cinnamon, ginger and hazelnuts which had greeted her earlier that morning. 'Christmas coffee', she murmured. 'Maybe she bought it by mistake, not knowing it contained nuts...'

But the grains in the jar smelled only of ordinary coffee and she frowned. 'This is not the coffee Dena was drinking.' She looked up at him doubtfully. 'So you expected someone to come and clean up.'

'Yes but I was too late,' he refused to meet her eyes. 'I mean, none of us liked her but I'd never hurt anyone. That was the one thing I did know. The only thing.'

'Oh – ' she sat down suddenly, feeling her cheeks flush. 'You think I did it. You think I brought coffee with nuts in for Dena...'

'I know the Worcester porcelain basket has gone missing.' Simon broke in, his voice wretched. 'And you've been keeping it quiet for three weeks.'

The terrible fogginess in her brain threatened to engulf her and, for a moment, she wondered if she had stolen the items. Maybe it had been part of the illness. 'I simply thought I'd mislaid them and they would turn up,' she said, her eyes on the scarred linoleum floor. 'After all, the storeroom was a complete jumble when I came back.'

'You should have told me. Or Dena. Even though you didn't like her.'

'I was scared of her,' Naomi whispered. She looked up. 'Why didn't you tell her if you knew?'

'I was waiting to talk to you first,' he sighed. 'But you always avoided me and shut yourself in the storeroom.'

'I was just making sure... I couldn't believe they were gone.'

They fell silent for some minutes and then he said. 'You're right, I should have said something earlier. I should have been braver too.'

'It was up to me and I should have spoken up. But I didn't do anything to harm Dena. You can disbelieve me if you want but, like you, I know I am telling the truth.' As she faced him over the old plan chest, she felt a new sense of certainty. 'We know that someone has been in here to cover their tracks. What if it is the same person who stole the artefacts from the storeroom while I was ill? Maybe they knew it would come to light today...'

'I've thought about this and done some digging,' he said. 'It must be Kevin, who took the china basket and the other things. His family are antique dealers so he'd know what to take and how to get shot of it.'

She was both surprised and sad that Simon had also been stewing about the lost artefacts. Aloud, she said, 'I know Kev expected to take charge of the team after Dena. He told me so just now. So he probably hoped he'd be able to cover it up.' Naomi paused and bit her lip. 'I thought for a while it might be Fitzy,' she admitted. 'Maybe taking some things that had memories for her. You know, a private collection. But then, as I compiled the inventory, I realised this is not a sentimental collection. These are valuable items that could be sold into the export market.'

'Well, that fits with Kevin.'

She crossed the room to the brass hooks on the panelling

where they all hung their belongings. She placed her hand on the gap. 'And Kevin came up and fetched Dena's coat for her. He must have taken the EpiPen out of her bag.'

Simon nodded quickly, surprising her again. 'I've already checked the bin. There's nothing much in there except the coffee grounds.' The doorbell sounded from downstairs and he gave a loud sigh of relief. 'The police will search anyway now so they will find them and any other evidence. We don't have to do anything.'

'No,' she contradicted him. 'I have to do something. I want to make sure everyone knows what I've been hiding.'

Downstairs, two uniformed officers, one male and one female, had arrived, both dusted lightly in snow. Surrounded by Fitzy and Kevin and the small crowd of volunteers, they made an odd spectacle in the 18th century hallway. The Christmas tree shivered beside them in all its decorated glory and green garlands filled every archway and mantelpiece. Kevin was leading the officers towards a seat in the dining room when Naomi spoke up. 'No, you need to come to the staff room upstairs,' she said and the little procession came to a halt. Standing in the same spot as Dena earlier, she went on, keeping her voice steady and clear. 'But first I've got something to confess.'

Simon stood at her back and Fitzy close to her side as Naomi told them about the missing items and her weeks of anxiety. The volunteers and even the police officers stood in silence and Fitzy patted her arm.

'There's no need to distress yourself, dear,' Fitzy said. 'We all know you care as much about the place as any of us.'

'Yes there is. I should have spoken up earlier. If I had then maybe Dena would not have died.' She turned to the officers and pointed towards the staff room. 'There is something you need to see – or rather smell.'

Kevin, moving quickly, managed to jostle to the front, holding out a palm to the police officers as if to lead the way and

Fitzy limped after him. Naomi glanced at Simon in alarm, 'No,' she began, 'Just the police...'

But the little group was already moving past her and Naomi stood, stock still, her eyes resting on the neat packing crates, now stacked behind the tree. Someone had tidied them into a dark corner. She thought of the rinsed cafetiere on the draining board and the neatness of the refilled coffee jar. Neatness was not Kevin's style.

She walked slowly down the stairs and in a kind of trance, she began to sift gently through the raffia and tissue paper in the empty packing crates. One crate was not empty. In a shallow tray, amongst the aged strands of raffia and shreds of tinsel lay one slim translucent tube: Dena's EpiPen.

As Naomi lifted the tray to the light, she saw that Fitzy stood alone on the stairs. 'It wasn't stealing,' the older woman said. 'I was only returning some precious things, which used to belong to the family. They supported me and my family in past years and this was my way of helping them out when they needed it. A family like theirs should not have to live hand to mouth. Not after all they've given.'

'The family have long ago given these things up. And were compensated too,' Naomi said quietly, still kneeling among the boxes.

'I knew it would come out today because of the Christmas opening and that Dena would show no mercy. You and Simon are different. You two would understand. Kevin is too stupid to care and, as long as we said he could be in charge, he'd agree to anything. But Dena was heartless so I had to get rid of her.' Fitzy sighed and there was a dreadful appeal in the lines on her face. 'Let's be honest, she never belonged with us.'

Naomi got to her feet and was at the woman's side before she spoke. 'I do understand,' she said, 'better than most. But I've also realised that, although some things are precious, they are not worth someone's whole life. ' She gently turned them both to face the staff room. As they climbed slowly towards it, the door opened and a police officer stood silently, taking in the scene. Naomi felt numb as he walked towards Fitzy, led her into the room and firmly closed the door.

Naomi was standing by the tree looking out through the long windows when Simon appeared by her side. The familiar court-yard was made magically different by early dusk and snow-heavy trees. She heard him approaching but didn't turn round.

'I was wrong,' he said. 'So much for my detective work.'

'So was I,' she sighed. 'Wrong in different ways.'

He leant over her shoulder to peer out at the snow-covered garden. 'The police have said the volunteers can go home. They'll be relieved, it's starting to get dark already. I've been feeding them more tea and mince pies,' he added. 'Sherry didn't seem quite right.'

Naomi turned to face the twinkling tree, its topmost branches stretching past the oil paintings to where the tinsel star shone at the top. She could pick out individual decorations she remembered. Beside her, Simon also gazed up at it, arms folded. 'The volunteers said something while I was pouring the tea,' he said. 'They asked me to tell you that they thought you had been very brave.'

Naomi looked at him. 'Thank you. That matters.'

'Maybe we can even have carols and sherry,' he said.

'Yes, we will,' she said decisively. 'On Christmas Eve.'

BIO

Linda Mather is the author of the Jo and Macy Mystery series. The books are *Forecast Murder, A Sign for Murder, Murder as Predicted, The Hanged Man* and *A Future Murder,* all published by Joffe Books and available on Amazon. They feature Jo Hughes and her private investigator boss David Macy. Jo is an astrologer, who also works as a PI and whose tenacious inquiries lead her to twisty resolutions.

Linda lives in Worcestershire, England and sets all the Jo and Macy Mysteries locally in the West Midlands and Cotswolds. The ideas for the latest book 'The Perfect House for Murder' came to her during lockdown on many canal walks. The cottages with their flower-filled window boxes and the idyllic pubs along the canals looked so pretty and pastoral that nothing bad could ever happen there. Linda took this as a challenge.

Linda is currently writing a police thriller set in the New Forest to be published in 2025 and also has plans for the next Jo & Macy Mystery.

https://www.instagram.com/lindamather.writer

Chapter Twelve

MOTIVE FOR MURDER

Gillian Duff

Nora McKenzie knows the signs. Her sister, Mavis, may have retired from the police force, but her appetite for justice remains. When Lenny the Lip, a one-time informer and small-time crook, is sentenced to life for poisoning his wife, Mavis knows he didn't do it. Someone got away with murder, and she's determined to find out whom. The Historical Society's winter retreat to Cairncross Castle brings the suspects together over mulled wine and mince pies. But can the sisters unmask the real killer before it's too late or will the murderer strike again?

'So, is he guilty or not?' Nora set a plate of mince pies on the coffee table. Following her difficult afternoon, her sister would need fortification.

'He may be guilty of something, but he isn't guilty of that!' Mavis sat heavily on the settee and removed her hat. She pushed the hatpin into the felt and laid it on the armchair. 'I'm not saying Lenny the Lip is an angel, but he didn't kill his wife.' She peeled off her leather gloves and popped them into her handbag which she shut with a snap.

Nora laid out cups, saucers and side plates from their mother's best china. She'd used special Christmas napkins but paper ones rather than linen. She waited for Mavis to complain about 'standards' but if she noticed, she didn't say.

'He was found guilty though, wasn't he?' Nora asked, pouring her sister a cup of tea.

'Yes, he was, but he isn't a murderer.' Between slurps Mavis said, "He adored Gladys. He was punching above his weight, and he knew it. Besides, she had a good income as a private secretary. Why would he kill the golden goose? His words, not mine.' She helped herself to a mince pie, smothered it with brandy butter, then popped half of it into her mouth.

'An unsafe conviction?' Nora said, using a phrase Mavis knew only too well.

'Absolutely, and, if that *is* the case, then a murderer is still at large. Of that I am quite sure.' She swilled the last of the mince pie down with the remainder of the tea.

'What are we going to do about it?' Nora knew the signs. Since her sister retired from the police, they had apprehended a jewel thief and exposed an official document as a forgery. They weren't Pinkerton's, but they were getting damn close.

'We'll unmask the killer and, perhaps, prevent another murder.'

'*Prevent* a murder?' Nora wasn't following.

'Think about it, Nora. It's the only thing that makes sense. Why would anyone kill Gladys?' Mavis said, as though stating the obvious. 'If Lenny didn't kill her, and no-one had a grievance against her, she may not have been the intended victim. And if not her, then who?'

'Who indeed?' Nora said. 'What more did you find out?'

'Gladys ingested some sort of poison, according to the post-mortem, though the source wasn't identified during the trial.' Mavis knew about that sort of thing. 'Not likely to be Strychnine as her muscles didn't convulse. Ricin or Thallium are colourless and odourless. She could have ingested them without being any the wiser. Lenny thinks it must have been administered during the Scottish Historical Society's summer outing, the day before she died. According to him, she ate nothing when she came home but complained of stomach-ache and started sweating profusely. Apart from a couple of boiled sweeties, she'd eaten nothing more than a green salad with a rather tart dressing on the trip, whereas everyone else ate roast beef sandwiches. Gladys had a moral qualm about eating animals, if you can imagine such a thing.'

'Very unusual but hardly grounds for murder.' Nora topped up her sister's teacup. Mavis required lubrication when in full flow.

'Exactly,' said Mavis. 'There *was* something unusual, however. She kept repeating, 'It wasn't mine in 39,' as she drifted in and out of consciousness. Lenny thought she was making no sense. But what if that was the only thing that *did* make sense? What if she were trying to tell him who had poisoned her and why?'

'It wasn't mine in 39,' Nora repeated in a voiced whisper.

The statement hung in the air.

'Something connected to the war?' Nora ventured, pouring herself another cup.

'Perhaps,' conceded Mavis. 'According to Lenny, she didn't do anything remarkable. Gladys was a land girl or some such, which accounts for her strange eating habits, but she wasn't in posses-sion of state secrets. She joined the bank after the war and never progressed beyond record checking and taking phone calls.'

'So, we're looking for a salad-wielding murderer with a grudge against the telephone?'

'Doesn't sound likely, does it?' Mavis gulped another mouthful of tea then said, 'The police made a thorough investigation, of course, but couldn't find anyone who had a better motive than Lenny... and he had no motive at all.'

'How many people were on the trip?'

'Eight. Nine if you count Gladys. They'll all be on the Christmas outing. The Hunters, he's the organiser, Major and Mrs Carruthers, Mr and Mrs Anderson, and one other couple – not married.' Mavis underlined the 'not married' with plenty of disapproval while cutting into another mince pie.

Nora ignored her sister's prudishness. 'I take it the police investigated everyone?'

'They did, but we'll need to investigate them again,' Mavis said, devouring another mince pie.

'That goes without saying,' Nora said, taking the empty cup from her sister's outstretched hand. 'What's your plan?' Nora might be the elder sister, but Mavis was in charge.

'The Scottish Historical Society has two new members for their winter retreat. I've already purchased tickets. We are going to Cairncross Castle. We'll find out as much as we can about those who were on the summer trip and make an arrest before Christmas.'

Later that week the McKenzie sisters found themselves on a small luxury coach winding their way through the wilds of the Angus countryside.

Nora wiped the mist from the window and looked up. The snow was falling in fat white flakes, and the pines were frosted and glistening.

Between the trees, she caught a glimpse of red sandstone

battlements flanked by two towers. 'Look, Mavis. That must be it. Cairncross Castle.'

'And not before time,' Mavis said, looking out, though the building disappeared as the coach rounded a corner.

Behind them, an angry voice complained, 'You promised we'd arrive before lunch! At this rate, we'll be lucky if we make before Christmas.'

'Nearly there,' said Nigel Hunter, 'Right, driver?'

The driver ignored both men, as another passenger offered some boiled sweeties.

'We've been on this coach for hours. A handful of sweeties isn't going to fill the gap!' It was Lance Giddings. Nora would know that voice anywhere and nudged her sister.

'Do you really need to be so loud? You're upsetting my wife.'

'Major Carruthers' wife is not having a good time of it,' Nora whispered. 'That spider this morning nearly sent her through the roof.'

'Boiled sweetie?' One of the women was trying to placate the irate passenger, but Nora couldn't identify the voice. She was about to turn around when her sister grabbed at her arm.

'Don't draw attention to yourself. I can see in the driver's rear-view mirror. That's why I chose these seats. Camel coat.'

In the mirror, Nora could see a paper bag in an outstretched hand, and the cuff of a camel coat.

'No, thank you. I'm diabetic!'

Nora nudged her sister again. 'Lance Giddings, the film director,' she whispered. 'Diabetic. You wouldn't think it to look at him.'

Mavis shot her sister a look that would have chastised a Mother Superior.

The single decker bus turned off the main road and trundled up the winding gravel drive of Cairncross Castle, deep in the Scottish countryside. The driver, in the dark blue uniform of Alexander & Son's Coach Company, crunched the gears twice in close succession as he negotiated the slope. Sweat trickled from beneath his patent peaked hat, but at last he stopped outside the castle entrance and pulled on the handbrake. Perhaps such a remote location had been a mistake midwinter. But the driver had taken it slowly, negotiating the glen road with grim determination.

Mavis was first to alight. She pulled her tweed waistcoat down and rebuttoned her jacket. 'Well, that was quite the journey!'

'It wasn't so bad,' said Nora. 'I like the twists and turns. Always a new view. The driver did rather well.'

'He did rather well for himself. Did you see the cost of fuel at Brechin?' She tapped the side of her nose in a knowing fashion. 'Just four shillings and eight pence a gallon, yet I noticed the receipt he got stated it was five shillings and six.'

'You and your eagle eyes! That's not what we're here to investigate,' Nora whispered, pulling her sister away from the coach door as the driver appeared. He pulled his hat low over his eyes and saluted the male passengers as they disembarked.

'So many old soldiers are still struggling now,' Mavis said with rarely exhibited compassion. 'I overheard someone at the depot saying, 'Oh, Ned, how long have you been out now?' He said it had been ten years but that the experience still haunted him, and he was finding it difficult to hold it together.'

'It's been fifteen years,' Nora stated. 'He must have stayed in after the war. A career soldier was always going to find civvy street a challenge.' They stood remembering the day the bombs fell silent. 'Still, it's a new decade soon, and the sixties are going to be the best yet.'

Mavis shrugged. 'Not if the state of this place is anything to go by.'

Nora looked up at the building and had to agree. Cairncross Castle was down on its luck. Paint was peeling from the window frames, and the oak door was missing a metal stud. The battlements were covered in lichen and slates had fallen from the turret roofs. At the top of the main building, just visible from the courtyard, was an empty flagpole. 'No Royal standard flying, so none of the royals are here.'

Mavis looked the building up and down like a headmistress checking the uniform of a wayward schoolgirl. 'They'd not be seen dead in a place like this.' She took her sister by the elbow and whispered, 'Stand by the coach and match the luggage to its owner. We'll need to check each of the bags if we get the chance, though poison could be kept about their person. I'll hover by reception and commit each room number to memory. Do you remember who was on the summer trip?'

'Of course. My memory's excellent. Remember in '49, I took over the role of Portia. 'The quality of mercy is not strained...'

'We've no time for that, Nora. Look sharp. They're pairing up.'

Mavis disappeared into the foyer leaving Nora in the cold watching the luggage being lowered to the ground. Her younger sister had the knack of getting the easier role, but Nora accepted it. Mavis was the brains behind the operation, and this was their most dangerous case to date. Someone outside Cairncross Castle waiting to claim their suitcase had committed murder and might be planning another.

The hotel owner appeared with a young porter in tow. After a brief introduction, he said, 'I'll get the guests settled. Park the bus round the back. Come to the kitchen when you're finished. I've a job for you, Ned.' He scurried off into the hotel, clipboard in hand.

The driver nodded, then said, 'Right, lad, let's get the luggage down.' He urged the young porter onto the top of the bus and instructed him to remove the canvas tarpaulin and unload the suitcases.

The Andersons were first in line. Mr Anderson looked peaky. 'Travel sickness,' his wife said, by way of explanation. 'He'll be fine now we're on dry land.' They travelled light with only one carpet bag between them.

'Mr Giddings,' Nora gushed as he came forward to claim their luggage, 'Can I just say I am a great admirer of your work.'

'I'm on holiday,' he growled.

'Oh, don't mind him,' said his companion, the stunning Beverley Dallas. 'He's always like that when he hasn't had a drink. And we've been on the coach for hours.'

Nora was about to disagree – they'd boarded the bus at 10am and it was only just after lunchtime – but she decided against it. Who would have thought Lance Giddings and Miss Dallas would be on the same bus tour ...' Nora stopped herself. What *were* people like that doing on a trip like this? It certainly didn't fit with their Hollywood lifestyle. She'd see what Mavis thought.

The last luggage to be claimed was a set of brown leather suitcases with brass buckles, buffed until they shone. Major Carruthers tapped them with the wooden baton he carried under his armpit. 'What does he use that for?' Nora wondered.

The Major's wife, a Russian heiress if the newspapers were to be believed, wrapped her fox fur tighter around her shoulders and swept into the foyer without a backwards glance. No doubt she was used to servants fetching and carrying.

Nora struck up a conversation. 'Major, do you need a hand? Can I carry your wife's vanity case?'

'Better not. She can be touchy.'

'Because of the awful business in the summer?' Nora said, hoping her reference to the murder didn't come across as crass.

He bristled. 'You heard about that?'

'Oh yes, the organisers had to tell us. Did you know the deceased well?'

'No better than anyone else. Seemed a nice sort. Strange eating habits though. Wouldn't eat meat, apparently.'

'So I heard. A picnic, wasn't it, in the summer?'

'Yes. At the Airlie Monument.'

'Who prepared the food?'

Major Carruthers tilted his head in a quizzical way. 'Look, I'd rather you didn't talk about this in front of my wife. She's sensitive.'

'Sensitive?' Nora's ears were still ringing from her high-pitched Little Miss Muffet scream.

'Highly strung. It took me a long time to persuade her to come on this trip. She called it cursed.'

'She's Russian, your wife?'

'Yes.' His lips tightened.

'You met in Russia?'

He bristled again, as though privacy and politeness were in conflict. 'London.'

'I speak a little Russian, you know,' Nora said. 'I performed at the Moscow State Theatre. Chekov's Three Sisters.'

Major Carruthers was clearly not impressed. He bowed slightly, probably out of courtesy, stuck his baton beneath his armpit, and picked up the three cases at once. Nora couldn't help but be impressed. He was clearly a strong man. More likely to beat a woman to death than to poison her. Poison was a woman's weapon, wasn't it? Boiled sweeties could be an effective weapon. She looked around for the camel coat but couldn't see it. Could it have been Beverley Dallas?

Later, in the safety of their room, Nora sprawled on one of the twin beds watching Mavis fold a piece of paper and place it beneath the leg of the writing desk in the bay window. 'I mean, this doesn't seem the kind of trip, to the kind of place, with the kind of people, that you'd expect would appeal to showbusiness royalty.'

Mavis lifted the piece of paper and folded it again. 'Perhaps they are history buffs and need a little bit of anonymity. I mean, there's Russian royalty on this trip, so why not showbusiness?' When she was satisfied with the stability, she sat at the desk and took out her notebook. 'But you're right. There is something amiss. I'll make a note.' She scribbled in her book with the stubby pencil she always had to hand. 'Did you know, the Scottish Historical Society has existed for over a hundred years, apart from a short hiatus during each of the wars?'

'Hiatus is such a funny word, don't you think?'

'Focus, Nora.' Mavis continued. 'The remit of the society is simple: visit local landmarks and engage the services of a local history buff. Sometimes there's a quiz, though I doubt there'll be questions about the stars of the silver screen.'

'Who gave the talk in the summer?'

'Good question. The Lord Lieutenant.'

'Is he above the law?'

'Probably, but he isn't visiting this time, so we can ignore him for now.' Mavis turned back to her notebook. 'Let's compare notes: Major Carruthers and his wife Natalya – Room 1, right next to the stairs. Suitcase long enough to hide a sword in?'

'Bayonet, maybe.'

Mavis scored through something on her list then said, 'I checked the Major's war record. He was hospitalised in '39, but Gladys wasn't a nurse so I can't see them being connected. Mind you, Cairncross Castle was a convalescent hospital during the war. I'd better check where he recuperated.' She made another scribble in her notebook, then looked up. 'Next is Nigel Hunter and his wife?'

'Before we move on, Mavis, an observation, if I may...'

'Proceed.' Mavis put down her pencil and turned to her sister.

'Natalya is a Russian heiress, right?' Nora said, enjoying her sister's full attention for a change.

'By all accounts.'

'You don't think she could be a secret agent, do you? I could talk to her in Russian, pretend to be her handler. Isn't that the word?'

'Now let's not get fanciful,' Mavis said.

'When we toured Chekov between the wars, Georgi said my accent was impeccable.' Nora demonstrated. '*Schell dozhd you sneg*. It's from the Three Sisters. *It was raining and snowing.* There was snow in Moscow, and we had just—'

'You were saying something about Natalya ...' Mavis said.

'Oh yes. If Natalya is a Russia secret agent, perhaps Gladys outed her. If she were in the secret service...'

'There's no evidence of that.'

'Of course not. It wouldn't be much of a secret if everyone knew about it.'

Mavis considered this. 'Fair point!' and wrote 'Natalya' in the column under 'Suspect' and 'Foreign agent?' under the column titled 'Motive'. Now we need to check her for the 'Means' and the 'Opportunity'. Right, who's next?' Mavis looked down her list. 'Nigel Hunter and his mouse-like wife, Edith.'

'Ah, the society chairman.'

'And Gladys's boss, don't forget.'

'Any suspicion he and Gladys may have—' Nora stretched out on the candlewick bedspread in a seductive pose, 'known each other as well as worked together?'

'Nora! Decorum. He's a bank manager.'

'He's a man. The sins of the flesh...' Nora said, knowingly. 'If they were having an affair, he might have wanted to prevent a scandal.'

'By murdering her?' Mavis was not convinced. 'Use your charm on him, Nora. Let's see if he is the straying type or if his wife is jealous.' Mavis returned to her list. 'The young honey-moon couple, Mr and Mrs Smith, weren't on the summer trip.'

Nora said, 'No but the name's suspicious for a start.'

'Someone has to be called Smith.'

'They didn't look at each other once on the journey. I was watching them in the driver's rear-view mirror. Definitely not the picture of young love.' Nora knew about these things. 'And their suitcases didn't match. One had the initials C.D. and the other had the initials M.B. Definitely not Mr and Mrs S.'

'Newly-weds wouldn't have matching suitcases. They did

hang about the foyer rather a long time. Reluctant to go upstairs. First night nerves, I imagine.'

Nora was sure her sister couldn't imagine but didn't say so.

'The Smiths weren't on the summer trip, so we can ignore them. The only other couple was Lance Giddings and Beverley Dallas.'

'Something happened in her past...' Nora stood, as though movement might entice the information back to her. 'She was in a horrific accident. Hit and run. The scars on her face are not nearly as bad as I imagined.'

'Giddings is quite the Casanova from what I gather,' Mavis said.

'Yes, he is.' Nora thrilled at the thought of a weekend in Lance Giddings' company. 'I can investigate him.'

'No,' said Mavis decisively. 'I'll do it.'

A gong sounded somewhere downstairs.

'Ooooh, showtime!' said Nora, smiling at herself in the mirror. Her skirt was a foot shorter than her sister's, but Mavis had never followed fashion. She was still wearing the tweed three-piece suit and sensible brogues she travelled in, reminding Nora of Agatha Christie's Miss Marple.

Downstairs, Christmas carols were playing on a scratchy '78 from a gramophone almost as old as the castle itself. The management had pushed the boat out by having a uniformed waitress in the foyer holding a tray of eggnog.

'Don't mind if I do,' said Nora, whipping a glass from the tray and taking a sip.

Mavis checked her watch and tutted.

'It's Christmas, Mavis. We're allowed a tipple in the afternoon.'

'A sherry might be in order, but that looks unnatural!'

Nora took a second glass and handed it to her sister then whispered, 'It's traditional! You might like it. Besides, it's an amazing prop. Wander upstage right to find a coaster and eavesdrop on the Major and his wife. Cross downstage left to get a refill and see what Mrs Hunter is rooting around for in her bag.'

'That reminds me. Who had the camel coat?'

Nora looked at her sister in a quizzical fashion.

'The boiled sweeties?'

Nora flushed. 'I can't remember. It could have been Mrs Anderson.' She looked across to see Mr Anderson holding his wife's arm as he shuffled along beside her. He was still looking distinctly under the weather. 'Can't still be travel sickness,' Nora whispered. 'Do you think she could be poisoning him right under our noses?'

'It's possible. But what would be the motive, and why do it here? She could do it in the privacy of their own home if she wanted.'

'You're right,' said Nora. 'Besides, I can't imagine Gladys having an affair with Mr Anderson. He's thirty years her senior. So, if we discount him, that leaves Lance Giddings, Major Carruthers and Nigel Hunter.'

'If it is an affair. We have no proof of that. Come on, let's see what we can find out.'

A fire had been lit in the drawing room but hadn't taken the chill off the room. A thin holly garland had been strung across the mantelpiece and two red candle sticks placed at either end, though neither of the candles had been lit. In the bay window sat a squat fir tree, too small for the space it occupied, a few fake presents beneath its lower branches.

Major Carruthers, in full uniform complete with medals, stood beside the fireplace and his wife in a gauze and satin puffball dress, sat gazing into the flames. Nora stopped as she passed the Contessa and whispered something in her ear. The woman smiled and raised her glass which Nora clinked saying, 'Za zdorov'ye!'

'She's about as Russian as I am,' Nora reported when she reached her sister's side. 'I knew she was acting, and not very well either.'

'How can you be sure?' Mavis asked.

'I told her, in impeccable Russian, that a spider was sitting on her shoulder, and she didn't react. And if she isn't Russian, I imagine she's no heiress either.'

'Interesting,' said Mavis, in a rare note of approval. 'Perhaps Gladys found out and was murdered to keep her secret.'

'She wouldn't want the Major to know. I'll speak to the kitchen staff. Find out if she could have tampered with the picnic. No doubt the police interviewed them at the time.'

'Yes. But no-one said anything to help poor Lenny. Let's hope we can put it right.'

Mavis still hadn't touched her eggnog, so Nora took her glass. 'You said yourself that Lenny was guilty of something.'

'Yes, but police informants get treated abysmally inside. If they think he killed his wife too, he could be in real danger, and I don't want that on my conscience. Lenny the Lip was valuable to me and my career. I cannot let him suffer unnecessarily.'

Nora downed the eggnog in one, then said, 'Be right back. I'll drag Nigel away with me – see what you can find out from his wife.' She winked at her sister then set off.

Mavis watched her sister shimmy across the drawing room floor and exit stage left with the banker in tow. Backstage was Nora's happy place, and a man on her arm made it even better. But would she find out anything useful? Only time would tell.

Mavis eyed the tiny canapes being served and wondered when they were going to be fed proper food. Or at least mince-meat pies.

The newly married couple were eying up the rest of the room rather than one another. Mavis followed the woman's eyeline. She was watching the famous director Lance Giddings as he threw himself into an armchair and pulled the actress on his arm into his lap. He seemed the type to have an affair but could have his pick of Hollywood beauties. The wedding picture Lenny had shown Mavis suggested Gladys was rather plain and not Lance Giddings' type. She scolded herself. Gladys was dead and as such demanded a certain level of respect.

Nigel Hunter was a different kettle of fish. Lenny's trial proved he knew Gladys through his work as well as the Historical Society, though there had been nothing in the news about an affair. If Nigel's wife were responsible for Gladys' death, might she pretend they hardly knew each other? Mavis needed to find out.

With her husband out of the way, Mavis sidled over to Edith and drew her away from the other guests on the pretext of asking her about the parcels under the tree.

'Oh, I am sure they are empty,' she said, picking one up and shaking it. She offered it to Mavis who declined. 'Why risk the contents being stolen!' She dumped the parcel back beneath the tree.

'I imagine it must be difficult, given what you've been through in the last decade,' said Mavis.

Edith blinked twice but remained silent.

'The bank,' Mavis said. 'I ...read about the embezzlement in the papers.' No reason to tell her she had been in the police, though she hadn't been involved in that case.

Edith flushed. 'Nigel trusted that odious man. It took years for the bank to recover.'

'An employee, wasn't it?' Given what Edith said, it made sense. Now to turn the conversation to Gladys.

'Charles Kelly. I'll never forgive him. We almost lost everything. After that, Nigel was edgy, distant, careful who he trusted.'

'And Gladys?' The moment of truth. Mavis monitored Edith's face closely.

'Gladys?' Edith flushed further. 'Yes, poor Gladys. Another disaster for Nigel.'

'It wasn't great for Gladys either, to be fair.'

'Of course not. She didn't deserve that. Her husband. How could he? I never met a sweeter, more honourable woman.'

Edith clearly bore Gladys no ill-will. 'It wasn't her husband,' Mavis confided. 'I'm certain of that.' She leant in as though to impart something in confidence, and Edith followed suit. 'For a long time, he was my...' she searched for the right word... 'researcher. I cannot imagine he murdered Gladys. But I wonder...' A thought which struck Mavis earlier now solidified. 'Could it have had something to do with the business at the bank?'

'She discovered the fraud,' Edith whispered.

'She did?'

'Her signature had been forged on one of the records. She maintained the ledger, all the transactions, rows and rows of them and cross checked them against the teller receipts. She was incredibly neat, and very mindful of detail. That's what Nigel liked about her.'

'It wasn't mine in '39.'

'Right. It wasn't her signature...' Edith looked askance. 'How did you know about the ledger?'

'Her husband told me. She repeated it over and over when she was delirious,' Mavis said. 'I thought it had a war connection. But I see her meaning now. Record 39. It wasn't her signature. And this Charles Kelly, he was imprisoned, wasn't he?'

'Yes, for ten years. He must be due to be released soon.'

'Of course, Ned Kelly, the Australian outlaw,' Mavis exclaimed.

'I beg your pardon?' Nigel Hunter said, appearing at his wife's side.

'Oh dear, I'm afraid someone is in incredible danger.' Mavis hurried off, leaving Edith and Nigel Hunter looking perplexed.

The kitchens of Cairncross Castle were not what Nora expected. No shiny copper pots hanging from the roof. No kitchen maids in uniforms. No chef that she could see. Simply the waitress, the bus driver, and the porter unpacking boxes of food.

'Not freshly prepared?' she said, by way of making her presence known.

'You shouldn't be in here,' said the waitress. 'Staff only.'

'It looks like you need a hand.' What can I do?'

The waitress hesitated a moment, looked at the progress they were making and said, 'Help Charlie here. We need to serve dinner at 6pm pronto.'

Nora looked at the old soldier, wearing a flowery pinny and no hat. He wasn't nearly as old as she'd imagined. 'Hello, Charlie.' Hadn't the hotel owner called him Ned? Nora couldn't be sure, but she rolled up her sleeves and started work.

'Don't forget, Charlie, Nigel Hunter doesn't like cranberry jelly. He will be having the redcurrant jelly instead. A little unorthodox but I am sure it will taste just fine.'

Charlie was busy tidying up the redcurrants stalks when Nora asked him, 'Were you in the army a long time?'

'No longer than I had to,' he replied. 'Why?'

'No reason,' Nora said. 'If your name is Charlie, why do you get called Ned?'

'You ask a lot of questions.'

'Just being friendly.'

Charlie dipped a teaspoon into the jam pot, turned away, fiddled with something in his pinny pocket, then turned back and offered Nora a spoonful of redcurrant jelly. 'Taste this for me.'

Mavis hurried into the kitchen shouting, 'Nobody touch anything.' She rushed across the room and swiped the spoon of redcurrant jelly out of Charlie Kelly's hands. 'Here! Evidence!' She handed it to the young married couple who had appeared in the door of the kitchen. 'You *are* undercover police, are you not?'

They looked a little dumbfounded, then nodded.

Charlie Kelly lunged for the door, but the Smiths grabbed him and wrestled him to the ground.

Mavis continued. 'He's the one you are looking for. Charlie Kelly, an ex-employee of the National Bank. He murdered Gladys in cold blood and was about to do the same to Nora and to Nigel Hunter.'

As they slapped the handcuffs on him, the newly-wed husband said, 'I'm Detective Day and this is Detective Brash. An anonymous tip suggested the conviction was unsafe and that we should come on this trip to find out more.'

'The tip was from me,' said Mavis. 'I'm no longer in the police and didn't fancy making a citizen's arrest.'

Detective Brash said, 'Well, we're glad you did. But how did you know the bus driver was the killer?'

'He saluted the men as they came off the bus. He wasn't being respectful. He was hiding his face behind his hand in case Nigel Hunter recognised him. He embezzled money when he worked at the bank and was caught. Gladys knew her signature had been forged in record 39, and that Charlie Kelly was responsible. I heard someone calling him Ned, and then he fiddled the receipts when we stopped for fuel at Brechin. That was what first alerted me to his true nature.'

'Charlie 'Ned' Kelly?' said the policewoman. 'Like the outlaw. Caught for the sake of a few shillings.'

'Once a thief, always a thief. He served a decade in prison for the embezzlement but never forgave those who put him behind bars. He blamed Gladys and Nigel, and so plotted his revenge.'

'And now he will serve life for murder. Who would suspect the bus driver had poisoned the food?' said Nora.

'Poison?' The hotel owner went pale.

'With Gladys it was the salad dressing. This time it was the redcurrant jelly prepared specially for Mr Hunter.' Mavis pointed to the board where the redcurrants stalks lay like fallen soldiers.

'And here is the poison.' Mavis pointed out the traces of white powder on the chopping board.

'This is all the evidence we need.' Detective Day lifted Ned's redcurrant-stained fingers while Detective Brash placed the white powder in a small evidence bag.

The undercover police officers looked relieved to stop pretending to be newly-weds and shook the owner by the hand. We will head off now, if you don't mind. Her Majesty's constabulary will foot the bill for the room.'

'No need. It's on the house,' said the owner. 'I am just thankful that no-one else was harmed.'

They bundled their prisoner into the back of a black police van which trundled off down the drive. Charlie 'Ned' Kelly would soon be back behind bars where he belonged, and Lenny the Lip would be released.

Later, in the drawing room of Cairncross Castle, with a generous fire in the grate, the hotel owner handed out sherry glasses filled to the brim with amber liquid.

'Merry Christmas, everyone,' said the owner. 'Here is to a fantastic festive season and to a great decade to come.'

'Ah,' said Mavis. 'A cream sherry.'

'Just the job!' replied Nora. They clinked glasses. 'Merry Christmas.'

BIO

Gillian Duff is a graduate of Dundee University's Crime Writing and Forensic Writing and won their Val McDermid prize for her first novel, Crossing the Line. Her second novel, Act of Betrayal, won the Scottish Association of Writers' Constable Stag. Her thrillers are fast-paced and twisty with unique protagonists and a strong forensic streak, while her cozy mysteries set in the '50's and '60's hark back to a more genteel time. When she is not writing, she can be found curling or hill walking in the Angus countryside.

https://www.instagram.com/gillianduffauthor/

Chapter Thirteen

DECK THE HALLS WITH YULETIDE SMUGGLING

Melicity Pope

E very night, Victoria Winters sneaks out of the naval-port-town hotel where she's been spending the Christmas season of 1802 with her mother and sister, desperately trying to track down the blackguard who ruined her family's fortunes. But when her inquiries lead to a young lieutenant's life hanging in the balance, and with the threat of her sister's happiness being set adrift, can Victoria uncover both a would-be murderer and a thief before the HMS Dominant weighs anchor and all her hopes are lost at sea?

The seaside was eerily calm in December's early twilight.

Was that man watching her? No, he'd only paused for a pinch of snuff.

Calm yourself, Victoria.

Ever since she'd been posing as a tavern maid at The Captain's Dog, she'd been looking over her shoulder. But she couldn't stop now.

Now that she was so close to finding it.

She tightened the neck of her pelisse against the bitter wind.

'Victoria Winters, there you are!'

Victoria's younger sister, Evalene, hurried up the promenade, pebbles and bits of sand crunching underneath her slim leather boots.

'Everyone's waiting for you at The Grande. Mama will be beside herself if the first course isn't served by 4 o'clock.'

Victoria scanned this way and that in the gathering dark. It wasn't like Lieutenant Rogers to be late. What if something had happened to him? What if...

'Victoria!'

Victoria bit her lip, then donned a bright smile for her sister.

'Yes, alright.' She threaded her arm through Evalene's and pulled her toward their hotel.

'You're spending an awful lot of time by the sea lately. How can you stand it this time of year?' Evalene shivered and drew Victoria closer as they sped along.

'Where's your scarf?' Victoria asked, slightly out of breath as the intricate wrought iron balconies of their hotel came into view. 'It's not a wonder you're freezing.'

'Don't change the topic. You're up to something. Mama will catch on soon enough if you're not careful.'

Evalene had a point. But Victoria was doing this *for* Mama. For all of them. And if she succeeded, they'd understand.

The moment they entered the festively bedecked lobby, Mrs Winters' voice rang out. 'At last!' But then she caught sight of her eldest daughter's windswept appearance. 'Oh, Victoria, I despair.

Sir Francis doesn't like to be kept waiting and as we are especially dependent upon his generosity, I mean to respect his wishes.'

Victoria's blood boiled at the thought of being beholden to such a man as Sir Francis Radcliffe. The unsavoury way he ogled her younger sister was simply beyond the pale. She had to find the ruby or Mrs Winters would inevitably sacrifice Evalene on the altar of financial comfort. Even being a lonely governess was more preferable to such an alliance, though Victoria had no intention of either of them experiencing these undesirable futures.

'Well, go on,' her mother pressed, scrutinising Victoria's dark blonde curls with distaste. 'Get upstairs and see if you can't do something to tame that mop. And for heaven's sake, use a looking glass! You may not have Evalene's delicate features, but you could at least make an effort. Think of the navy, dear. We're not spending the holiday season in a port town for nothing. And it was your idea after all.'

Victoria pursed her lips in exasperation and strode toward the sweeping marble staircase until she caught sight of Sir Francis' corpulent figure emerging from the private parlour.

'Sister, I beg you would assist me!' Victoria clasped Evalene's hand and hurried up the stairs.

"I'm grateful to you,' Evalene breathed as they arrived on the second floor. 'Mama continues to force me into conversations with Sir Francis.'

'You leave Mama to me.' Victoria gave Evalene her most reassuring smile.

But her smile faded as they rounded the corner and her gaze travelled to the end of the hall. Who was that woman in the vivid blue gown coming out of their rooms? Victoria's eyes widened.

Was that...? No, it couldn't be her!

Before Victoria could entirely make out the woman's features, the lady ran to the opposite end of the corridor, rounded the corner and vanished out of sight. Victoria hastened to catch her, yet by the time she'd rounded the corner herself, the woman was gone.

Lieutenant Rogers had uncharacteristically failed to meet her at their appointed time. Now a strange woman had gained entrance to their rooms and had run off rather than make herself known. Such a curious course of events. Lost in thought while retracing her steps down the corridor, Victoria stumbled a little on an uneven piece of carpet. She checked her foot. Not carpet. A piece of fabric. A handkerchief with the initials F.R. embellishing a corner. Frederick? Why would this woman be in possession of Lieutenant Rogers' handkerchief? It was streaked with a sticky redness that almost made her release it in disgust. Had the woman dropped this in her hurry?

Evalene's panicked crying out shook Victoria from her ruminations. She stuffed the handkerchief into her reticule and hurried to find her sister trembling in the doorway.

'What is it?' Victoria demanded, but Evalene merely stared into the room, her mouth agape. When Victoria squeezed her way past, her heart leapt into her throat at the sight.

A man lay splayed out on their sofa, rivulets of red running down the buttercream-coloured material, gathering in pools on the oriental rug below.

'Who... who is he?' Evalene gasped at length.

It was Lieutenant Rogers. And he was barely breathing.

'Tell Mama to have someone fetch a doctor. Evalene! Make haste!'

That last outburst roused the young woman out of her frozenness and she dashed away on unsteady legs.

Victoria knelt down and took the bleeding man's hand in hers.

'Lieutenant Rogers? Frederick? Can you hear me?'

His eyelids flickered, but didn't open.

'Miss Winters...' he rasped.

'Yes, Lieutenant, I'm here.' Unbidden tears blurred her vision at the sight of his white shirt soaked crimson. 'How... Great God, whatever happened?'

He squeezed her hand, now slippery with blood. 'I had it, Miss Winters. Had it in my grasp.' He took a wheezing breath. 'Meant to bring to you... was followed...thought to hide it here...'

Lieutenant Rogers' head lolled to the side.

'Who did this? Frederick?'

She jostled his hand, but to no avail.

Just then Victoria heard a veritable stampede approaching.

'Out of my way, girl!' a man commanded, his old-fashioned wig pitching sideways as he leaned over the lieutenant.

While Mama declared to anyone within earshot that she was in a swoon and the hotel manager stood wringing his hands, muttering, Evalene took Victoria's elbow.

'Who is he, Victoria?'

Never taking her eyes off the wounded man, Victoria whispered, 'His name is Lieutenant Rogers. He's... my friend.'

'Is this why you've been spending so much time walking? Victoria, have you formed an attachment? Oh, Mama will be thrilled. Provided he does not die.'

Victoria felt the air leave her lungs.

'Oh, forgive me,' Evalene squeezed Victoria's arm. 'I wish I could weigh my words more carefully, as you do. However, I think you must tell me now what you've been about.'

Instead of responding, Victoria watched as the doctor stemmed Lieutenant Rogers' bleeding.

At length, the doctor sighed and stood.

'It would be best not to move him. I will stay the night to monitor his progress.' He addressed Mrs Winters. 'If that is acceptable to you, madam.'

Mrs Winters recoiled. 'Oh, well, I don't know. It's only... he's quite in the way there...'

'Mama!' Victoria chided. 'Yes, of course, sir. Whatever you think best to aid his recovery.'

'But where are *we* to go, my dear?' Mrs Winters dabbed her

eyes. 'Alas, 1802. The year we were turned out in the streets at Christmas!'

The manager cleared his throat. 'Madam, if I may? As you no doubt understand the establishment's need for discretion, I would be happy to place you and your daughters in The Rose Rooms, which have lately been vacated by Lord and Lady Burtwater.'

'The Rose Rooms!' Mrs Winters exclaimed in awe before remembering herself. 'Well, it is most inconvenient, but I suppose that would suit.'

'But the extra charges may not, Mama,' Victoria cautioned in low tones.

'Hush, child! Sir Francis would be only too delighted—'

'No extra charge, Miss Winters. Though the Burtwaters had to depart suddenly, they are paid up until the new year.' The man leaned forward conspiratorially. 'I believe Lord Burtwater is in poor health, for he's never stirred outside their rooms.'

'That is very generous, sir,' Victoria replied.

'I only ask that we keep this matter...' He gestured with a shudder to the blood-soaked sofa and the man upon it. 'Confidential.'

Victoria nodded. 'We understand completely.'

Worse things could be imagined than being accommodated in luxurious rooms in exchange for their silence. The manager showed Victoria's mother and sister out, however she approached the settee.

'Will he survive, doctor?'

'He's young. If he makes it through the night, I have hope for him.'

'Thank you, sir.'

Victoria turned to go, but the man stopped her.

'Miss, I don't like to pry, though if I'm not mistaken, that's a lieutenant's uniform and I'm sure his ship will note his absence. A stabbing will in all likelihood require an enquiry, no matter what the proprietor of this fine hotel wishes.'

'Is it your duty to alert the authorities?'

'Not as such, no. Men are ever brawling in these seaside towns. But do you not wish to bring this culprit to justice?'

'Most definitely, sir! I will see his ship is notified and determine what they wish to be done.'

The doctor gave her a short bow and she found her way to The Rose Rooms.

After Victoria scrubbed her hands at the basin, Evalene ushered her toward the sumptuously decorated sitting area of their new accommodation and poured two cups of tea. 'Will you now tell me what's happening?'

Victoria inhaled deeply, the fragrance of clove and bergamot soothing her after the sight of poor Lieutenant Rogers.

'This is about The Heirloom Ruby,' Victoria began in hushed tones.

'You found it? Mama will be in raptures! I'll never forget her shock when we tried to sell it and the solicitor told her it was a counterfeit. Oh, Victoria! However did you manage it? Where is it? Can I see it?'

'Wait, just listen. Against Mama's wishes, I went through Papa's papers. I learned he had the ruby appraised and when the appraisers returned it to him, he took it to a second appraiser to be sure of the value. But he was informed the first appraiser returned a counterfeit jewel to him.'

Evalene sucked in a sharp breath. 'He gave the appraisers the ruby?'

'They apparently came highly recommended by Mr. Rushington.'

'Papa's friend who owns all those mills?'

'Yes. At any rate, Papa had been trying to track the ruby down when he died. So, I contacted Mr. Rushington, who admitted he was mortified he'd recommended someone who ended up a swindler, and had been attempting to locate the man. But—'

'But?'

'But when he found the appraiser, he was in hiding from the bailiffs and claimed to have never even met Papa. And indeed he had not. Someone had been intercepting the man's correspondence and impersonating him to new clients.'

'Good God, Victoria!' Evalene took a calming sip of her tea. 'Was he telling the truth?'

'According to Mr. Rushington, he was about to be sent to debtors' prison over the affair, which is why he was in hiding. And now we come to it.' Victoria glanced up to make sure they were still alone and leaned in closer. 'Through one of Mr. Rushington's contacts, Papa discovered a man working for the government tasked with tracking this thief, and this government man was posing as the tavern owner at an establishment called The Captain's Dog—'

'The one here in Churchgate?'

'The very same.'

'Oh, Victoria, please don't tell me this is why you were so insistent Mama bring us here and why you allowed Sir Francis to bear the expense.'

'I could not think of any other way to raise the funds necessary, our financial picture being what it is.'

Evalene set her cup down with a clatter and bit her bottom lip. 'How very like you not to share any of this with me.'

Victoria winced. Her sister saw her secrecy as a failing.

'Go on,' Evalene sighed.

Victoria inhaled deeply. 'Well, according to the man at the tavern, as this is a major port town, the false appraisers frequent Churchgate to get their stolen goods to the continent, but they continue to elude capture. The Captain's Dog is apparently the hub of a whole smuggling ring with operatives on The HMS Dominant, which happens to be the ship Lieutenant Rogers serves on. Lieutenant Rogers has been trying to unearth the smugglers himself, so offered to help me in exchange for anything I might overhear in the tavern.'

'Gracious! Victoria, this is terribly dangerous. And foolish!'

'Would you rather end up on the stage? Or worse? Would you rather become the next Lady Radcliffe?'

'What? How could you ask such a thing? There's no question of my marrying such a man as Sir Francis. He's odious. And old as Papa!'

'Why do you think he's been hanging about? Buying us presents? Bringing us here at no little cost to himself? Make no mistake, Evalene, Mama is planning even now to make the match between you by Christmas.'

'That's only two days' time! But I thought he sought Mama as his future bride. For they are both widowed and...'

Victoria snorted into her cup. 'Oh, my sweet sister. Think so if it gives you comfort.' She touched Evalene's smooth satin sleeve. 'This is why I'm trying to find that ruby. To secure our fortunes, to give us our independence and some day to allow us to marry the men of our choosing, if we choose to marry at all.'

Evalene set her jaw. 'You mustn't bear this burden alone. How can I help?'

'I must get a message to The Dominant. The captain needs to know Lieutenant Rogers' whereabouts. If you could make my excuses to Mama and Sir Francis? Say I have a headache from the shock and wish to lie in quiet.'

'Mama is going to insist the doctor attend you next, for I've pleaded a headache for you these past seven nights while you were, I now learn, at the tavern. Besides, you cannot go alone to the docks in the dark of night! Only see what they've done to that poor lieutenant!' Evalene protested.

'I won't go alone. Naturally, I'll procure one of the hotel servants to accompany me, as I have been doing all along.'

At that moment, Sir Francis entered the room. 'I hope you ladies are ready for a feast. Just the thing to, er, calm the nerves! Unfortunately I have unexpected business with my man this evening, but I've arranged a lovely supper for you all.'

'Oh, Sir Francis, I doubt I could touch a morsel,' Mrs

Winters announced as she sashayed into the parlour. 'It's been a most distressing hour.'

'Now, now, madam. You must keep up your strength. Think of the solace you provide your daughters.'

Victoria and Evalene exchanged a nod and with a hand to her forehead, Victoria stood. 'I beg you would excuse me, Mama. Sir Francis.'

'It is one of her headaches coming on, Mama. She must lie down immediately.'

Victoria hastily retreated to her bedroom and changed into a cheap brown woollen. When certain the coast was clear, she flew down the servants' stairs, following the aroma of spit-roasted meat to the kitchens.

'Ah, there you are, miss!' came the cheerful call of Jimmy, the young man of about fifteen who'd been accompanying Victoria to The Captain's Dog, and fetching her again every night if Lieutenant Rogers was unable to escort her back.

'My apologies for detaining you.' Victoria pressed a coin into his palm. 'We've had... some excitement abovestairs.'

'Yes, miss. We heard you was moving rooms an' all, though nobody knows why.'

They stepped into the frigid December air and carried on to the coastal promenade, Victoria's mind racing for the right excuse.

'A mouse,' she blurted.

'A mouse, miss?'

'Indeed.'

Though Jimmy gave her a sidelong glance, he let the matter drop.

The Captain's Dog was lively this evening. Victoria ignored the pungent odour of too many bodies and made a beeline for the hook behind the counter, dodging all the spots she knew mistletoe was hung. As she tossed an apron over her dress, she greeted the surprised older man wiping glasses.

'Wasn't expecting you tonight, miss. Thought your business

here was all sewn up,' the incognito government man said with a nonchalant air.

'I'm not staying, Dave, however I needed to speak with you.'

In between serving patrons, Victoria explained everything that had transpired.

'And now the ruby is gone again, and I have to find a way to let Lieutenant Rogers' ship know he can't be on board tonight.'

Dave whistled through the gap in his front teeth.

'Have you seen any sign of the men we've been watching?' Victoria asked, peering around the heaving room.

'Not been in. Most likely on account of The Dominant setting sail tonight.'

'Tonight?' Victoria's heart plummeted. If her suspicion was correct and the ruby was on that ship, she was about to lose her only hope of a respectable future for her family. 'We have to get there before it's too late!'

'Not I, I'm afraid. Think some of the men are getting suspicious and I daren't leave tonight. But take this.'

Dave sank down behind the bar for a moment and then reappeared with a folded piece of parchment, fastened with a wax seal. He quickly shoved it underneath her apron.

'Sir!' Victoria gasped.

'Now, none of that, if you please,' Dave urged in lowered tones. 'This is the report I was meant to give to Lieutenant Rogers tonight.'

'And you want me to deliver it?'

'Seeing as you're going that way.' Dave winked at her.

How could he be so glib about something so dangerous? Then again, this must be how Evalene felt when Victoria divulged what she'd been up to.

The parchment was too large for her tiny reticule, so hiding behind the bar, Victoria lifted her skirt and shoved the paper into the top of her ribbon garter. She gave a quick nod to Dave who wished her luck and weaved her way through the crowd to where Jimmy sat warming himself with a bowl of stew. She joined him and leaned close.

'I need your services once more, Jimmy.'

'Off to The Grande, miss?' Jimmy scraped the last bits of mutton into a spoonful.

Victoria shook her head. 'To The Dominant.'

Jimmy coughed. 'Begging your pardon, miss, but a ship of lads is no place for a lady such as yourself.'

'Be that as it may, the ship is where I must go with all speed.'

The docks seemed as cold and empty as the promenade had earlier, with only an intermittent bell toll and a distant sailor's voice calling to his mates to break the misty silence.

'How will you know which one it is?' Jimmy asked, casting nervous glances at the men watching them go by.

'It's fifth down the line.'

When they arrived at The Dominant, Victoria advised Jimmy to return to the hotel. There was no sense in him waiting in the cold and the last thing she wanted was for him to be pressed into naval service. Jimmy shifted from foot to foot, but she assured him one of the officers would see her safely back and urged him again to leave.

'And where do you think you're going?' came a marine's rough voice behind her as she was about to embark.

'I'm here to see Captain Mayhew on a matter of urgent business.' Victoria began lifting her woollen skirts to access the report, yet only too late thought better of it.

The marine's expression changed as he approached with one of his shipmates. 'Captain's a married man, but we're sure we could find you some urgent business.'

Victoria drew herself up to her full height. Dressed as she was and about to lift her skirts, what else might he expect?

'My name is Victoria Winters, the grand-niece of Lord Hector Winters, Earl of Wesley, and my family are guests of Sir Francis Radcliffe at The Grande. My business with Captain Mayhew is at the request of Lieutenant Frederick Rogers. If you would take me to your captain at once, I may not mention how you waylaid a lady of quality with your unbecoming behaviour.'

Though her hands shook, she raised her chin defiantly.

'Alright, miss, I meant no offence. A lady such as yourself might be surprised how many unchaperoned women of ill-repute hang about the docks. It was an honest mistake an' all.'

'To Captain Mayhew, if you please.'

'Yes, miss,' the marine mumbled.

He led her through a rabbit warren of hallways to the captain's dining room. When they entered, the captain looked up in surprise. 'Yes? What is it?'

'Begging your pardon, sir. This, er, lady says she has urgent business with you regarding Lieutenant Rogers.'

'Well?'

Victoria took a deep breath to still her nerves. 'My... My name is Miss Victoria Winters of the Wesley Winters and what I have to say is for your ears alone, captain.'

Captain Mayhew sat back as he considered her. 'Leave us.'

'But, sir...'

'I said leave us!'

The marine slunk away and shut the polished wooden door.

As Victoria was about to speak, she was distracted by a fir tree in the corner strung with a garland of berries, nuts and ribbon, tinging the air with its pine scent. 'How lovely!' she remarked.

'Yes, my wife insisted. If it's good enough for the king and all that. Now Miss Winters of the Wesley Winters, what is this about?'

Victoria reached under her skirts and, ignoring the man's raised eyebrows, retrieved Dave's missive.

'This is the report from Dave at The Captain's Dog. He feared he wouldn't be able to get away and keep his cover intact, so he asked me to bring it to you.'

'Taken you into his confidence, has he?'

'Indeed, sir. Lieutenant Rogers—'

'Yes, where is my second lieutenant? I have men searching for him even now.'

'I regret to inform you he's been injured and is at The Grande. Recovering, I hope.'

'Injured?' Mayhew clenched his fists, though kept his expression pleasant. 'What do you mean, injured?'

'Stabbed, sir. I saw a woman in a blue dress fleeing right after it happened. More than this, I do not know. The truth is, alongside his assignment to uncover the smugglers on board this ship, Lieutenant Rogers has been assisting me in my recovery attempts of a rare family heirloom... a large ruby I have on good authority is one of the items being moved by this smuggling ring.' Victoria glanced down at her hands. 'I believe he found my ruby and was stabbed for it.'

A knock rattled the door and the captain's steward appeared. 'Your dinner guests have arrived, captain.' He gave Victoria a once over. 'Or shall I give you a moment?'

'No, no, show them in. But send for Dr Fen. Lieutenant Rogers is wounded at The Grande. This young lady will show him where.'

Victoria curtsied to go, right as Mayhew's guests entered the room.

'Ah, Lord and Lady Burtwater, apologies for keeping you waiting...'

Victoria gasped.

There before her stood none other than Sir Francis and a woman in an unmistakable vivid blue dress.

Victoria's heart thundered in her ears. 'Aunt Minerva?'

Sir Francis sputtered. 'M-miss Winters! What... what are you doing here?'

'I could ask you the same thing, sir!' Victoria faced a stunned Captain Mayhew. 'These two are not Lord and Lady Burtwater. This man is Sir Francis Radcliffe, and this woman is Minerva Hart-Gibson, my mother's estranged sister... The person who stabbed Lieutenant Rogers and stole The Heirloom Ruby!'

Aunt Minerva's nostrils flared. 'How could I steal something that was rightfully mine? Nevertheless, you have no proof.'

'You are wearing the same blue dress as the woman I saw. And how convenient Lord and Lady Burtwater had to leave The Grande so suddenly! And more to the point, nobody had ever seen Lord Burtwater because of his ill health. Once you had your prize, of course you'd want to get away as quickly as possible. Securing passage on the ship with your smuggling companions would make perfect sense.'

Sir Francis stood dumbly wiping his profusely sweating forehead with a monogrammed square of material from his coat pocket. All of a sudden, Victoria remembered the handkerchief she'd gathered up from the floor when chasing after the woman in the corridor. F.R. didn't stand for Frederick Rogers! She plucked the blood-stained cloth from her reticule and held it aloft. 'You dropped this during your escape, ma'am. Note the F.R. For Francis Radcliffe, I presume?'

All eyes travelled from the material dangling between Victoria's fingers to Sir Francis' hand seemingly frozen on his brow. The embroidered monograms were a perfect match.

'Guards!' Captain Mayhew bellowed.

'They'll be no use to you,' Minerva said, cocking the small silver pistol she'd produced from her own reticule.

The door burst open then, but instead of marines, two armed sailors emerged. Minerva smiled triumphantly at them.

'You will hang, all of you, by God!' Mayhew growled.

'Close the door behind you, lads.' Minerva ordered and then gestured at Victoria with her pistol. 'Be so good as to stand next to the captain.'

'Why are you doing this?' Victoria asked.

'It's quite simple, really... Did you not know I was once betrothed to your dear Papa? It was I who was to be mistress of Winter Manor. And it was I who was to have The Heirloom Ruby bestowed upon me on our wedding day. But my jealous younger sister just couldn't keep her mouth shut about my...

indiscretions and went telling tales to your father. Of course, she had recently come out, so was in the perfect position to accept his offer only days after he threw me over.'

Victoria stared at her aunt. 'So this is about revenge?'

'This is about justice!' Minerva spat. 'And how I've had to make my own way in the world these thirty years.'

Victoria took in Minerva's expensive satin gown. 'You seem to have done very well for yourself.'

'Yes, I have built a profitable enterprise—'

'My dear...' Sir Francis put a cautioning hand on Minerva's elbow.

'Oh, be quiet, you fool,' she barked at him. 'They'll both be dead soon and we will be gone.'

'Dead? You never said you planned to harm your own niece.' Sir Francis let out a whimper.

Minerva's mouth twisted. 'I will do whatever it takes to get what is mine.' She scowled at Victoria. 'Now stand over there.'

Victoria did as she was bidden while Minerva instructed one of the sailors to tie them up. But as Victoria rounded the far edge of the dining table, she grabbed a knife and wielded it at the sailor. He lunged for it and a great boom shook the room. The sailor sank to the floor, while Minerva's gun billowed smoke.

'Damnation!' she said under her breath. 'You are either a very lucky or very foolish young woman. The next bullet will hit its intended mark if there are any more tricks.'

Victoria swallowed hard as she stared at the body at her feet. With a shaking hand, she dropped the knife back on the table and glanced at Captain Mayhew. She couldn't imagine how infuriatingly helpless the decorated captain must've felt to be held at gunpoint by a deranged woman on his own ship. Inching past the decorated tree, Victoria drew closer to him.

'You're not going to get away with this, you harridan.' Mayhew's voice was gruff and low as he glared at Minerva. 'The sound of the gunshot will bring my men upon you.'

'Yes, my dear,' Sir Francis pleaded. 'You must get away before you're captured.'

'I?' Minerva dragged the word out with a tone of incredulity.

'Well, I did not just shoot a man.'

Minerva regarded him coldly, her eyes almost slits.

'Hold this.' She held the pistol out to Sir Francis and he took it. Then she began to scream for help.

Sir Francis stared down at the weapon in his hand as realisation dawned. 'What... What are you doing? Now see here, Minerva...'

The other sailor, understanding Minerva had betrayed them, mumbled an epithet and made his way around the room to the exit.

'Not so fast!' Mayhew shouted to the sailor. He grabbed a fine china plate and hurled it at the young man. It crashed hard into his shoulder and shattered on the wooden floor.

The pistol slipped from Sir Francis' trembling, sweaty grasp and he hurtled toward the door. 'S-s-stand aside, woman,' he squeaked.

Victoria had to stop them. In a desperate move, she toppled the tree, knocking the sailor and Sir Francis down and trapping them within its branches and garland. In the chaos of the tangle, Minerva slipped out, her shouts for help echoing down the passageway.

In the next moment, Dave and Jimmy tore into the dining room, a handful of armed marines at their sides. They surveyed the scene.

'It appears you could use some assistance, Ned,' Dave remarked, his accent now crisp and polished as he grinned at the captain. 'Good thing this lad fetched me.'

'It's that bedevilled woman!' Mayhew bellowed. He then commanded the marines to find her and bring her to him at once.

'She wouldn't leave without the ruby!' Victoria called out. 'I must get to her quarters.'

Victoria sidestepped the struggling men underneath the tree and headed for the door, only to be stopped by Dave.

'You don't need to be chasing any more criminals, miss. Let the men handle it.'

'Sir, Minerva Hart-Gibson would drop that ruby to the bottom of the sea rather than release it into anyone's possession. I have gained and lost it once today. I refuse to lose it again. And I will not let Lieutenant Rogers suffer for nothing.'

Dave shot a look at Mayhew who nodded.

'Then I'll accompany you,' Dave said.

'And I, miss!' Jimmy shouted.

Mayhew instructed one of the marines to show the group to Minerva's quarters with all haste. Many twists and turns later, they found her holding several marines at bay, wielding a plank of wood with two nails protruding from it, her eyes as wild as her tumbled down hair.

'Stay back!' she screamed.

'It's over, Minerva,' Victoria declared. 'I'm sure if you give yourself and the smuggling operation up, it will go better for you at your trial.'

'Give up everything I've worked a lifetime to build? Never!'

With that, she let forth a crazed shriek and leapt at the nearest marine. A shot rang out behind Victoria, so close she thought for a moment she would find the bullet had made a home in her own body. But when she redirected her gaze to the scene, Minerva lay crumpled and moaning, a red stain blooming at her shoulder. Victoria pushed her way past the soldiers and knelt next to her aunt.

'Get away from me and let me die.'

'Not today, Ms Hart-Gibson,' came the commanding voice of Captain Mayhew.

Victoria whipped her head up to see him standing over them, musket in hand.

'You will answer for your crimes,' he announced.

While two men removed Minerva to a cell to await the

doctor's return from The Grande, Victoria received permission to search the room with Dave under Mayhew's watchful eye. Deep within Minerva's trunk was a small wooden box containing a black velvet pouch. Victoria reached inside and withdrew a hard oval object. The jewel in her hand gleamed all shades of red in the lantern light.

'I have it, Papa,' she whispered as a tear spilled over her lower lashes. 'I have it at last.'

An hour later, Victoria bounded up the stairs to their old rooms where she found Lieutenant Rogers lying peacefully, the first doctor sitting nearby.

'How is he?'

'Ah, Miss Winters. The patient has no fever and has been awake. Dr Fen and I believe he'll make a full and speedy recovery.'

'Can I speak with him?' Victoria asked.

'You may.' The physician returned to his notes.

Victoria knelt by Lieutenant Rogers' side. 'Frederick? Can you hear me?'

'Miss Winters?' he murmured.

'Yes, I'm here. We did it. We've unearthed the leader of the smuggling ring and I'm in possession of my family's ruby at last. The Winters ladies will be alright now.' She retrieved the shimmering jewel from her reticule and held it up for him. 'Thank you. Thank you for... oh, everything!'

She touched his forehead then, imagining the comfort this turn of events would bring to her mother and sister.

'I'm glad,' he sighed and with a slight smile, drifted off once more.

Victoria's face shone with joy and relief as she watched the steady rise and fall of his chest.

'Happy Christmas, Lieutenant,' she sniffed. 'Happy Christmas.'

❄

BIO

Melicity Pope is the cozy pen name for Melissa Williams-Pope. When not writing, she cycles through a variety of passions such as acting, singing and traveling the world fostering furry friends, while coaching other creatives to experience their own dream-come-true lives and businesses. She's a whimsical American, married to a down-to-earth Kiwi, currently based in the UK.

www.MelicityPope.com

SNOWBALL CHEESECAKE RECIPE

Ingredients

150g butter, melted
300g Digestive biscuits, crushed
600g full fat cream cheese
150g caster sugar
300ml double cream
2 packs Lee's small snowballs

Recipe

Mix melted butter and crushed digestives. Cover base of large spring form tin
Pour in fridge to set

Mix soft cheese with sugar and add double cream. Mix till thickens.

Add 1 whole pack of Lee's snowballs

Top the biscuit base with the cheesecake mixture and decorate with the other pack of snowballs.
Sprinkle with the leftover coconut from the pack and set in fridge till needed

COMING SOON

A Right Cozy Culinary Crime

A Right Cozy Historical Crime